Vet there be Love

ISLA GREEN

HarperNorth
Windmill Green
24 Mount Street
Manchester M2 3NX

A division of
HarperCollins*Publishers*
1 London Bridge Street
London SE1 9GF

www.harpercollins.co.uk

HarperCollins*Publishers*
Macken House,
39/40 Mayor Street Upper,
Dublin 1, D01 C9W8, Ireland

Published by HarperCollins*Publishers* Ltd 2026

Copyright © HarperCollins*Publishers* Ltd 2026

Isla Green asserts the moral right to
be identified as the author of this work.

A catalogue record for this book is available from the British Library.

ISBN: 978-0-00-881861-6

This novel is entirely a work of fiction. The names, characters and incidents portrayed in it are the work of the author's imagination. Any resemblance to actual persons, living or dead, events or localities is entirely coincidental.

Set in (Minion Pro) by (Amnet)

Printed and bound in the UK using 100% Renewable Electricity by
CPI Group (UK) Ltd

All rights reserved. No part of this publication may be reproduced, stored in a retrieval system, or transmitted, in any form or by any means, electronic, mechanical, photocopying, recording or otherwise, without the prior permission of the publishers.

Without limiting the exclusive rights of any author, contributor or the publisher of this publication, any unauthorised use of this publication to train generative artificial intelligence (AI) technologies is expressly prohibited. HarperCollins also exercise their rights under Article 4(3) of the Digital Single Market Directive 2019/790 and expressly reserve this publication from the text and data mining exception.

1 3 5 7 9 10 8 6 4 2

To June

1

There was nothing wrong with the day to begin with, but nor was there anything particularly right with it. Amy had grown so used to days like this, they barely registered. As usual, she took the tube from her home in Camden to the veterinary practice in Archway. She was always the first vet to arrive for her shift, and staff-wise she was second only to receptionist, Ruby. Ruby had long purple hair worn in dreadlocks, a stud piercing her nose and a sleeve of tattoos. Amy had no desire for any of the above, but she admired Ruby's devil-may-care attitude and outgoing nature. A down-to-earth East Ender, she was popular with both staff and customers.

'How was your weekend, Rubes?'

Ruby was brewing coffee in the kitchen while washing a couple of dirty mugs. She grimaced as she thrust the one with a thick layer of mould caking the bottom under Amy's nose. 'Look at that! You could grow something interesting in there, I'm sure. But would it harm them to wash up before they left?'

Amy pulled a sympathetic face, safe in the knowledge that Ruby would know she was not guilty of the offence.

'My weekend?' Ruby returned to the question. 'Aha! I had a fabulous one! Luke and I went to see Excess Baggage at the Palace. They're local – have you heard of them? Fantastic! Sort of Arctic Monkeys but a real Seventies vibe?' Ruby often made her statements sound like a question. 'We went for dinner at Gregorio's after. Yesterday, I cooked dinner for all my clan. The whole bleedin' lot of them! My sister's kids ran riot, Mum moaned but didn't do much to help, Nan was going on about her new hips. Families, eh?'

She had scrubbed out the mugs by now and set them down beside the coffee machine with the others. 'Coffee's on its way. What about you? Get up to much?'

'Oh, this and that.' She had read, then cleaned and tidied her flat, but none of these tasks seemed worth mentioning. 'I went to Camden Market though,' she remembered.

She hadn't perused the stalls for long before losing her patience. Had it always been so busy? It felt as if everyone in North London had descended on it that morning. It wasn't much fun shuffling from one stall to another, all the while keeping a hand on her bag in case of pickpockets. Amy had lived in London for the past ten years, ever since she left home in a village near Guildford to study at the Royal Veterinary College. She considered herself a Londoner now – or as much as anyone could be, with its continually shifting population. She had rarely gone back to Guildford apart from holidays and the odd weekend. When she spoke to her parents and her old friend Penny, who had stayed close to home, she extolled the benefits of London living – the concerts, the museums, the art galleries. But when had she last visited any of them? Had she been to a gallery since she met her mother at The Tate for her birthday last year?

'Cool! Did you buy anything?'

'No. Not this time. Nothing took my fancy.' She picked up her mug. Ruby had poured the perfect splash of milk. 'Thanks for the coffee. Better get on. Another busy Monday, no doubt.'

Twenty minutes later, the rest of the staff had arrived. Veterinary nurse, Sam, who was working with Amy that morning, had also been to see Excess Baggage, and eaten out, as well as managed a trip into the West End.

'There was an amazing magician at Covent Garden yesterday. He was asking the crowd for money and making it reappear in the most ludicrous places. Would you believe that one woman found the five-pound note in her shoe? I kid you not. Maybe she was a plant? I hope not. He seemed genuine. And I'm off to see *Les Mis* tonight. I must have seen it twenty-five times now!'

'Well, I'm glad some of you are having such a good time.'

Amy realised her comment sounded more sarcastic than she had intended.

Sam cast her a slightly hurt look. 'You OK?'

Amy sighed. 'Sorry, it wasn't meant to come out like that. Let's get ready, shall we. We should check on the inpatients.'

Amy was happier when she was working. She didn't really want to hear about how wonderful everyone else's social life was, particularly when her own was sorely lacking. It hadn't always been like that, though. When she had been going out with Jake, her days and nights were always filled with exciting activities. Nine months had passed since then; it felt both like yesterday and a lifetime ago, and though she relished her newfound freedom, just occasionally, when she saw a happy couple, she couldn't escape the feeling that there was a hole in her life that only another human being could fill.

The day began with routine check-ups and vaccinations, after which the day's emergency patients began to arrive. Amy went to call her next patient. She preferred to do that personally – to greet the animal and its owner in the waiting area; to walk them to her consulting room and ensure everyone felt calm. Most customers used the main waiting room, but there was also a smaller one for very nervous or more unusual pets that might spook or be spooked by the others.

A handsome tabby called Tiger had been frightened by a noise in the street, shot back into the house through the kitchen door, leapt onto one of the kitchen cabinets, then fallen into the gap between it and the wall, landing awkwardly and crushing his tail in the tight space.

'It took ages to get him out,' said his owner, a young woman of a similar age to Amy. 'My partner rang me in such a state and I dashed home from work to help her. We had to take everything out of the cupboard to move it, and poor Tiger was just making this really pathetic miaowing sound. It broke my heart.' She looked close to tears.

'Once he was out, we thought he was OK, but now I'm not so sure. His tail looks a bit wonky.' She bit her lip. 'Has he broken anything?'

Amy examined Tiger gently. 'You're a beautiful boy, aren't you? And so placid.' She carefully felt his tail. 'Yes, it does feel a little crooked right here – sorry, Tiger, I won't touch it again – but nothing seems broken. We're also at the tip of his tail so I'm keen to see if we can get this to settle. It'd be another story if it were higher up. I'll give you some anti-inflammatory painkillers, and they should do the trick.'

Apart from the odd mew of pain, Tiger's eyes were half-closed in bliss as he wallowed in the attention. The women laughed.

'I bet you've got lots of pets, Miss Ashton,' said her customer.

Amy shook her head. 'No, I live on my own in a flat. It wouldn't be fair.'

Amy had begged her parents for a dog or cat when she was growing up. Her father softened to the idea, but her houseproud mother was adamant. In the end, she had been allowed a rabbit, Thumper, which lived in a hutch in the garden. He had lived for seven years, a long life for a rabbit, and she had been heartbroken when he died. It was thanks to Thumper that Amy had made up her mind to become a vet. She was going to take care of animals just like her beloved rabbit. Her parents – who had expected her to become a doctor, like her father – had assumed it was a phase she would grow out of, but nothing could dissuade their daughter from that path.

Tiger and his owner left, both of them happier than they had been when they arrived. It had been a successful morning.

Lunch was a hastily eaten sandwich and an apple. Passing reception on her way back to her consulting room, Amy could hear someone querying their bill.

'Three thousand pounds? Where do you think I'm going to get that sort of money from? It's a scandalous amount!'

'It was a very difficult procedure, and an expensive one, I know. Mr Richards told me he had explained it to you before the operation. But he'd be happy for you to pay in instalments.' Ruby was doing her best to placate the angry pet owner.

'Well that's good of him, but it doesn't make it any more affordable. You lot must be millionaires charging those sorts of figures.'

Amy closed the door of her consulting room. There wasn't much she could do. She sympathised with the pet owner, well aware the cost of treating a sick animal could be very expensive these days. But taking out insurance was expensive as well. She seriously wondered how some people could afford to own a pet.

It was a long afternoon, with a succession of dogs, cats, a pet rat, a terrapin and a pygmy goat. Amy was looking forward to her evening run. Funny how she could feel weary and jaded, but once she started running she found a new energy. It was like turning on the engine of a car – a bit bumpy in first gear, but by the time she got to fourth, she was coasting!

Only one more patient to go … Amy knew what the problem was as soon as she set eyes on the guinea pig. The poor creature was limping. It held up one of its legs in a pitiful effort to avoid putting pressure on it. Closer examination revealed a lesion on its front right foot that had become infected. The other feet, though not as bad, also bore red, inflamed patches. To cap it all, the guinea pig was obese. You didn't have to be a vet to see that.

'Poor Larry,' said his owner. 'He's such a happy chap, but he's a bit out of sorts right now.'

He's more than a bit 'out of sorts,' thought Amy, as she popped him on the scales, checked his heart rate with a stethoscope and took his temperature, while he was gently restrained by Sam. He had a fever and was clearly in pain. Amy asked the woman what she was feeding him. The woman had a thin face and wore what looked like a homemade knitted hat, with long flaps that covered her ears, even though it was a hot day. There was an air of eccentricity about her, though by London's standards it was probably fairly low on the scale.

She looked affronted by the question. 'What I've always fed my guinea pigs. I've had guinea pigs for years, I really don't think I need *you* to tell *me* what they should be eating.'

'I'm sure Larry eats very well, but sometimes what suits one animal doesn't suit another. Larry would benefit from a stricter diet, especially while he's recovering from this nasty infection. We call it bumblefoot. You've probably heard of it.'

The woman didn't respond. She glared at Amy, her mouth set in a hard line.

'Might he be eating a lot of fresh food?' Amy tried to lighten the tone. 'I know how much they all love apples and bananas, but they do contain a lot of sugar. We recommend that seventy per cent of their diet should be made up of hay, ten per cent dry food and twenty per cent fresh.'

'What I'd like to know, is why we're talking about Larry's diet. I've come here with concerns about his feet. If you can't help him, I'll have to see someone else.'

Amy was aware of Sam shuffling awkwardly beside her.

'I can help Larry, of course. I think a topical antibiotic should do the trick on treating his foot. I'll take a blood sample, just to rule anything else out. However, I must also tell you that a dietary supplement would be a good idea.' She added, cautiously, 'Hygiene is more important than ever too. You need to ensure that his cage is regularly cleaned down. Is his –'

The woman didn't wait to hear her question. 'Are you here to treat my animal or to pass judgements on me? First diet, then cleanliness!' She pulled her wire-rimmed glasses down over her nose and peered at Amy. 'Are you even qualified? You look very young to me. I saw Mr Richards last time and I'm in a mind to see him this time too.'

Amy thought it best to ignore these remarks. 'Shall I ask the nurse to hold him while I treat his feet, or would you prefer to?'

The woman gave a terse nod to indicate that Sam should continue to hold Larry. Unlike her pet, she was skinny. Amy had a mental flash of her seated at the dining table with a giant Larry sitting opposite her, as she fed him from her own plate.

'Increasing his exercise can help too,' Amy added, as she gently bathed Larry's feet. 'Larry should have some toys to play with and time to explore outside his cage in a safe environment.'

Amy was well aware that every utterance annoyed her customer further, yet she felt compelled to continue.

'The fact is, he's a bit on the heavy side, and it doesn't do him any favours.'

Could she have been more sensitive? Probably, but the animal's health was her main concern, not the wounded pride of its owner. She would have liked to label the blatant overfeeding 'cruel', but knew that was a step too far.

The woman opened her mouth, closed it, then opened it again. Her face, which had been very pale, flushed a deep shade of red. 'How rude! I shall be speaking to your superior. I have never met a vet who knows so little about animals, or one so ill-mannered.' She jabbed a bony finger at Amy. 'I hope, for everyone's sake, you find yourself another calling, young lady.'

She snatched Larry from Sam, returned the poor animal to the box she had brought him in, and marched towards the door. After a brief pause, she turned to say, 'I shall take the prescription for the antibiotic, but I will be waiting in reception for it.' Then she was gone.

Amy let out a sigh of relief that was short-lived, as a few seconds later she returned. 'I'll have you know that not only have you insulted me, but you have also insulted Larry – and that, I can't forgive.'

When they were sure she wasn't flouncing back for round three, Amy closed the door, leant against it, and breathed deeply. She forced a laugh, but it didn't sound very convincing. Sam cast her a sympathetic look.

'She's a daft old cow. Don't let her get under your skin.' She tutted. 'Poor little fellow. Let's hope she puts that cream on him sharpish. Honestly, some people shouldn't be allowed pets.'

Amy nodded gratefully, but found she was unable to speak. She crossed to the basin and washed her hands even more thoroughly than usual, as if she was ridding herself of the stain of the encounter.

'You weren't rude, either. Just saying things as they are. I'll back you up.'

'Thanks, Sam. I'm not taking any notice of her, anyway. You get all sorts, don't you?'

'Yes, and fortunately her type is few and far between.'

***

As if things couldn't get any worse, Amy returned home after her run to hear pounding music coming from the building her flat backed onto. It was a sultry evening in August. A variety of cooking smells drifted through her open windows. She didn't mind them; it was intriguing to wonder what dishes were being concocted that produced the fragrant spicy aromas, but other people's noise was a different matter. *Boom! Boom! Boom!* The walls of her flat seemed to vibrate with the deep bass notes.

As if everyone shares your awful taste in music, Amy thought to herself, as she examined the contents of her fridge. She had been vegetarian in her early twenties. It had lasted for a few years but, to her surprise, she had found herself craving meat, even though she had eaten it only rarely before. Now, she ate it when she felt like it, which still wasn't often. Today she baked a salmon fillet with some fennel, boiled half a dozen new potatoes and some broccoli. Healthy, but delicious! She did also smear a generous dollop of butter on the potatoes – life was too short to skimp on the little pleasures.

Amy naturally had a slim build, and her passion for running had continued to keep her fit. The regular exercise was part of her life now. She felt twitchy if she went more than a couple of days without it. When she had insisted on going for a run while spending a weekend with her parents, her mother had voiced the opinion that she might be a bit *obsessive* about it. She had tipped her head to the side and stretched her lips in a look that Amy knew only too well – one masked with concern that really said, 'I think you'll find that I know what's best.' Well, she probably *was* obsessive, but it was beneficial. Running gave her the opportunity to unclutter her head, and though she tried not to dwell on things that were bothering her while she ran, she often found that she came home to clear solutions. Or at least, she was able to put them into perspective.

She usually sat at the table to eat, but after today's fiasco, she needed to melt into the comfort of the sofa. Fork in one hand, her phone in the other, she absent-mindedly scrolled through a cycle of Facebook and Instagram. Amy rarely posted anything herself, but it was interesting to see what others were doing. Old school and university friends shared photos of meals out with boyfriends or day trips to Brighton, Whitstable or the New Forest. Someone had been proposed to in Mauritius. She would have to add her congratulations later. She cleared the dishes, dumped the bin bag in the communal waste bin outside and had a shower. There was always something to watch on TV or Netflix these days, but today she just wasn't in the mood. Amy picked up her novel, read a few pages, then put the book down. Images of obese guinea pigs, some as big as small dogs, floated into her vision. Damn that woman! How dare she speak to her like that!

Amy, she's a sad old bat, don't waste your time dwelling on it.

Robert, her boss, would want to have a word with her tomorrow. Even if he didn't take the woman's side, he would tell Amy she ought to have been more diplomatic. Amy pictured the poor, overweight creature, who must have been in considerable discomfort. Animals and their thoughtless or incompetent owners sometimes kept her awake at night. But was that all that was bothering her?

The cooking smells had now been replaced by a whiff of cannabis wafting up from the garden of the ground-floor flat next door, accompanied by the voice of her neighbour, who seemed to spend most of his time bellowing into his mobile phone. She had taken in a parcel for him a couple of weeks ago, and been surprised to deliver it to a smartly dressed man wearing a suit and tie, appearing the model image of respectability. Meanwhile, in the flat upstairs, a woman she had never seen – she knew her name only from her post in the mailbox downstairs – skulked around at strange hours of the night, while the couple directly below argued constantly, usually kicking off when Amy was getting ready for bed. She had once loved London for these very reasons: the luxury to do your own thing with carefree anonymity. But had she finally outgrown that stage?

If she could live anywhere, where would she go? The Highlands of Scotland? Beautiful, but too remote. Wales? The north of England? A placement in Northumberland was part of her training, working in a veterinary practice in Hexham. It was the first time she had been 'up north' apart from a school trip to York visiting the Jorvik Viking Museum when she was twelve, and a weekend with her parents to Edinburgh to see the castle and the Tattoo. A lot of the work in Hexham had been on farms, so she had felt out of her depth at first.

Cattle, sheep, horses. She was actually a little afraid of horses, finding them skittish and unpredictable. She had spent the evenings with her nose in a textbook, brushing up on her knowledge of farm animals. Her boss had been delighted with her progress. 'I wish all the students we had were like you. You don't fancy coming back here, do you, when you've completed your degree? One of my team might be retiring soon, so if the timing's right …'

She had been flattered, but she still considered herself a city girl at the time.

She browsed the vacant posts out of habit, really – the way some people were always eyeing property, even though they had no intention of moving house. An advert on the site of a veterinary group she belonged to caught her attention.

'We are seeking an enthusiastic veterinary surgeon to join our small team in Grassdale, North Yorkshire. As a veterinarian at our independent country practice, you will be diagnosing, treating and caring for both large and small animals.'

Grassdale! Forget the job, even the name sounded idyllic! She pictured a village nestled amongst rolling hills. There was probably a stream running alongside the main road, brimming with ducks. The houses would all be quaint cottages with slate roofs and roses planted in the front garden. The advert stated that the ideal candidate would have about ten years' experience. Amy sighed; she'd only been qualified for five. She continued scrolling. Jobs in London, jobs in the Midlands, jobs in the West Country. She googled Grassdale, and found that the village itself wasn't so different from how she'd envisioned it, bar the stream running along the high street, though there was a river at one end, crossed by a humpback bridge. It was as pretty as a picture, lying in a valley in the Yorkshire Dales cradled by hills and moorland. White-washed cottages interspersed with buildings of biscuit-coloured stone trailed one long road. There was a pub, looking as quaint as a country pub should, with a white-washed frontage and pretty sash windows painted bluey-grey, a patch of grass in front set with wooden tables and chairs. Imagine living in such a place! Imagine running on those moors!

Her feelings caught her off guard. She enjoyed the countryside as much as anyone; she had even joined her parents in rented cottages in Devon and Dorset – her father embarking on long walks, her mother joining him reluctantly but preferring to potter round pretty villages with antique shops. But she had never felt a great pull to actually *live* in the country. So why was this place toying with her emotions? She had no idea, but she returned to the advert. Was she even qualified for the job?

As the music from the house behind cranked up another notch, Amy formed a new idea. Feeling as if another person had hijacked her body, she began typing. Her CV would need updating, but that wouldn't take long. Her qualifications spoke for themselves: one A and three A stars at A level, a first-class degree in veterinary medicine, as well as the prestigious Sir Leonard Blackwell award for outstanding student in her year. Amy had spent her childhood trying to earn her parents' approval. That award finally did the trick. Watching from the audience as she collected it onstage, her father had looked as delighted as if he had won it himself. Amy considered it the only time he actually congratulated her for anything. Their expectations had always been high. 'You must have impressed them all,' he'd said. That meant more to her than winning the award itself.

She would emphasise her experience at the Northumberland practice. In all honesty, it was a few years since she had been anywhere near a cow, but she doubted their anatomy had changed much since then.

She finished tweaking her CV, adding new referees, and had just completed the accompanying email when the couple below started their nightly slanging match. She scanned over it all one last time. Was she really going to send it? Had she thought this through?

Before she could second-guess herself any further, she pressed 'Send'. Too late: it was gone! The wonders of the internet!

It was bonkers, really. She was surprised at herself for acting so impulsively. Being qualified was one thing, but having the relevant experience was another. And could she really hack it in a country village anyway? It might look idyllic, but actually *living* there? She wouldn't know where to start! It was a far more terrifying thought than the familiarity of a city. She consoled herself with the knowledge that it hardly mattered anyway. She wasn't going to get the job – not in a million years!

Though it was quite a thrill doing something so wild.

2

Amy had practically forgotten her application by the next day. Life was too hectic to focus on anything other than the present. Two colleagues were on annual leave, which meant an even busier workload than usual.

'She said you belittled her,' said Robert Richards, after he'd asked Amy for a quick word about yesterday's difficult customer. 'I know, I know,' he raised his hands as if to fend off her forthcoming protest. 'She's a tricky one. I've known her for years. We just have to bite our tongues sometimes.'

Amy folded her arms. 'I don't mind biting my tongue, but the animal's welfare is my priority. The poor creature was obese.'

'A little overweight, perhaps.'

'Obese for a guinea pig. And in pain!'

'We do our job, and we don't judge.'

'Judge? Robert, I—' She averted her gaze and stopped herself from saying any more. This was her boss she was talking to. She wasn't an argumentative person – in fact she hated confrontation of any sort – but where her work was concerned, she possessed a confidence that she lacked in her personal life.

'Sorry, Robert. I didn't mean to upset her.'

He nodded. 'I spoke to her this morning and I gather the foot is already showing signs of improvement.'

'That's great!'

Amy managed a smile as they went their separate ways. She was fighting a losing battle here. Best to save her energy for the day ahead.

***

A young brother and sister brought their Labrador puppy in for its first injections. The boy was struggling to hold it. The dog would have leapt out of his arms if Amy hadn't intervened.

'He's so wriggly!' The puppy had given the boy a light nip in the process. 'It didn't hurt!' he said, looking at his mother, clearly worried the dog would get into trouble, and Amy felt her heart squeeze.

'It's like having a new baby in the house,' said the mother. 'We're all very new to this. The kids were desperate for a dog but I'm afraid he's been a shock to the system.'

Amy helped the boy lower the puppy carefully onto the floor, then crouched down beside him. 'He needs to feel secure. He could hurt himself if you drop him or he jumps down.' She showed the three of them the right way to pick him up, with one hand under his chest and the other supporting his rear end, keeping him close to the body.

'He's very young, he'll calm down. The best thing you can do is give him lots of handling. Let him grow accustomed to having his ears touched and his paws lifted. That will make it easier for all of us if you need to bring him to the practice in future.'

'You hear that?' said the children's mother. 'Are you listening to the vet? Remember our agreement?' She looked at Amy, and raised her eyebrows. 'He's their responsibility supposedly. We'll have to see how long that lasts.'

After checking him over, Amy asked the boy to hold the puppy while she injected him under the skin on the back of his neck. He didn't budge.

'He's really beautiful.' Amy was rewarded with some rough licks on the back of her hand. She tickled him behind the ears. 'I know you're going to take care of him and that he's going to be so happy with you. What a lucky dog.'

When Amy saw children and their parents, she often dwelled on her own childhood. Had it been a happy one? She wasn't really sure. When she heard other people reminiscing about their parents – special memories of doing things together – it made her wonder if she had missed out. She knew she was loved; not that her parents ever told her outright, but she assumed it to be the case. She had rarely wanted for anything – though she wasn't spoilt, given daily chores that must be done just so before she would receive her pocket money. Her mother inspected her bed every morning to ensure it was made properly, and it was Amy's job to dust and hoover her bedroom every Saturday morning, whatever her plans might be. If she was meeting friends, she simply had to get up earlier to ensure it was done before she left the house.

One day, when she was ten years old, not long before she sat the entrance exam for Blake's, a girls' fee-paying academic institution, she came home from school to find that her dolls had all disappeared. 'You're too old to play with them now,' said her mother, when she went running to ask where they were. 'No need to cry – you've got a cupboard full of things to play with.' An array of toys and games disappeared on her mother's whim at other times too. (Fortunately, her teddy bear, Bingo, was never touched.)

Her father, Tim, was a cardiologist, one of the top in the field of interventional cardiology. He came from a well-off family, following his father's footsteps by attending an elite boarding school where, at his own admission, he was one of those 'annoying boys' who excelled at both sports and academic subjects. He met her mother when he was a registrar on his way up the career ladder.

Judith Smith was a nurse, who had grown up as the bookish daughter of a grocer and his wife, the only one of their four children to pass her Eleven Plus and attend a grammar school. Although highly intelligent, and drawn towards the sciences, she had been steered – like most of the girls at her school – towards the arts. With neither the confidence nor the encouragement to consider applying for university, she instead opted for nursing – it was that or secretarial work. By the time it dawned on her that she was at least an equal in intelligence to the doctors she worked alongside, it was too late for a career change. She had a house and a husband by then, and her only child would soon be on the way.

Frustrated by her own thwarted ambitions, she pushed Amy hard, often more vocal about her objectives than her husband. Sometimes it seemed as if nothing could meet her impossible standards. When Amy sailed through her local junior school, consistently getting excellent reports and regularly commandeered by the teacher to help her with some of the less able pupils, she assumed she would shine at her next school, too. And she did – but competition was fierce, as there were other very able pupils.

One of them in particular was always snapping at Amy's heels in the mid-term tests and end-of-year exams. Even so, when Jess beat Amy by one mark in the maths exam, Amy couldn't help but admire her adversary. But her mother was appalled. Doubly so when Jess was made head girl and Amy her deputy. She demanded to know if it was a mistake. Wasn't it supposed to be the other way round?

The three of them had gone for a meal in the clubhouse at her father's golf club to celebrate her A level results – A stars in biology, chemistry and maths, and an A in English literature – and acceptance at her first choice of university, the Royal Veterinary College in London. By then, Tim and Judith had come round to their daughter's choice of career. Perhaps for Amy, the thought of being compared to her father for the rest of her career was too much to contemplate.

Amy had felt a sense of freedom as soon as her mother left her that day in her north London hall of residence. She loved everything about the course: the lectures, the practical assignments, the essays. She loved the diverse mix of students and teaching staff, who came from all over the UK and overseas. Even without her parents breathing down her neck, Amy was as driven as ever. She couldn't help it. That determination to come top never left her. And come top she usually did.

She loved having London on her doorstep – even if, in truth, she preferred to spend her time working. When she did allow herself a break, she found she preferred to be alone instead of joining her new friends in the pub or at a party. The first student shindig she attended had horrified her. People getting blind drunk, smoking weed, disappearing into bedrooms. Students who usually seemed so serious when she sat beside them in the lecture theatre, talking to her overenthusiastically with flushed, slightly manic faces. She was still invited to parties, but went to few. If she wasn't studying, she was happy reading, a passion borne from a young age and one she could thank her mother for.

And then a new love came along.

Amy had never considered herself a natural athlete when she was at school, and was often picked last when it came to choosing teams. After one humiliation too many, she had rather lost her confidence in any sort of sporting activity, reserving the competitive side of her nature for the classroom. She had therefore been surprised to discover how much she enjoyed cross-country running when the opportunity to do it came along, but sadly that had only been an option for one term. Then, during freshers' week, she'd lingered for just a second too long by the stall, and had been convinced to join the running society. 'You look like a runner,' the society president had told her, and with her tallish, lean frame and long legs, Amy wondered if she should try it.

That was it. She was smitten.

After joining the group for a few runs, she found she actually preferred her own company. She discovered Hampstead Heath, and as she ran past ponds and through woodland, could hardly believe such idyllic sights were still in the heart of London. It did get busy, but she learnt to avoid weekends, setting off as early as she could. On summer mornings, she often aimed for before six, enjoying the relative peace, though even at that hour there were a few other keen souls. She could never resist lingering over the view of the city skyline from Parliament Hill. It was almost too perfect – like a painted backdrop in a film. *I will never tire of looking at that*, she thought.

***

There was no time to run over the next few days. Not only were two vets on holiday, another was on long-term sick leave, and Robert wasn't always able to find locum cover. After her shifts, she was often on call for the rest of the evening, and once was asked to remain on call all night. This meant that she was effectively on duty for thirty-six hours. Fortunately, her services hadn't been required, but she had found it hard to sleep, waiting for the pager beep that never came.

She accepted it without fuss, but Ruby voiced her complaints.

'What happened to work-life balance?' Ruby said to her one morning. 'Yesterday I had a woman who insisted on an appointment even though everyone was fully booked. I said – *very politely* – that she would have to wait until today, but she starts throwing her toys out the pram, insisting she speaks to the boss. Well, Robert only goes and starts looking through the diary, seeing who can squeeze her in. I said I'd already done that! He ended up seeing her himself, but only because you lot were run off your feet already.' She shook her head. 'It's not right. No wonder Suze hasn't come back to work yet. Between you and me, I don't think she will.'

Suze was the vet who was on sick leave. No one had spoken about it much, but everyone knew that she had been suffering from stress.

'It's not much fun for you either, Ruby. I couldn't do your job, that's for sure.'

Some days were OK. On others, Amy went home wondering if she had done enough. If she could *ever* do enough. One day she saw a young Cocker Spaniel with an injury that she suspected might have been inflicted by its owner. The man was pleasant, affable, even, but something about his manner and the evasive way he answered her questions stirred her suspicions. When he had left, she asked Sam what she thought. Sam wasn't sure, but admitted to something feeling 'a bit off'.

Amy vowed to speak to Robert, but with back-to-back appointments that afternoon and the following days little better, it wasn't until a week or so later that she remembered. She was disgusted at herself. How could she have allowed so much time to elapse? Robert didn't think he could report anything from what she had told him, but promised to flag the owner if he came in again. Amy felt dissatisfied, both with herself and her practice.

***

After a rare day off, Amy was about to go to bed when she remembered an email from her boss that she'd purposely delayed reading. She opened it, finding it was a thank you to the team for all their hard work. Robert assured them he was well aware that they were all taking the strain at present, due to absent colleagues, but asked them to be patient for just a little longer as he was hoping to recruit not one but two new vets along with two more nurses.

Amy sighed. It all sounded good on paper, but would it even make much of a difference? Wouldn't it simply mean a greater number of customers rather than a more manageable workload for each vet? Only time would tell, but she didn't feel very optimistic about it.

Another email informed her a subscription to *Runner's Weekly* was renewed, one was from her mother, attaching a link to an interview with her old schoolfriend, Jess, now working for Médecins Sans Frontières; yet another was from a name that sounded only vaguely familiar.

Amy spotted the word 'Grassdale' in the subject line. Of course! That was the village where the veterinary practice she had applied to was based. She could see, even without opening the email, that it began with, 'I am delighted to—' Oh heck, they must be offering her an interview. Would it really be worth trekking all the way up to Yorkshire for a job she was unlikely to get? It might just be a telephone interview, though, or on Zoom. Well, that could be worth a shot, if only to satisfy her curiosity …

She opened it. The email was from Mark Jeffreys, the practice owner, who said how impressed he had been with her application. There was no mention of an interview; nor, it seemed, was there any problem with her lack of experience, but instead he asked if she would complete an attached questionnaire.

She opened the document and scanned it quickly; it looked straightforward enough. There were some multiple-choice questions first, the tricky sort in which more than one answer could be correct, but she knew where the traps lay in answering those. Then there were some case studies providing various symptoms for her to diagnose. That section was followed by a couple of scenario-based problems, one involving a farmer and another a difficult pet owner. Ha! She certainly knew all about the latter. There was a final section, which seemed to test her interpersonal skills and ability to work within a team. She knew she wasn't always the best team player, but she could be when push came to shove.

Although she was still not entirely sure why she had applied for the job in the first place, and even though it was late, and she had been on her way to bed, she found herself completing the questionnaire. As far as Amy was concerned, if you were going to do something: do it properly. She focused her mind as if she was resitting her final exams. It took a little longer than she'd expected, but she was happy with the result, and fired it off before she could talk herself out of it. Then she went to bed, with visions of farmyards and country lanes dancing around in her brain, which was now too active to allow her to fall asleep as quickly as usual.

By the time she returned home the following day, Mark Jeffreys had already replied. She opened the email. Her eyes widened. She had to read it two or three times over to be sure she'd understood.

'Dear Ms Ashton,' it began. 'I am delighted to offer you the position of veterinary surgeon in our practice here in Grassdale. We are a small team, so it is important to us to ensure we've found the right candidate. Please ring me as soon as possible if you would like to accept the offer, or if you have any outstanding questions.'

It went on to include further details, and to state that a start date as soon as possible would be ideal, although they would understand if she had a notice period.

Amy could feel her heart racing. She went to fetch a glass of water from the kitchen, then sat down and read the email again. There was something a little too perfect about it. Was it all too good to be true? But then, who would play a practical joke on her? Who even knew that she had applied? No one. All the same, she scrutinised the email address, checked every dot and every letter in case it was a scam, but it looked legit. She felt excited and terrified at the same time. She didn't think she had a hope in hell of getting this job, and now that she had been offered it, she had no idea what to do.

Something still seemed strange. Why were they so desperate? Surely it was most irregular to be offered a job without both sides meeting each other first? Was something fishy going on? Perhaps they were building a nuclear power station at the bottom of the village? Perhaps the practice owner was a tyrant who made Robert look like Mother Teresa?

Her imagination spun into overdrive. She googled Grassdale again, this time scouring news instead of pretty pictures, and found a local website run by someone called Mary. There were photos from the church summer fair, a 'polite' notice about parking outside the store, and a warning to the persistent offender who was not picking up their dog's mess. 'Special measures' would be taken if this continued.

Amy uttered a dry laugh as she wondered what these measures might be. A team of vigilantes patrolling the green? DNA testing of all the dogs in the neighbourhood? However, if this was the biggest problem in the village, there seemed little to worry about. There was no mention of the veterinary practice, other than a listing in the 'Useful Addresses' section.

Trustpilot reviews of it were uniformly excellent.

'Mr Jeffreys showed great compassion in treating my old dog, Rufus. I can't recommend him or his team highly enough.'

'Damian has such a lovely manner! Poppy absolutely adored him!'

The local newspaper was based in a town about ten miles away. Its lead story covered the prize winners at the agricultural show the day before. It was illustrated with several photos, including a bizarre one of sheep that looked as if they had spent the day at the hairdresser's, their wool dyed in blues and reds, and one of a man holding a homegrown carrot whose shape resembled Bugs Bunny. She googled 'Mark Jeffreys' on the paper's website. There was nothing related to his work as a vet, but a man of the same name – she assumed it was him – said that new ringers were always welcome at St John the Baptist's Church in Grassdale.

Nothing irregular – although she wondered, as she browsed, what North London folk would make of gundog parades or a ferret roadshow.

So it was a genuine email – *had she secretly hoped it wasn't?* Her mind was running wild with conflicting thoughts. One voice said, 'We're in a rut. We've gotta get out of here and this is exactly what we need!' while another, just as convincingly, said, 'Hold on a minute! Isn't this all a bit drastic? We've rarely stepped foot in the countryside other than the odd weekend away, now you're seriously considering living there? Besides, do you even want to join a new practice?'

She debated calling her best friend, Penny. They had met at primary school, after which Penny had gone to the local comp while Amy went to Blake's. But they had remained close. Twenty years later, Amy still felt grateful to Penny, who had picked her as a partner for a class project when they were seven years old. She hadn't been able to believe that this popular, exuberant girl had chosen her, and that she remained her friend ever since.

She picked up her phone, but hesitated. She was pretty sure she knew what Penny's reaction would be. Penny would think it was crazy, totally out of character – and therefore totally the right thing for her to do. 'Go for it, girl!' she would say. But suppose she objected? Suppose she threw a list of practical things at Amy to consider? She didn't want to be swayed by such logistics right now. She knew deep down what her decision was. She was ready to throw caution to the wind. It had all begun that day with the guinea pig woman, but really, she had known in her bones for a while that she was ready for a change – that there was no point in living in the capital when she was no longer reaping the benefit of everything the big city had to offer. All that London-living meant to her these days was an astronomical rent and selfish neighbours.

She drained the remains of her glass of water as if she was knocking back a shot of vodka, then plonked the glass down at her feet and drew a deep breath. She had nothing to lose. She had never turned down a challenge yet. She pressed 'Reply' and started typing.

She finished the email, hesitated for a few seconds, then pressed 'Send'. She closed her laptop and gazed out of the window for a while before she went to cook her tea, wondering what on earth she had done.

3

'Oh no! You can't go!' Ruby pulled her into a hug in mock outrage when she told her of her plans, after discussing her notice period with Mr Richards. 'I won't let you!' She added, 'It sounds exciting, though. The countryside! I'm dead jealous!'

Amy wondered if she really was. It was hard to picture Ruby in a rural setting, what with her concerts and posh meals and addiction to matcha lattes. Her boyfriend had recently taken her to a restaurant that had just been awarded a single Michelin star. She said it was delicious, but she could have eaten both their portions and still been hungry.

She cast Amy an odd look. 'You are sure it's *you*, though, aren't you? I mean, won't you miss all … *this*?' She waved an arm around, indicating not only the practice, but the wider world outside. The buzz of the city.

'Well, I'll miss all of you lot,' Amy admitted, while thinking that 'you lot' encompassed only two or three of her colleagues.

Sam was even more practical in her reservations.

'Isn't it a different kind of work there? Farm animals rather than pets?'

'Well, actually, a bit of both, I think.'

'Freezing cold cow sheds in the middle of winter? Sheep stuck in snowdrifts? Rather you than me!'

Amy, who had been in Hexham in the summer, hadn't really considered that.

The next day, Sam said to her, 'I looked that place up, Amy – Grassdale, you said? It's in the middle of nowhere! Blimey! You *are* brave!'

Amy shrugged. 'It doesn't have to be forever.'

***

She was surprised how little sorrow she felt as she started to pack up her belongings in her rented flat. Everything she was taking had to fit into her little peppermint green Fiat 500, which meant leaving expendable items behind, some of which she was able to drop off at her family home in Guildford a few days before leaving. Despite having owned the car for a couple of years, she had rarely driven it, even preferring to take the train to visit her parents when it was feasible. Not that she minded London traffic; with all the stopping and starting it simply required copious amounts of patience. But would she be nervous on motorways and country roads? These were questions she hadn't considered before.

Her parents had been as astonished by the news as her colleagues. After offering somewhat muted congratulations, there had been the expected comment on whether Amy was wasting her top-class degree and expensive education. Well, they may not have actually used the word 'expensive', but it was implied. Amy knew she'd had opportunities not available to everyone, and was grateful, but hated how she felt obliged to justify the decisions she made, even now.

She told her parents that as far as she was concerned, she was advancing her career, not hindering it.

'The work will be more varied. I'll have experiences I'd never have in London.'

'But darling,' her mother persisted, 'where is this place? What will you do for a social life?'

They were drinking their coffee on the patio, overlooking the garden. The outdoor space was the pride and joy of her parents. The large lawn was dotted with circular, beautifully tended flowerbeds. The dahlias appeared magnificent: one bed of delicate pastel shades, another flaunting deep red and burnt orange pompoms. Since taking early retirement a couple of years ago, Judith spent most of her spare time in the garden. On Sundays, she and her husband worked there together if he didn't have research to do or lectures to prepare; he cut the lawn, tidied hedges, pruned and weeded, while she completed more of the intricate jobs, and planned for the next season.

Amy couldn't admit to her mother that, despite living in one of the coolest parts of London, she didn't have much of a social life these days. Somehow she had fallen out of the habit of accepting invitations. She was sociable enough; despite her naturally reserved nature, people liked her. (Well, everyone apart from the guinea pig woman!) Her ex, Jake, had always been organising something for them to do together. It had been overwhelming, at times. Smothering, even. In the end, though he had been the one to leave, she had practically pushed him out the door. Now, a combination of an exhausting job and no one to boss her around meant that she was getting used to spending most of her free time on her own.

'I know you'll think I'm silly ...' her mother looked at Amy, then focused on something at the far end of the garden, 'but at your age you do have to think about things like young men and ... romance!' She gave an embarrassed laugh. 'If this village you're off to is full of old farmer-types, you might find yourself, well, stranded.'

'Oh, Mum, who said all farmers were old men? Anyway, it's easy enough to meet people these days.'

Her mother studied her over her coffee cup.

'You know, apps and what-not.'

Her mother put her cup down sharply on its saucer. 'Darling, I don't think a girl like you would *ever* need to resort to that sort of thing.'

Amy shrugged. She had never used a dating app herself, but that was simply because she had neither wanted nor needed to. Even if she had been eager to meet a new man, there was so little time in her life these days, what with work, and running, and the further studies that were required to stay up to date with the latest developments in veterinary medicine. The whole effort of assessing someone's compatibility from a few words and a photo, deciding to meet, getting to know them – those hours of small talk – felt like simply too much investment for what would probably lead to nothing.

Thinking she was on safer ground, she added, 'Anyway, I've seen pictures of the area and it will be a wonderful place for running.'

Her mother gasped. 'You'll have to be *so* careful. You must have seen these television programmes where people have to be rescued because they've fallen and broken a bone in some godforsaken place. I don't want to be hearing about you on the news.'

Amy glanced at her father. He hadn't said much. Not that he often did, preferring to let his wife do the talking (or lecturing, as Amy often felt). He had become adept at cutting a diplomatic path between his wife and his daughter, trying to keep both of them happy – occasionally succeeding to do neither.

'Anything to add to that, Dad? Rabid sheep? Farmers with shotguns? Wild bulls?'

Even her mother managed to laugh, flapping her hand at her daughter's nonsense.

'Your mum's right, in a way; people *are* different in the country, especially ones who've been born and bred there. But we know you have to forge your own path, and you're young enough to try something new. Find out if it's for you or not.'

He stood up. 'Delicious coffee, dear. I'm going to pick some apples now. Fancy giving me a hand, Amy?'

Amy wondered if her father would impart any words of wisdom while they were together, but he said very little. She asked how he was getting on with his research, and he muttered about the lack of NHS funding not helping things, a common gripe of his.

Amy had insisted that she had no use for three carrier bags full of apples, but they were just a tiny portion of that summer's crop and she had ended up taking them back to London anyway. She was a competent enough cook, but she rarely ate puddings, and there was no point in filling her small freezer with sliced apples or apple puree when she was about to move. After taking a bag to work for her colleagues to help themselves to and leaving another on the doorstep of the rowdy couple downstairs – perhaps this act of generosity might calm them down? – she decided to take the remaining ones with her. Who knew, she might be about to turn into a domestic goddess in her new surroundings.

Amy closed the door to her flat for the last time. Her car was packed to the brim. There had been leaving drinks at work and she had received a generous book token, but there were no neighbours to say goodbye to and no one watched her go. As she left Camden and drove through Kentish Town and Tufnell Park, she felt a hint of sadness at leaving this part of London, which had been her home for several years; everything she could possibly need was on her doorstep or a short tube ride away. One place merged seamlessly with the next. Shops selling food from every nation, as well as endless coffee shops, nail bars, hair salons and tattoo parlours. A concert venue she had frequented in her student days, which had closed its doors after Covid, looked shabby and rundown.

When Amy approached the road where her old workplace was situated, she deliberately didn't look. She didn't want to start feeling nostalgic now. She'd taken the plunge, done something no one there expected her to do and deviated from the path her parents were so keen to pave for her. Perhaps – apart from her decision to study veterinary medicine in the first place – it was the first time she had done something solely for herself?

At Archway she picked up the A1. She would stay on this road for most of the journey, until she took a turning close to the city of Ripon and headed into the Dales. There were places she could have visited en route, but she would have to save them for another day. She didn't fancy leaving all her worldly belongings in the car just so that she could mooch around Peterborough or Stamford, though when she caught a glimpse of the latter, looking like a miniature medieval city with its golden church towers and steeples poking up through the other buildings, she made a mental note to visit another day.

The London traffic gave way to faster moving vehicles. Had there always been so many lorries on the roads? Amy's heart lurched when one of them indicated suddenly before pulling straight out in front of her. She was left with only a second to react and let out a yelp as she created space for the driver in front.

Relax Amy, she told herself. And after a while, she did. She found herself starting to anticipate the other drivers' moves more easily, though having two pairs of eyes would have been helpful at times.

It was lunchtime when she pulled into the service station near Cambridge to stretch her legs and buy a sandwich. Not fearful of being judged while eating alone, Amy was used to doing things on her own, and plonked herself in the seating area of the large food court. Casting her eyes over the other travellers, she wondered who they could be and where they were going.

Was anyone else making a life-changing journey like she was? It was September, and a lot of the other people were older couples, probably taking their own vacations now that the school summer holidays were over. Some were chatting quietly, others eating in companionable silence. A surprising number were as glued to their phones as teenagers might be.

She wondered if she would be half of a long-married couple by the time she was their age, but dismissed the thought. It was hard to imagine meeting anyone she would want to spend the rest of her life with these days. She could blame Jake for that. Thanks to him, marriage or a long-term relationship had started to look more like a tether than a partnership. *Surely it doesn't have to be like that, though?*

While Amy enjoyed people-watching, she knew that she'd better get a move on. There was still a long way to go, and the journey was less straightforward when she left the A1.

It had still felt like summer in London, but there were more signs of autumn the further north she drove. Sometimes a stray flash of red in a tree peeked out amongst otherwise green leaves, while others had turned copper all over. A sign reading 'THE NORTH' in bold capital letters gave her a pang of trepidation – a reminder that she was heading for a different land, perhaps one where southern city girls would not be so welcome.

In an area close to Sherwood Forest – had she even known it was real, and not some mythical place from British folklore? – the traffic ground to a halt. After half an hour vehicles started to move again, trickling slowly along until the three lanes filtered into one as they passed a jack-knifed lorry. It was a long delay, meaning that it was late afternoon when she reached her turn-off. Thank God she'd stopped for food.

She had studied the map before setting off again, noting a couple of road names, fairly confident she had the route visualised in her head. (Amy was very much her father's daughter and preferred an old-fashioned map to Satnav.) But after driving for what felt like hours down a B road, with no familiar names on the signposts to gather her bearings, she realised that she must have made a wrong turn somewhere. She had to drive another mile at least before she could find somewhere safe to pull in and consult her road atlas. She backtracked for several miles before finding the turning she had missed. It was after six, and she wanted to arrive while it was light. When *would* it get dark? She had no idea.

Her relief was enormous when she came to the large village of Crowdale and saw the name Grassdale on a signpost for the first time. Beyond Crowdale, the road became narrower. In one or two places, it didn't look wide enough for two-way traffic. She wondered what she would do if she met a vehicle coming in the opposite direction. The grassy verges were tight, flanked by unforgiving drystone walls. She supposed that two cars could pass each other, at a squeeze, but what if she met a tractor? She felt relief at the sight of every passing place, and lingered on each one, though as the road was winding, she couldn't see oncoming traffic until it was almost upon her.

In the end, the only other traffic she encountered – apart from a couple of cars which she found she could navigate easily thanks to the neat size of the Fiat – was a couple of heavy-laden bicycles. Wobbling all over the road, their riders waved at her, gratefully, when she slowed down as they passed. Ten minutes after leaving Crowdale, she arrived in Grassdale. Lauren, who owned Ivy Cottage, the place she was renting, had explained how to find it.

'Make sure you turn left as soon as you get to the junction; the cottage is the first building on the right on the main street, several metres back from the road. If you miss it and carry on over the crossroads, you'll be out of the village almost as soon as you've arrived.'

She recognised the cottage instantly. It looked smaller than in the photo she had seen, but just as pretty. A solid, low-lying white-washed house, set behind a wide strip of green that ran down the middle of the road. It was rather like a child's drawing of a house, perfectly symmetrical, with two small deep-set square windows on the first floor, two slightly larger rectangular ones on the ground floor, and a solid wooden front door. She parked the car on a patch of gravel at the side of the house.

She remained in the car for a couple of minutes. She was here. She had done it. She had never embarked on such a long drive on her own, and was pleased with herself, if slightly frazzled. But there was a niggling feeling too, knowing that she was actually at the beginning of a journey, not the end of one.

It was starting to get dark now, so she decided she'd better unpack the car while she could see what she was doing.

Lauren had told her where to find the key – round the back, under the large stone beside the door of the conservatory. The wooden gate that led into the garden was stiff, but opened with a sharp shove. The garden was fairly large with a lawn and borders round three sides. She'd not had a garden to call her own since living with her parents. She almost laughed when she saw a low-hanging, gnarly tree, laden with tiny red apples. At this rate, she'd be eating apples for ever more! Amy located the key and thirty seconds later opened the door to her new home.

A hallway with a flagstone floor in soft shades of brown and pewter led to the other downstairs rooms: a long narrow kitchen on the left, running the length of the house; the conservatory – clearly a more recent addition, still warm from the day's sunshine – at the back; dining room/study and living room on the right. She poked her head very quickly into each before heading back out to empty the car.

The village was deserted. The shop on the other side of the road – signposted 'Grassdale Store' via a large green board above the door, in elegant lettering – was closed. Well, it would be – it was nearing six-thirty. No twenty-four-hour corner shops or branches of Tesco Metro here. She heaved a suitcase out of the car and lugged it into the house, leaving it in the hallway. As she was returning from the car carrying her next load, a cardboard box containing books and papers far heavier than she remembered, she spotted a lone figure striding up the road, walking pole in each hand. The person was so swaddled in their woolly hat and waterproofs that she couldn't tell if it was a man or a woman. Amy removed a hand supporting the bottom of the box to offer a quick wave; it was awkward, but felt the right thing to do, especially as there appeared to be no one else around other than the pair of them. As she did, the bottom of the box split open and most of the contents thudded onto the ground, while some of the apples – which were in a carrier bag in the same box – skittered away from her down the sloping road.

Damn!

The walker raised an arm back and carried on, oblivious to her plight, as Amy crouched down to pick everything up. A couple of books were battered, and some cuttings and loose papers had blown onto the grass verge. She consoled herself with the thought that at least there had been nothing breakable in the box. But now, someone else was approaching. A man walked towards her on the narrow cobbled pavement that ran along the front of the houses on this side of the road. He must have come from one of the cottages further down.

Some of the apples rolled towards him and he bent to pick them up before heading to the green, where he began to gather up the papers. He wore an off-white baggy T-shirt and tracksuit bottoms, and had an old-fashioned pudding-basin haircut. He smiled, without quite making eye contact, as he put the items back in the box. Holding the bottom of it securely, he nodded towards the door before carrying it inside for her. She allowed him to do it, even though she found his silence slightly unnerving.

'Thank you!' she gushed, when he came out, 'I really appreciate it.' He nodded with a tight smile again, and headed to the open boot of the car to fetch another box. Amy tried to dissuade him, but the man seemed compelled to help her. He continued to do this, ensuring he retrieved all the heavier loads, stacking everything neatly in the hall until the car was empty.

'Thank you so much!' said Amy again.

He had a solemn face, but she thought she detected a hint of amusement.

'You're welcome,' he said in a gravelly voice, and continued on his way before she had the opportunity to properly introduce herself.

What a strange man.

Now that it was all piled up together, she was surprised to see how much stuff she had brought. It took up most of the hallway. The cottage was fully furnished and equipped with everything she would need, but she had packed spare bedding and extra towels to be on the safe side – and because she was fussy about good-quality cotton sheets. She had also brought her fancy coffee machine, as she couldn't find one on the list of kitchen appliances.

The kitchen was sleek and surprisingly modern – cupboards and drawers in beige wood with brushed steel handles, a granite work top, and the same matching flagstone floor as the hall. She filled the kettle and located her teabags, which she'd kept handy in a small rucksack. She hadn't brought much in the way of food, other than a few tins left over from her larder in Camden, reasoning that she would stock up on fresh goods when she arrived. But she had purchased a small carton of milk on the journey. She could smell it as soon as she opened it. How had it gone off so quickly? She looked at the date. Not yet up to its 'best before', but something had made it turn. She cursed under her breath. She had been dying for this cup of tea. She tipped the milk down the sink and sat down at the kitchen table, grimacing at her first sip of black tea until, slowly, it became more palatable.

As she drank, and heated a ready-meal from the motorway services in the microwave, she read the folder containing the house instructions. Ivy Cottage had been a holiday home for a few months before Amy took out her twelve-month lease. She had understood from Lauren, during their brief email communication, that the cottage once belonged to her grandparents and she had spent much of her childhood with them. Lauren was now married, with a child, and lived in Crowdale, the place Amy had driven through. Her grandparents had both died within a few months of each other a couple of years back.

After eating, Amy examined the rest of the house. She could see that Lauren had spent a fortune renovating it for visitors. The bathroom was as high-spec as the kitchen, with a powerful shower and a freestanding bath. The dining room was small and functional, but would be perfect as an office. It contained two bookcases, one of them crammed with books. The living room had a cosier, more old-fashioned feel, with an open fireplace, a faded leather settee and two armchairs. Fairy lights were strung on a tree-like structure in the corner of the room. Both the kitchen and living room had seats built into the deep windows overlooking the road. The cushion covers for these seats were embroidered with small birds and flowers. They were beautiful, if slightly faded, and Amy wondered if Lauren's grandmother had been the seamstress.

She decided to have a shower and go to bed early, remembering, just before undressing, that her sponge bag was in the footwell of the passenger seat. She had kept it handy so that she could freshen up on the journey if she needed to. She opened the front door and was shocked to see total darkness. There were no street lights, with not even a flicker of light from another house visible. She unlocked the car from where she stood, seeing the vehicle headlights blink in the darkness, but hesitated before she ventured further. Who knew what was lurking round the corner …?

Don't be an idiot, Amy. You've got this.

She forced herself to walk to the car, not daring to glance sideways or behind her, knowing that every shape she saw would take the form of some ghoulish apparition. An animal yowled somewhere in the distance. She opened the car door, grabbed her sponge bag, and hurried back to the house.

Welcome to the countryside, Amy! she thought to herself.

4

When Amy woke up, at around her usual time of six-thirty, for a couple of seconds she had no idea where she was. She had slept soundly, despite the strange room and new bed, but it had been unnerving, at first. The silence in the room had been startling to her ears. In London, it was never quiet. Even at night, she heard traffic on her road, people talking in the street outside, comings and goings in the neighbouring flats, not to mention the bickering couple downstairs. And with no artificial light stealing through her curtains, the blackness made her panic, to the extent that she had switched her bedside lamp back on, got out of bed and opened her curtains slightly, leaving a gap of a few inches, so that the early daylight would seep into her room.

Her bedroom, with its walls thick like a cave's, felt cool, but not uncomfortably so. The duvet was thick, feathery and warm, and after her little adjustment, she had fallen asleep almost instantly.

Her bedroom was at the back of the house. She went to the window and saw the view in daylight for the first time. A large field on which sheep were grazing in the misty early-morning light blurred into rougher moorland which rose to a purple-coloured top. The sky was a perfect blue. After dressing and going to see what she could have for breakfast – bemoaning her lack of milk – she opened the fridge to see a pint of semi-skimmed milk and a small pack of butter. She could have had her tea with milk after all! On a small table in the hallway, leaning against a pot which contained a spare set of keys, was an envelope with her name on it. Inside was a note.

Dear Amy

A huge Yorkshire welcome from my family and me to Ivy Cottage! I hope you have everything here that you need, but should there be anything I can provide to make you more comfortable, please let me know.

You'll find tea and coffee in one of the cupboards, also a locally made cake (not by me, I'm afraid!), a loaf of bread and some jam. There's milk in the fridge. I bet you'll be desperate to put your feet up with a cuppa after your long journey!

We all wish you a very happy stay. I look forward to meeting you soon.

Kind regards

Lauren

Why didn't I see this last night? She could have kicked herself! She would have loved a proper cup of tea and a slice of the scrummy-looking lemon drizzle cake after the uninspiring microwave lasagna she had eaten the night before. She managed to chuckle about it as she made toast, slathering it with the strawberry jam from the cupboard (also handmade, judging by the label), then sat in the kitchen window seat to eat it and drink her tea.

A group of walkers marched past from the higher part of the village on the other side of the junction. They were making an early start. She knew that the village lay just off the route of the Dale and Valley trail, a long-distance footpath that began in South Yorkshire and ended in the Scottish Borders. She was also aware that Grassdale was a popular place to break the journey.

She scoured the house details again: instructions for all the appliances, recycling information – there was a communal recycling centre behind the shop rather than the doorstep collection she was used to in London – a map of the village, a list of interesting places nearby, and other useful addresses.

The next time she looked up, she saw that the shop had opened. A car pulled up, its driver dashed briefly inside, emerged clutching a newspaper, and drove off. A man in a long brown apron came out of the shop, holding a large sandwich board which he propped on the pavement. Amy couldn't read what it said because of the angle at which it had been placed. He went back inside and returned with a small metal table, followed by two chairs. *Café society*, thought Amy, with a smile. *Wait till I tell Mum!* Next to arrive was a small delivery van with a Crowdale address emblazoned on the side.

At the junction itself, a few metres higher up from the store, was a building she knew to be Grassdale Veterinary Practice, her new workplace, although she could only see a side wall from where she was sitting. Fancy being able to see her place of work from her home! (She hoped, however, that it wouldn't be too close for comfort.) She had chatted a couple of times with Mark, her new boss, on the phone. She'd meet him and the rest of the team tomorrow. For now, there were other things to get on with.

Amy set to work unpacking her belongings and deciding where to store each. She was her mother's daughter, and a little obsessive about order and cleanliness, but the cottage was already spotlessly clean. The drawers in her bedroom – a solid, old-fashioned piece of oak furniture, with ornate metal pulls – were lined with rose-scented paper. She ran her finger along the tops of the doorframes – not a trace of dust to be seen.

She put her professional books and papers in the empty bookcase in the dining room, which she had now designated as her study. She kicked herself for not having bought some new novels with her book token before leaving London, as she preferred bookshops to online shopping and she was surely a long way from a chain bookshop here. Oh well, she supposed it would have to be Amazon.

Through the open window of the front bedroom, she could hear banging in the street outside. The noise continued. It took her a while to realise that someone was knocking at her front door. She dashed downstairs, but to her surprise the door opened before she reached it – had she really left it unlocked all night? – and a voice called out, 'Anyone home?'

Amy saw a tall, slim woman standing in the hallway. She was probably somewhere in her fifties, with reddish-brown hair scraped back into a ponytail. Her skin was tanned, with a few darker brown patches, and Amy was struck by her eyes, which were very blue. She was wearing jeans, lace-up leather boots and a long woollen plum-coloured jacket – shabby but good quality – over a V-neck olive-green vest top.

'Hi! Mary from next door!' The woman extended an arm. Her hand felt large for someone of such a slim build. Her handshake was very firm, her palm coarse. With her other hand she passed Amy an apple.

'Found it on your doorstep. Looked very symbolic – though I couldn't say what it means.'

'Err, cheers. I'm Amy.' She was almost too surprised to speak.

'You didn't mind me letting myself in, did you? I'd been banging for ages and I was getting concerned.'

Amy did mind, but seemed to be finding it hard to express her thoughts. Mary waved a key before Amy's eyes before slipping it back in her pocket.

'Lauren thought it a good idea I had the spare, as I'm so much nearer than she is.'

Ah, so she hadn't left the door unlocked. As if she would. Mary had simply 'let herself in' as if *that was normal*.

Mary surveyed the scene in front of her – the boxes yet to be unpacked were still stacked neatly, thanks to Amy's mystery assistant last night, but there were a lot of them.

'Let me know if you need a hand, won't you. But first, if you don't mind, I promised Lauren I'd explain the *dodgy* tap to you.' She pronounced 'dodgy' in a conspiratorial way, a glint in her eye. 'All these old houses have got their little quirks. A bit like me, ha ha! Though I'm not quite as old as they are!'

Before Amy could say a word, Mary had walked into the kitchen.

'Off, on, then off again. Not too tight. Otherwise it drips. Works every time.'

Amy watched the demonstration, but could only nod in reply. Mission accomplished, Mary leant back against the sink and smiled.

'Piece of cake. Talking of which, shall I put the kettle on.' She didn't really say it as a question, but held an imaginary cup in the air.

Still rather stunned, Amy said, 'It's fine. I'll do it. Tea? Coffee? Do sit down.'

'Tea please.'

Her neighbour sat at the kitchen table. Amy busied herself making the drinks while Mary continued to talk.

'You're a vet, Lauren said. From London? I was there myself for almost forty years, but I was born here. Only came back a few years ago. Still getting used to it. What do you think of this place?' She wafted an arm around to indicate the room and the rest of the house.

She continued, 'Lauren's done a great job, hasn't she? It must have cost a bit. It was hard for her, with the old folks passing on – and so close together, too – but that's life, isn't it? You have to move on. She had it on Airbnb for a while, then she had a film crew. You know that wartime series about the POWs on the farm? Can't remember for the life of me what it was called, but some of them stayed here. Mind, they left it in a right mess. Not particularly friendly, either.'

She gave Amy a quizzical look, as if trying to decide if she was going to be any better, before changing the subject.

'I thought you'd have pets. I don't have any myself.'

Amy placed two mugs on the table and sat down opposite Mary. 'I don't have any either. Too busy.'

'They're a tie, aren't they? My parents had a cat. She was almost twenty when she died, a housecat by then. I had to organise my life around her.' She abruptly sat up straight. 'Anyway, tell me what you want to know about your new home. All things Grassdale: I'm your woman! It helps having lived here and then away for so long.' She adopted a sinister tone. 'I see things the others don't. Ha!' She uttered a cackle. 'You look worried, Amy! Honestly, most of the folks here are lovely. They'd do anything for a fellow resident.'

'Thank you, Mary. I intend to have a walk around very soon and see the place for myself.' Amy hoped it might sound like a hint. She didn't want this woman sitting here all morning. 'It was getting dark when I arrived last night, so I haven't had the chance for a proper look.'

'I know, I was looking out for you in case you needed a hand. I promised Lauren I would pop over. But I had to nip into Crowdale and got back later than I'd intended. You must have arrived when I was out. Sorry about that. Is there anything I can do for you now?'

Mary watched her expectantly. Amy really just wished she would go away at this point. The incessant chatter was exhausting.

'Well, maybe after I've—'

'You'll be needing a hand with the garden, no doubt. Being a vet in a place like this is busy work.' She dipped her head towards Amy, acknowledging that she'd been listening to what she had told her. 'It doesn't look that big, but it's a lot for one person to keep on top of. Dan's the man for the job. You'll have better things to do than mow the lawn, as well as all the weeding. And I'm telling you, things grow like crazy here.'

She laughed, then stood up suddenly.

'Thanks a lot for the tea. I'll love you and leave you. You know where I am.'

Amy showed her to the door and breathed a sigh of relief as she closed it behind her. What a woman! She hoped everyone in the village wasn't quite like her. What a whirlwind!

After her early breakfast, she was starving. She'd go for a walk and buy some essentials from the store on the way back.

5

Most of the houses in Grassdale were situated on a road known as 'The Street', with a few others dotted in clusters behind it. Amy would soon learn that locals called the two parts of this road New Street and Old Street, or other times, just to confuse her, it seemed, Upper Street and Lower Street – as though they were interchangeable. Ivy Cottage lay on Old or Lower Street, the original part of the village, where a collection of workers' cottages had sprung up a few centuries earlier, close to a neighbouring farm. They had been joined over time by other buildings, almost all with slate roofs.

Mary's house next door was a detached property, similar in size and appearance to Ivy Cottage, but after it came a terrace of five houses built in a rich brown stone, their doors and windows – all painted in matching pale blue – so tiny, they looked rather like dolls' houses. At five feet seven inches, Amy thought she might have to stoop to enter them. Further down the road – which sloped towards the river – after a couple of much larger, detached houses, was the pub, the Fox and Ferret. It didn't appear to be open yet.

She crossed to the other side of the road where two women were busily loading laundry bags into the boot of a small car. Amy guessed that they were cleaners, preparing the property for a new rental. In the small front garden, a thick metal ring was attached to a heavy stone, while ancient-looking tongs hung on a nail at the front of the building, presumably for decorative reasons. 'The Old Smithy', read the sign on the door. Amy smiled and said hello to the women, who responded with a polite wave.

'Gorgeous day,' said an elderly man as he passed her a few seconds later, dipping his head in greeting. And it was. The sky was an unbroken blue, even the wind was mild. It didn't feel much cooler than the city she had left behind, two hundred miles south.

Her face broke into a smile when she came to a bookshop. Really? She had somehow missed seeing that in her earlier research. She looked at the display in the window. Hardbacks of newly published books by big-name authors; books about the history and geography of the Yorkshire Dales and North Yorkshire Moors, including one about lead mining in the area; walking guides for the Dale and Valley footpath; a cookery book called *Autumn Feasts*. It also stocked second-hand books. In the window of the porch there were several notices about forthcoming events: the book group, the monthly meeting of the local history society, the screening of a film in the village hall. Another was about donations for the local food bank.

'Even in our beautiful part of the country, hunger is a problem for some. Please drop your fresh and dried goods off at Warren House and I will be happy to take them to the food bank in Crowdale. Much appreciated. Mary.'

One rather tatty notice, adorned with accomplished line drawings, said, *'Come and join us in The Snug for coffee while Tizz talks about his new book, Postmen of the Dales. Betty is making her famous parkin! Profits from book sales split between St John's bell fund and the food bank.'*

Postmen of the Dales! She must remember to tell Penny about that fascinating read! That would amuse her. *And what on earth was parkin?*

A larger window gave a partial view of The Snug, a coffee area in the bookshop, accessed through an archway and dotted with leather sofas, armchairs and low tables. One of the sofas was occupied by two women, and, realising that she now appeared to be staring straight at them, Amy hurried past, not wanting to seem nosy.

At the bottom of the road ran a narrow river, crossed by a picture-perfect humpback bridge, wide enough only for one car. Amy was thankful to only be driving her little Fiat on these roads. Beyond the bridge were a few more houses, most of them far larger than the others she had seen. This road was called Church Lane. The first house was The Old Rectory. It had a look of faded grandeur, its appearance spoilt somewhat thanks to the construction of half a dozen modern houses in its grounds, which must have been very extensive at one time. The church, which lay opposite it, was a very old one, possibly Saxon, thought Amy. Her father had enjoyed looking round old churches during family outings, something that had bored her stiff as a child. As an adult, she could understand his fascination.

Beyond the church were a few more houses, before the road petered out into a single-track lane that ran along the bottom of the hill overlooking the village. There would be time to explore there later. First, she wanted to see the rest of Grassdale.

She turned back the way she had come, passing the same buildings and her new home, and carried on over the crossroads to Upper Street. Here, each side of the road contained grander, Georgian-style houses. She saw from the signs in the windows that some of them were holiday homes, and two were bed and breakfast establishments. She guessed that the walkers she had seen earlier had come from one of these. One smart, three-storey house had an antiques shop on its ground floor. This road was steeper than Lower Street, and continued to rise as it wound away out of the village into the distance. There was a wide green down the middle of the road, with two wooden benches. A rope swing hung from a large tree.

She passed a young woman walking a dog, more hikers, some of them wrapped in waterproof coats and woollen hats, despite it being a warm day. An elderly couple, who looked like tourists, gazed through the antiques shop window before shuffling off down the road.

Turning back, Amy caught her first proper view of the veterinary practice, facing her at the crossroads. She had seen a photo online, so shouldn't have been surprised, but it looked smaller than she had anticipated, more like someone's home than a business. She knew that Mark, the owner, lived upstairs. Three cars were parked in front, and a sign indicated further parking behind. Not wanting to run into anyone just yet – she would be meeting her new colleagues soon enough – she didn't linger, heading into the village store.

The store occupied a corner position, and Amy could see now that the side of the building facing the main road contained a café, which had its own front door as well as being accessible through the shop. Two coffee establishments in a place this size wasn't bad! The table she had watched being put out earlier had been joined by a few more, one of them occupied by a hiker who appeared to be checking his feet for blisters.

In the store, the man in the apron she had seen earlier was stocking shelves. He turned round to say good morning as Amy entered. On a table in front of her was a collection of crates and wooden boxes of varying sizes. Displayed on these were jars of locally made jams, marmalades and sauces, bars of exotic-looking chocolate and packets of biscuits containing delicacies such as stem ginger and rose petals.

On a table to the side were wicker baskets of freshly baked bread, and boxes of eggs – not just hens' eggs but large goose eggs. Bunches of flowers stood in metal buckets on the floor. A rack of baskets on the back wall contained a wide array of vegetables, while pine shelving stocked more run-of-the-mill products.

There were also chill cabinets with both well-known and fancier brands of ready meals and frozen goods. At the right-hand end of the store was a small deli counter, while facing it at the opposite end was a Post Office sign, with stationery, newspapers and magazines on shelves beside it. Above an opening at the back of the shop, a sign read 'Community Café this way'.

'Can I help you, duck?'

Amy realised that she was standing there staring, like an idiot – *gosh, is my mouth hanging open?* She hadn't expected the store to be as well stocked as this, or anywhere near as fancy.

The woman who spoke to her was behind the Post Office counter. She appeared quite elderly – certainly old enough to be retired.

'Um, thank you. I'm not sure yet. I'm a little bit spoilt for choice!'

'We've got pretty much whatever you need.' It was the man who spoke now. 'Drinks are round the corner if you're looking for your favourite tipple. We're an off-licence too.'

'If you want something nice for your tea tonight,' said the lady, 'we've just had a delivery of some of Barry's steaks.' She spoke as if Amy would know exactly who Barry was. 'They'll go quickly, I'll tell you. Organic, you know.'

Amy – who almost never ate steak but was a sucker when she heard the word 'organic' – found herself strangely tempted by the suggestion. With a wicker basket on her arm – *had she picked it up herself or had it been foisted upon her?* – she perused the offerings, and found herself filling it with the same practised ease with which she filled her trolley on her twice-monthly trip to the supermarket in Camden. A few minutes later, it contained not one but two steaks, locally grown potatoes and corn on the cob, as well as various other groceries. At the last minute, she added a bunch of pink and yellow roses from one of the metal buckets – there was no one else to buy flowers for her these days, she reasoned, so why shouldn't she treat herself?

The assistant moved out from behind the Post Office counter to serve her at the other end of the shop. 'On holiday, duck?'

'Actually, no, I've just moved here.'

'The new one in Ivy Cottage?'

'That's me!'

'Well we're happy to have you, duck. Oh, and while you're here—'

She felt around in the vast pocket of her apron and pulled out a slip of paper which she handed to Amy.

'Something to explain how we operate.'

'Val, let her be! She's only just arrived,' scolded the man. In an apologetic tone, he said to Amy, 'The café is run by the locals, so we always need volunteers. But beware: she'll have you signing your life away if you're not careful!'

'If you want owt done, you have to ask for it,' said Val. 'We don't make a lot, but any profit goes back into the community so we all benefit. It's a good way of meeting new people too.' She gave Amy a meaningful look.

Amy took the slip of paper, paid for her groceries and thanked them both politely, before making a quick getaway. Her bags were heavy, and she was starving. That was potentially going to be one of the disadvantages of living here, she mused, thinking wistfully for a second of London: people were so involved in their own lives that they left you to your own devices in the city. It had always rather suited her.

As she walked up the path to Ivy Cottage, seeing it illuminated by daylight for the first time, Amy considered how pretty it was. It made her think of the cottages she'd read about in fairytales. In her mind, she pictured Lauren's grandparents, the previous owners, as the old-fashioned couple in one of her favourite childhood stories, *The Elves and the Shoemaker*. She wouldn't have been surprised to see a woman in a white bonnet peeking out through the kitchen window, and the shoemaker himself bent over his work table, at the other window. And yet it was her new home. She breathed a sigh of contentment as she went inside. She was excited by this fresh start.

***

After a cheese salad sandwich, Amy sat in the back garden sipping her herbal tea, enjoying the peace and quiet before setting off for her run. She'd spotted that there was a small metal bench outside her front door, but she knew she would feel too conspicuous sitting there. She wasn't quite ready for the number of people she expected to stop and talk to her; she might end up cornered by Val again, persuaded into something she didn't want to do! She made a mental note to buy more bird food for the feeder hanging from one of the trees. The birds were keeping their distance now that she was outside, but she had observed several different species from inside the house, a far larger and more varied selection than she ever saw in London.

***

Leaving a decent interval after her lunch, she set off for her run. She chose to turn right down Lower Street and head towards the river. She spotted Val from the shop in the front garden of one of the large houses over the bridge, after the church. Amy raised her hand in greeting, and while the lady looked confused at first, she waved anyway with a smile. Amy realised that Val probably didn't recognise her from earlier, now that she had donned her running gear. Her long strawberry-blonde hair was scraped into a low bun, which poked out of the back of her pink New York Mets baseball cap, a present from Jake after he had gone to the States on business. After their break-up she'd completed the ceremonious 'clear-out', but she couldn't quite let the hat go. These days the sentimental connections to it had withered, but it was still the perfect cap for a run.

The September sun was warm – almost too warm. She could hardly believe what a perfect day it was. All those misery guts in London telling her how cold it was 'up north'. *Well, I'm having the last laugh now.* The road narrowed, and soon became little more than a track. A sign warned of oncoming farm vehicles, but there was no trace of any traffic today.

As if channelling Amy herself, a deep peace seemed to have descended upon the valley. Down below, on her left, ran the river, partly hidden amongst the trees on its banks. To her right, an expanse of gorse-covered moor rose, steeply in places, to Ram's Seat. She could see some well-trodden routes heading up to the summit. The paths looked rocky and grew steeper the higher they got, but the summit appeared to be a long, flattish ridge. Amy had read in an online article that it was popular with runners, though care had to be taken as the ground was uneven. She would save that for another day. For now, she was keen to immerse herself in the surrounding nature and enjoy the downtime before starting her new role.

After a couple of miles on the track, Amy saw a gate ahead, with a sign reading 'Bottom Farm'. Unfamiliar with the route, she had no idea if there was public access through the farmyard. Fearing she may be about to trespass, Amy decided to find a way down to the river and return to the village following its course. However, while she could see a neat path on the other side of the water, the side she was on was overgrown and boggy. As her feet fell upon softer ground, she soon gave up and went back the way she had come in an attempt to save her trainers.

***

Amy returned from her run on a high, buzzing with exhilaration and the joy of her new surroundings. She could hardly believe that until now she'd endured running on crowded streets, breathing in noxious traffic fumes, having the odd near miss with entitled bicycle users who swore at her when she suddenly veered off in another direction as they came up behind her. 'Use your bell!' she'd yell at their backs after they almost collided. 'How was I expected to know you were there?!' Oh, and of course, the sheep wouldn't dare heckle the way the entitled men of the city would! *It truly is a breath of fresh air*.

As she drew closer, she saw someone hovering around the front of Ivy Cottage. The man crouched and peered through a window – *why is that the norm here?* – before putting something through the letterbox.

'Can I help you?'

He jumped when Amy appeared breathlessly behind him, panting from her exertions.

'Sorry! I didn't mean to startle you.' She was the one to feel guilty now.

'No bother. I'm Dan. You must be Amy. Mary said you might be needing a hand with the garden. I've got an apple-picker too. Saves faffing around with ladders. You can break your neck if you're not careful.'

When Amy didn't reply straightaway, he added, 'If it's not a great time, I can come back. I just happened to be passing.'

Amy suddenly felt claustrophobic. She'd so enjoyed being out in the open and running in peace. Now, with people appearing uninvited to her door, she felt irritated. She didn't remember telling Mary that she wanted a gardener. Mary may well have *suggested* it to her, but she had no recollection of agreeing. She had barely glanced at the garden besides her brief sit-down for an afternoon cuppa. Plus, she had never had her own garden, and the idea occurred to her that she might enjoy looking after this one herself. If she needed any tips, she could always ask her green-fingered parents.

'I'm sorry, but I think there's been a misunderstanding. I'm not looking for any help.' Then, catching her own tone and fearing it to be too harsh, she added, 'Not at the moment, anyway.'

She fished out her key. 'Thanks, though.'

'Well, if you change your mind, I posted you my card.'

She nodded with a tight smile and went inside, ensuring the door was firmly closed behind her. At least he wasn't as pushy as Mary. She'd envisioned him following her inside and making himself a cup of tea. She took off her shoes and put them in the conservatory to dry, then downed a large pint of water. *Is that banging on the door again? What the …?* Was there a sign on the door today inviting residents to treat this place like a second home? Sighing, she opened it expecting to see Dan. Instead, Mary was standing there.

'Hi Mary, look – I'm just in from a rather long run, but I don't really need any help with anything at the moment. Thank you.'

Mary looked bemused but took Amy's greeting in her stride. 'I took this parcel in for you before. It was left on your doorstep, which at one point would have been fine round here, but even Grassdale is changing now. In my parents' day, we didn't bother locking our doors. They once got home to find a stranger sitting with his feet up by their fire. Turned out he was visiting relatives in the village but had got the wrong house.' She bent down to pick up the box beside her and passed it to Amy. 'Hope everything's going well. You've certainly brought the good weather. Looks like you've caught the sun!'

Amy touched her face. She could feel it glowing. That was the trouble with having pale skin and reddish hair. She was the girl who used to go home from school with a pink nose after an afternoon on the hockey field in April. She was usually obsessive about wearing sunscreen at all times of year. Annoyed with herself for not being more careful and snapping slightly at Mary when all she really did was try to help, Amy sighed and thanked Mary for the parcel as she closed the door.

6

Amy's first day at the practice was finally here, beginning at eight in the morning. No excuses for arriving late on her first day – not that she had ever been late in London for any shifts, despite the odd bus strike or tube stuck in a tunnel. She simply had to cross the road, walk past the store, and the next building was Grassdale Practice, standing on a piece of land at the crossroads.

Mark, her new boss and the owner of the practice, had steely-grey hair, a ruddy complexion and a slight paunch. He had one of those loud, self-assured voices that was common in men of a certain class – her father was one of them – and an accent that sounded more Home Counties than Yorkshire. But that was where the similarity ended.

'Everyone's been dying to meet you,' he gushed, shaking her hand vigorously, his cheeks seeming to grow even pinker. He was as enthusiastic as a puppy. 'We don't get many newcomers here. Not in this part of the dale, anyway. I'm a southerner myself, but I've been here for almost twenty years.'

'You wouldn't think it, would you?' said a tall woman with curly fair hair and bright red lips. She winked a fluttery-lashed eye at Amy. 'I keep telling him he still talks like they used to on the BBC when I was growing up. But we'll make a proper Dalesman of him one day.'

Mark introduced the blonde as Donna, the practice manager and receptionist – 'Though we all take our turn on the front desk when needed.'

Donna was dressed in a pair of leopard-print-style leggings and a black woollen jumper. Round her neck she wore several gold chains, one of them with her name engraved on a small bar, and another with a charm on it in the shape of an elephant. It was hard to tell her age, but Amy presumed she was in her fifties. Clearly embracing her own style, Amy found comfort with Donna reminding her of an equally bold Ruby.

There were two veterinary nurses. Fran was petite, with a black bob and a pretty elfin face; Sophie was willowy and blonde. Amy was surprised to hear that Sophie, who she didn't think looked much older than her, was a mother of three, with her eldest just starting university.

'So, you're in Ivy Cottage,' said Donna. 'I've known Lauren since she was a child. Smashing girl.'

Amy agreed that Lauren sounded lovely on the phone.

'Do you all live in the village?' she asked them.

Donna looked most affronted. 'I live up the dale. Always have done. Fran lives down the dale. Sophie's a Grassdale lass, though.'

'Damian lives in Grassdale, too,' said Sophie. 'Just up hill yonder. You'll meet him next week. He's on holiday right now.'

Amy had seen his name on the practice website. Damian Lonsdale.

The other member of the team was Simon, Mark's former partner, now semi-retired, who was working that day and taking care of the morning appointments while Mark showed Amy the practice and its facilities. Simon was more Amy's idea of what a 'country' sort might look like. He arrived a little later wearing a waxed Barbour jacket and a tweed cap. He was about sixty, tall with grey hair, and rather handsome.

Mark told her more about everyone as they chatted that morning, including the absent Damian. 'He's been with me for a few years now. Grew up in these parts, studied in Edinburgh, then came back. It's got that pull, you know.'

Amy concurred, what she had seen so far was beautiful.

'There's nowhere like it, Amy. The scenery is the best in the country, and the people are, well, salt of the earth.'

And some of them are bloody irritating, thought Amy, remembering her new neighbour, but kept her mouth shut.

'Having almost burnt myself out down south, I set up this practice and resolved to do things differently. We're a small team, so we don't offer an out-of-hours emergency service. Those calls are directed to the bigger practices nearby. We open two Saturday mornings a month, and take a day off in the week in lieu. It all makes for healthier vets as well as patients.'

'I'm all in favour of that,' said Amy.

'They tend to get the bulk of the farming jobs in Crowdale, and they've got a couple of equine specialists there, so we don't see too many horses. But we do get our share of large animals too. Much as I hate to blow my own trumpet, I have to say that some of the farmers prefer us. That's what they tell us, anyway.' He shrugged, as if to absolve himself of immodesty. 'We give them a more personal service, I suppose.'

Amy learnt that mornings typically began with fifteen-minute pre-booked consultations. Emergencies could come in at any time and were to be attended to by whoever was free. Twelve till two was reserved for surgical procedures and diagnostic tests. Lunch was fitted in then too. Afternoons consisted of further consultations, reviewing test results and ongoing treatment. The surgery closed at five.

'Of course there are always exceptions. I'm not saying we never work late, but for most of the year we keep fairly regular hours. I'm afraid it rather goes out the window at lambing time, but that's to be expected.' Amy noticed that Mark had a rather disconcerting habit of closing his eyes for a few seconds at a time when he was mid conversation. He opened them now, regarded Amy and stroked his chin. 'I could tell from your application and our phone calls that you were on our wavelength.'

The staff popped in and out of the kitchen at lunch time. Amy hadn't thought to bring any lunch, but Donna went to buy sandwiches from the store. 'We're so lucky to have that place. We nearly lost it, you know, then John and his partner arrived. Some of the older folk were a bit funny about the idea of a couple of gays running it, at first. But once they got to know the pair of them, they all warmed quickly. Now their chuffing stupid opinions have changed. Plus, the shop knocks spots off the one we used to have. Most of the people here had never heard of sourdough in their lives! Now they're first in the queue before it sells out, and then they're in the caff ordering their lattes and cappuccinos as if they've gone out of fashion!' She chuckled, then looked at Amy sternly for a second. 'You will use the store, won't you? Use it or lose it is what I say to everyone.'

'I already have,' replied Amy, feeling smug, as Donna nodded approvingly.

In the afternoon, Amy saw her first patients: a dog with suspected diabetes, a cat with a sore patch on one leg and a white rabbit that had diarrhoea. Donna brought her a cup of tea between appointments, and thrust a tin of cookies at her.

'Take one. They're sublime.'

'Did you make them?'

'Me? No!' She scoffed at the idea. 'They're from Mary over the road. She's always baking something or other.'

'Mary who lives next door to me?'

'That's the one. You've already met her?'

Amy was tempted to reply, 'Yes, several times,' but she restricted herself to, 'She's very friendly.'

'Oh, she's a grand lass. She was at school with my older sister. I've known her all my life.'

And this is why we keep our mouth shut, she thought to herself.

Amy noticed that a lot of her customers, when asked where they had come from, replied with a simple 'up the dale' or 'down the dale' rather than a placename. All very confusing.

She told Donna, who laughed. 'I bet your head is pottered after all that.'

Amy didn't need to ask what pottered meant – she felt that it was quite obvious.

Although it had been a smooth introduction to her new job – the cases straightforward, the owners relaxed and friendly – Amy felt drained from the newness of it all when she got back to Ivy Cottage. A run would probably have helped to revitalise her, but she decided on a lazy evening instead. She cooked the other steak, and poured herself a glass of wine from the bottle Donna had given her as a welcome present. Her father would have insisted on red wine with steak, but she preferred white.

'I had you down as a Sauvignon Blanc girl,' Donna had said to her, mysteriously. 'Was I right?' Amy had wondered if it was a lucky guess, or if Donna had been stalking her on Facebook.

Although she usually preferred to shower, she ran a large bath, instead. The tub, for some reason, was on a small dais. She felt like the Queen of Sheba – one of her mother's expressions – as she lay back in the hot bubbles, surveying the rest of the room from her exalted position.

The window was set low in the thick wall and was very small, looking over the garden and fields. There was a curtain, but as there was no chance of being overlooked, she didn't bother to close it.

She might have stayed in the bath for another ten minutes if she hadn't heard her phone ringing from her bedroom. It paused, restarted, then stopped again. Perhaps it was important. She hauled herself out of the bath with a grumble, and almost tripped, forgetting there was a step to descend. It was her mother, though she didn't leave a message. She supposed she should call her back.

'Darling, how is it going? Are you having those terrible winds they're having in Scotland?'

'I'm in Yorkshire, Mum, not Scotland.'

'I know where you are, but it's not far in the grand scheme of things.' (Another of her mother's favourite expressions.)

'The weather's been beautiful. I can hardly believe it. It's like summer.'

She told her mother a little about her day.

'Well, I hope they realise how lucky they are to have you. I don't suppose they have any idea how qualified you are.'

'Of course they do, Mum! Why do you think they gave me the job? Anyway, I'm not here to be idolised, though everyone has been incredibly nice.' She swiftly changed the subject. 'How are you and Dad?'

'Oh, so-so. Daddy's very busy at work, as always. He still won't even talk about the possibility of retiring. Well, you know what happened with Uncle Paul.' (Amy's uncle had retired when he was fifty-one, also after a career in medicine. He'd had a heart attack and died a few weeks later.) 'I've got my book group tomorrow. My turn to host. I'm making a pavlova for them with the raspberries from the garden. I've never had such a good autumn crop before. Do you think they'll like it? It usually goes down well, doesn't it?'

'I'm sure they'll love it.'
'Have you made something nice with those apples?'
'Not yet, Mum. I've only just got here.'
'There was a lovely recipe in *The Telegraph* at the weekend. A cake that keeps for ages. I'll send it to you. Don't forget to keep an eye on the weather!'

Going to work was a doddle compared to keeping up with her mother's conversations.

7

Having started her job on a Wednesday, there were only two more days to go until the weekend. They passed quickly. Most of the cases were run-of-the-mill problems she had dealt with time and time again in London: stomach upsets, ear infections and skin irritations. Even the animals themselves were the same: dogs and cats of all breeds and sizes, as well as smaller pets like rabbits, mice and hamsters. A young boy and his mother came in with a goldfish in a small plastic tank. The boy was beside himself looking at the goldfish as it swam upside down.

The mother spoke. 'We thought he was dead at first. He was like this all day yesterday. I said to Archie, if he's still alive when you get back from school, we'll take him to the vet.' She offered an apologetic smile, then whispered to Amy, 'He adores that fish.'

Archie was almost too upset to speak.

'Ginger,' he managed to whisper, when Amy asked him what the fish was called. 'Will he be all right?'

'I think he probably has swim bladder disorder. See how his stomach is a bit swollen? He might have been eating too much. What do you feed him?'

After establishing that the fish's diet consisted mainly of flaky foods that floated on the surface of the water, Amy recommended that he fast for a couple of days before switching to a food type that sank to the bottom of the tank. This would prevent him from gulping too much air when feeding.

'We live in Crowdale, two doors from Lauren,' said the woman to Amy as they prepared to leave, the boy looking far happier. 'I'll tell her that we've met you.'

Amy was starting to wonder if everyone here knew everyone else.

An elderly woman and her adult daughter were her final clients of the week, bringing with them a tortoise suffering from a rather sore leg. The older woman told Amy that she'd had the tortoise since she was a girl.

'My father took me to the pet shop for my birthday when I was six years old. We lived in Leeds at the time. I was allowed to choose whatever I wanted. I was going to buy a cat, but when I saw Matilda, I knew that I had to have her.'

Her face grew animated as she relived her memories.

'Oh, that's wonderful!' said Amy, doing some swift mental arithmetic, but the woman's daughter was pulling a face at Amy behind her mother's back, and shaking her head.

'Mum, this isn't Matilda. Remember, Matilda died a long time ago. This is Octavia.' She said under her breath, 'Mum's starting to get a tiny bit forgetful.'

'Well, whoever she is, I love her! And she's got a wonderful name! Now, let's see what your problem is, Octavia …'

Happily, Matilda/Octavia's problem was as straightforward as a thorn that had become embedded in the fleshy part of her foot. It appeared to have been in there for some time, becoming infected. Amy managed to extract it, then applied an anti-bacterial cream. The tortoise bore the process stoically.

'Oh, thank you, doctor!' said her owner. 'And Matilda says thank you, too. I do hope we see you again. Perhaps you can come for tea one day. We'd both like that very much.'

'Mum lives in Church Lane,' said her daughter, slightly apologetically, as they left. 'Her name is Betty.' She touched Amy's arm. 'But don't feel obliged.'

Amy left work on Friday evening feeling elated. She might have been at the practice for only three days, but she knew already that she had made the right decision. Perhaps being a country vet wasn't so different from being a city vet after all. Her job was to diagnose illnesses and afflictions in animals, so why should that be any different here?

As for their owners, well, people were people wherever they happened to live. Some were more difficult than others, true, but that was understandable under stressful conditions. British pet owners were renowned for treating their animals like members of the family, which meant high expectations and – occasionally – a reluctance to accept difficult decisions.

She'd warmed to her new colleagues, too. At first, she was in awe of Donna, despite her down-to-earth tone and friendliness. She was extremely efficient – in a way that made Ruby back in London seem like a hopeless scatterbrain, which she wasn't at all. Donna spoke to everyone in the same straightforward manner. She was a no-nonsense woman, but could clearly adapt to handle each and every one of the customers. One minute she was sympathising with an owner over a sick animal, the next, she was talking about the weather or the DIY her live-in boyfriend was supposed to be tackling but never getting round to. Amy could see that the customers liked her.

Fran and Sophie seemed nice, though she didn't know them as well yet. Sophie talked about her children a lot – as well as the university fresher, she had a three-year-old and a ten-year-old. 'And all by the same father!' she quipped to

Amy, who, blushing slightly, realised she had been silently wondering just that.

All the same, being the 'new girl' was exhausting. Amy decided to put off a run until the next day. The forecast was good, with the beautiful weather set to continue.

It was warm enough to have breakfast in the garden on Saturday morning. Amy found that if she sat very still, the birds still came to the feeder. She had become very fond of the nuthatch – she'd had to look it up – a plump little bird with a blueish upper body and chestnut belly, a dark stripe across each eye. And – oh my gosh, what was that on the wall? She froze, unable to believe what she was seeing. A bushy greyish-brown tail was being held up in the air like a question mark before it curled back over the delicate body of a red squirrel that was scampering over the drystone wall at the end of the garden.

Having never seen a red squirrel in the wild, nor been aware that they were found in these parts, she had doubted her eyes for a second. It was dainty and pretty, far smaller than the grey squirrels she was used to seeing in London. Another one appeared, and, as if for Amy's benefit, stopped to nibble whatever it held in its tiny paws. It was beyond cute. She quietly picked up her phone and snapped it.

'What do you think of my new neighbour?' she WhatsApped her mother.

A reply came back, almost instantly. 'What a beauty! I've just chased one of its horrible grey cousins off the bird feeder. The pest!'

'Book group OK?'

'Yes, but Tasha wants us to read one of those Tok Tik books next, something about spicy romance? Anyway, I think Marion will die at the rude bits ha!' She followed that with a winking face emoji.

Amy rolled her eyes and laughed to herself. 'That's TikTok, Mum.'

***

After doing some more unpacking, Amy was making a sandwich for lunch when her phone rang.

'Hello, Amy, this is Lauren. Welcome to Grassdale!'

'Lauren! Gosh, hi! I should have been in touch before now to thank you for the groceries – and that delicious cake! That was so kind of you.'

'Oh, you're OK. I like to make my guests feel at home. How are you settling in? Is there anything you need?'

'I love this place,' Amy gushed, realising as she said it just how true it was. She had taken the phone into the conservatory, where she noticed how the cushions on the wicker chairs were all beautifully embroidered, just like the ones on the window seats. 'It's perfect for me, Lauren – modern and cosy at the same time. I can't believe how at home I feel already. And I wasn't expecting to find such a well-stocked library!'

'They were Nana and Grandad's books – Grandad's mainly. I'm not much of a reader myself, but I didn't have the heart to get rid of them. They'll be useful, right? The local ones, anyway. Grandad was a true Dalesman and a great outdoorsman. He belonged to all the societies round here. There's a full set of Wainwrights, if you're interested in the Lakes. Sorry about all those political biographies, though! They looked a bit heavy to me but you never know what other people like, do you?'

Amy heard the sound of a child in the background.

'Sorry, that's Aidan, my little one. He's reminding me that it's lunchtime. I really should run now, Amy, but I'll pop round the next time I'm in the village, and do call if you need anything at all. Oh, and there's Mary next door? Worth giving her a knock. She'll be able to help with most things if you do get stuck.'

'Yes, we've, er, already met.'

'She's wonderful! She did so much for Nana and Grandad in their last years. They'd have had to go into a care home long ago if it hadn't been for her.'

It sounds as if the whole world loves Mary. Amy resolved to give her the benefit of the doubt and to try harder with her neighbour.

'Oh, Lauren, while I remember. Where's the nearest garage? I should fill my little Fiat up.'

'Woody's, by the bridge.' Lauren sounded surprised. 'You haven't seen it?'

'Must have missed it.'

The child screeched. 'So sorry, Amy! Hope that didn't deafen you. Speak soon.'

***

The garage was indeed beside the bridge. Amy supposed that the reason she had missed it was because it didn't really look like a garage. True, there were a couple of petrol pumps close to the road, but they looked more like stage setting than actual pumps – like the sort you would see in a Sunday-night television drama set in the 1950s. There was also a large stone building, a bit more modern than most of the houses in Grassdale, and a yard with various outbuildings. Amy was just wondering why the pump with unleaded fuel wasn't working, when a man in a blue boiler suit came ambling over from the other side of the yard, wiping his hands on a rag. He pointed to a sign on the wall that read, 'Ring for service'.

'Ah! Sorry! I didn't see the bell.'

He hummed to himself unselfconsciously as he started to fill the tank. Amy stood there awkwardly beside him, looking around. Her eyes landed on a sign that read: 'Wood's taxi. Booking essential. No further than Hebden.' And another that read, 'Logs sold here'.

Feeling the need to say something, Amy opened her mouth, but before she had chance to speak, he stopped humming and said, 'Nice day, but it's definitely getting a bit back-endish at night time'.

Amy was unsure what 'back-endish' meant, but agreed that it was lovely for September. 'I'm starting to think you have your own little microclimate here!'

He grunted in reply.

While she was waiting for him to finish, Amy fished her purse out of her bag. He shook his head when he saw her take out her bank card, and pointed to a sign she hadn't read.

'I only do cash or bank transfer. But don't worry, if you can't manage that right now you can pay me another time.'

Amy was horrified. 'Oh, I couldn't do that! Let me see.' She rarely had much cash on her in London, but had withdrawn some money at the services on her way up, as a precaution.

The man – she later learnt that everyone called him Woody, after his surname – went into the house to gather her change, and beckoned her to follow. She found herself in a large hallway with dark wooden furniture including a grandfather clock, a cabinet containing family photos, and a large desk.

As he unlocked the top drawer to get her change, he saw her looking at the photos. 'Four generations on that one,' he said, pointing to one of them.

The photo showed three men and a child standing side by side – two of the men in dark suits, with big Victorian whiskers, a third in casual workman's clothing, and a boy of about five, gazing in awe at the oldest man. 'That's me, me dad, me grandad, and his dad. All of us born in this house.'

'That's amazing,' said Amy, who didn't think she knew any adult who still lived in the house where they had been born, let alone the one their ancestors had been born in. 'Are there a lot of people in Grassdale with history like yours?'

As he handed her change over, Amy noticed a shift in his previously indifferent expression. At the mention of his family, the man's voice became softer and amused-sounding now. 'Not so many these days. World's a different place, eh?'

Amy learnt that Woody wasn't just the owner of the garage and the village taxi driver, but a mechanic and odd-job man too.

***

Running here wasn't like running in a big city, she reflected, as she set off half an hour later. Back in London, you were just one of a thousand runners pounding the city's streets; no one gave you a second glance. Here, Amy felt more conspicuous. There were more people out on this sunny Saturday afternoon, including a few tourists wandering aimlessly between Upper Street and Lower Street, and many of the pedestrians ogled her, as if they hadn't seen a runner before. She waved at the two old men sitting on a bench near the pub. Both waved back, and one said something she couldn't quite catch. Oh blimey, that was Mary coming towards her. She raised her hand in a 'hello-but-I-can't-stop' gesture, which, fortunately, did the trick.

'Better you than me!' Mary shouted after her and Amy chuckled to herself. Maybe the woman would grow on her after all.

She saw the garage as she approached the bridge – it was obvious, now that she knew – and smiled as she remembered her meeting with Woody. She started framing the story in her head for her future audience. 'And, would you believe it, he told me I could pay him another time. He didn't even know who I was! Imagine that in London!' Her father would probably think he was an idiot; her mother would say how wonderful it was to think that such trusting people still existed.

She decided that she liked Woody. There was definitely a twinkle in the eyes of that otherwise lugubrious face. Plus, it sounded as if he would be useful to know, and on hand to help in a crisis. She'd have to ask him abo-

Amy, chill!

She really needed to learn how to switch off. To silence that constantly chattering brain.

Enough planning and thinking! Enjoy the moment!

If she had thought she could slip straight out of her city mindset when she moved to the countryside, she had been very much mistaken.

In London, Amy had usually listened to music when she ran – it helped to transport her from the chaos of the streets, with their constant refrain of tooting horns or people shouting into their phones. But she had decided to shun her running playlist for now. She wanted to hear the pounding of her feet on the ground, to feel the reverberations in her body, to drink in her surroundings. As she crossed the bridge onto Church Lane, birdsong and the distant hum of farming machinery were all she could hear. She felt alive. It was glorious!

The clock on the church tower suddenly struck the hour: three o'clock already. The day was speeding by. (*Relax, Amy! There's no rush!*) Someone had left a box of apples on the wall beside the lychgate, along with an ice cream tub for donations. Mark had told her about the fundraising appeal to replace two of the bells. She had made the mistake of telling him her grandfather had been a bellringer, causing his eyes to light up. 'Our current ringers are all rather elderly.' That enquiring look again. Perhaps she *would* give it a go. It might be in the genes!

Get real, Amy! You've got a million other things to do first.

She didn't continue on the road this time, but after passing the new houses, veered off to the left and went through a small gate into a field where a well-worn path led to the riverbank. The trail was baked dry, unlike the boggy mess she'd nearly run into just days ago. It hadn't rained for weeks. She'd even heard talk of the reservoir getting low amongst pet owners in the practice. Ahead of her, the sun lit up the leaves of the trees that lined the river – some a pale golden, others fiery red. Autumn had been less noticeable in the city other than a gradual need to wear a cardigan, then jacket, then coat again, after the summer. Here, she was reminded how beautiful it could be. Keats came to mind – she had studied him for A level.

Season of mists and mellow fruitfulness.

The morning had started with a low mist over the fields, which had burnt off quickly.

Close bosom-friend of the maturing sun;
Conspiring with him how to load and bless
With fruit the vines that round the thatch-eves run.

Her apple tree was burgeoning.

It all made sense now. Autumn was a season to appreciate in the countryside.

She had reached the river. Here the path changed direction to follow its course, the low-hanging trees and bushes forming a barrier between it and the greeny-brown water. She could hear her heart thumping in her ears.

She had been running on the riverside path for a few minutes when something caught her eye on the opposite bank. She stopped running, and saw a bird standing on a fallen tree branch. Long legs, long neck, long, pointed beak. Almost mythical in its stature. A heron. It was so still, that for a moment, she wondered if it was real. She knew that was ridiculous – whoever would put a statue on a riverbank? – but despite staring at it, she failed to detect the slightest movement. Then, as if it knew what she was thinking, it spread its magnificent wings and flew upstream, staying low over the water until it landed on another branch about fifty metres ahead. Amy started running again, and when she drew level with the bird, it took to its wings once more. She felt that it was playing a game with her.

Amy followed. Had she even seen a heron before? She wasn't sure. She hadn't taken a great deal of interest in birds, other than the ones she had tended to in a professional capacity. A few metres further on, Amy was completely entranced by the bird. No longer watching her footing, she failed to spot the gnarly roots of one of the low trees poking up through the earth. One foot sailed through the air, the other caught behind her. The next thing she knew, she hit the ground with a painful thud.

Amy had only fallen once before when she was running, when she had skidded on autumn leaves that were hiding a piece of wet cardboard on the pavement of Camden High Street. The effect had been like slipping on a sheet of ice. She remembered the embarrassed faces of the people at the adjacent bus stop, not knowing whether to help her or pretend they hadn't noticed.

After a second or two of total shock, she had started to clamber to her feet, but not before a teenager in her school uniform, seemingly engrossed in her music, had pushed back her headphones and asked if she was OK. She had felt a huge surge of affection for the girl, finding herself apologising for the accident that wasn't her fault and assuring her that she was fine. She would have glared at the people at the bus stop if she hadn't felt too embarrassed to look their way; she bet some of them would be sniggering to themselves at her misfortune.

Now, as she tried to stand up, a pain shot through her right ankle. She sank back down immediately, letting out a frustrated grunt. She tried again, but every time she transferred weight to her right foot, it was agony. *Dammit!* That was all she needed. Amy was in two minds about what to do next; she knew it was probably best to keep her foot within her shoe, but here on the track, alone, she needed to assess the damage. She unlaced her trainer, took off her sock and examined her foot. Flexing her ankle, Amy was satisfied that it wasn't broken, thank goodness, but it was starting to swell.

She would have to hobble back to the village. It was only a mile or so away. But there was no hurry, it would be light for a few more hours. She would try to get up again in a minute. The sun shone warmly on her face. The air smelt damp and earthy, of the river and the plants that grew there. Pungent, but not unpleasant. No traffic fumes to worry about here.

She had all the time in the world. No one was expecting her. It was both a liberating and slightly alarming feeling.

'Doing a spot of sunbathing?'

She hadn't realised anyone was approaching until the person was right beside her. She heard the clomp of footsteps and the slightly breathless voice that confirmed this person had been running too. She looked up to see a face towering over her, flushed from exertion. Black hair, slightly windswept. Very blue eyes. Late twenties, perhaps a bit older. Quite nice-looking, really. But the last thing she wanted was a good Samaritan.

Amy hated feeling vulnerable. She didn't like pity – her mother had taught her that early on in life. Even as a little girl, she wore a brave face when things went haywire. Most people were fooled. They didn't know that afterwards, she often cried in private.

'I'm fine, thank you, I just tripped and … well I'm fine.' She gave the man a strained smile. She wondered if he had seen her fall. *I must have looked a right idiot.*

He crouched down beside her, balancing on the balls of his feet. She saw the dark hairs on his legs, and strong, long-fingered hands, a fresh scar, about an inch long, on the back of one of them. 'You sure?' He pointed to her foot. 'You may have twisted your ankle. You don't want to go putting too much weight on it. Want me to have a look?'

She could feel the flush creeping up her neck. 'No thanks, honestly. I'm just going to sit for a while.'

He shook his head in mild disagreement and made a sort of tutting noise. 'You really need a chilled compress on it, sharpish. Some cold water will do for now though. Here.' He had a water bottle in one hand – why had she not brought hers? – which he held in front of her. 'With your permission?'

Amy nodded weakly as he tipped the contents of the bottle over her swollen joint. It felt good, but the relief was gone in a few seconds.

'There. How does that feel?' He didn't wait for an answer. 'You need more.'

He climbed to his feet, picked his way through the trees and bushes and disappeared from view for a few seconds. Then he was back at her side, emptying another bottleful over her ankle.

Amy spoke up. 'Honestly, I don't want any fuss. Thank you for what you've done, but really I'm fine. Please just carry on with your run.'

'I can run any time. Let me help you get up and walk you back to …' he squinted at the track behind them, 'wherever you've come from. Did you drive here to try out a local route?'

'No!' Amy hadn't meant to snap, but she was annoyed by his assumption and really wished he would go away.

'Look, I've run this route a hundred times over and not managed to take a tumble yet. Maybe it's best if you stick to the main roads, you know? The ground probably isn't as uneven where you're used to running.'

She wondered if he knew how condescending he sounded. She could already tell, *one of those men who always thought they were right*. Amy just wanted to be left in peace. She would find a branch to use as support if she needed one. The last thing she wanted was to return to the village hobbling on the arm of some smarmy know-it-all.

To show him that she had no need of his services, she started to stand, but couldn't contain an involuntary yelp. He stretched out a hand, but she shook her head furiously as she propped herself up against a tree.

'Please leave me alone. I just need time.'

'I think you—'

'I didn't ask for your thoughts, did I!'

'OK, OK.' He held up his hands, palms facing her, in surrender. 'I get the hint.'

'Took you long enough.'

'Cutting!' He pretended to look hurt, but he was smirking. 'Well, enjoy the rest of your run, or should I say, hobble. Don't stay out too late. It's going to be a cold one tonight.'

When he had gone, disappearing round a bend in the river as it flowed towards Crowdale, Amy wondered why she had been so hostile. It didn't take her long to realise what it was. He reminded her of Jake. He wasn't *that* similar in appearance – Jake's hair had been lighter, and his eyes darker – but something about that 'sticking to the main roads' comment. Yes, that was what it was. Jake always thought he knew better too. Was always trying to take control, tell her what she should and shouldn't do.

She'd despised him for that in the end. Still, it hadn't stopped her from missing him hugely when they had split up. Maybe a part of her still did.

***

Amy had somehow hobbled home to Ivy Cottage – yes, hobble had indeed been the word. Despite the relatively short distance back, it had taken ages. Whenever she caught sight of someone, she straightened up and tried to walk normally, but it hadn't been easy. She felt like an idiot. It seemed such a cliché. She could hear how the conversations might go in the pub that night: 'You heard about the Londoner in Ivy Cottage? She goes running, would you believe it? Only went and face-planted herself on the riverbank. Typical city sort!'

She'd stuck her foot under the cold tap in the bath as soon as she was in, and held it there for ages, but it was probably too late to do much good by then. She needed to get it better for work on Monday. Panic rose as she imagined having to phone in sick for her first full week. She couldn't let that happen. She kept her leg raised as she flicked through the TV channels that night, eventually deciding on a light romantic film on Netflix. She remembered about halfway through that it was one she had watched with Jake about a year ago, not long before they split up, and suddenly didn't feel like watching it anymore.

The next morning, she ate her breakfast in the conservatory. It was getting cooler in there, and especially at that hour, before the sun was high enough to warm it. When she saw the dainty red squirrel on the wall again, she couldn't help smiling. Her foot was still swollen but less painful than the day before. Best to stay put and take it easy. Whenever she was sitting, she made sure she raised her leg higher than her body. She needed to be able to get her shoes on for work. Honestly, what timing! She could have kicked herself.

Ouch! Not a good idea either!

To cheer herself up, she rang Penny that afternoon.

'Heyy! How's it going?'

'Oh, Penny, it's so nice to hear your voice!'

'Steady on! You're not getting emotional, are you?'

Amy realised that her voice had indeed sounded rather shaky. She reassured her friend that things were fine, that work was fine, that she loved her new home.

'But?'

'Oh, I tripped when I was running and I'm sitting here like an invalid. I felt like a right fool. Some wannabe knight in shining armour came along, and—'

'What? You've only been there five minutes and you're already hitting it off with the local talent!'

'I was being sarcastic. But I could tell he thought he was God's gift.'

'So, what happened? Did you pull an Amy?'

'What do you mean, *pull an Amy*?'

'I *mean*, did you frighten him away?'

'Well, after he'd done his whole doctor act – as if he knew anything about medical matters – I thanked him and told him where to go. Not like that, of course.' She thought for a second. 'Well, a bit like that, actually.'

'Amy Ashton, I'm disappointed in you. You go out on a run and meet a man who clearly shares the same bloody interest as you, and you went and blew it.'

'Penny, I'm in Yorkshire, not on Mars. There are other men. Jeez, you're as bad as Mum.'

'Well at least be a bit more civil next time. There might not be a whole lot of eligible bachelors to choose from.'

'Who said he was a bachelor, or eligible? Anyway, I probably won't see him again.'

After their running disaster debrief, Amy asked Penny what she was up to, and how her extensive family were doing. She had always rather envied Penny for her five brothers and sisters, cousins who lived round the corner, grandparents in the next street, all of whom seemed to get along in a state of noisy, chaotic contentment. Going to Penny's house as a child had been unnerving at times. So many people, so many of them talking at once, boisterous but caring. She had never dared ask Penny what she made of *her* home, thinking that it must have felt so silent in comparison. She remembered a seven-year-old Penny, who had come for a sleepover for the first time, saying, 'Does anyone else live in this house with you?' Perhaps that answered the question.

Amy then told Penny about Mary, and Lauren, and the people in the shop – 'I'll probably be working there the next time you see me,' she joked.

Penny said, 'Blimey, Amy, it's a right social whirlwind there. I might have to move up myself.'

Amy had to cut their conversation short when she heard a muffled knocking that signalled someone was at the door. She said a quick goodbye to her friend, promised to be in touch again soon, and went to open it. Mary was standing there, a small paper bag in her hand.

'I thought I'd better check up on you. I hear you've hurt herself. This is why I don't run!'

When she didn't say anything, Mary thrust the paper bag towards her.

'I've just made these. Mini quiches. No meat though, just cheese and onion. I don't eat much these days. No one does, do they? Well, some of the folk here probably do. There's a farmer I know up the dale who has it with every meal – breakfast, lunch and dinner. He says no do-gooders are going to change his diet.'

Amy, almost lost for words, muttered a thank you, before saying, 'I twisted my ankle, that's all. Nothing serious. I really must go back to propping it up. I was in the middle of a phone call.'

'Sorry about that! I'll make myself scarce. Toodle-oo!'

Honestly, thought Amy, as she closed the door, and stood with her back against it for a second or two, did everyone know everyone else's business here? *This is going to take some getting used to.*

The packet felt warm in her hand. She had to admit, the quiches smelt delicious. No one had baked treats for her in London, or knocked on her door if they thought she was unwell. She ate three of them for her tea with salad and new potatoes. Her mood lifted instantly. She knew that her irritation with Mary and her annoyance with the interfering stranger by the river were really displacements for anger she felt at herself. She needed to 'take a chill pill', as Penny would say. Or 'snap out of it', as her late gran would have said. She had been very close to her grandma, her father's mother, when she was a child. Dad said she had been very strict when he was young, but she had softened in her old age. As the mother of boys, she had adored her only granddaughter. Amy missed her a lot. She'd paid heed to her wise advice.

Later, she plonked herself on the floor in the dining room to look more closely at the books there. Lauren's grandad had clearly been a great reader. One shelf was full of well-thumbed paperbacks, their spines wrinkled. A full set of Thomas Hardy novels sat next to a few by Dickens and the Brontës. She hadn't read Hardy since school. Perhaps she would read him again now. Yorkshire was probably very different from Hardy's Dorset, but it felt fitting to read a bucolic novel while living in a country village. There were also biographies of famous people: Martin Luther King, Gandhi, Alfred Hitchcock, Queen Victoria. She was going to be very well educated if she managed to read even a fraction of these titles! There was always CPD – Continuing Professional Development – reading to do as well, of course. *Who said that life in the country will be quiet?*

8

With her ankle much improved, though still limping slightly, Amy was determined to start the new week in a positive frame of mind. She'd made a last-minute purchase of walking boots before leaving London and thanked her lucky stars for the extra support they offered as she laced her feet into them. She gave herself a talking to in the hallway mirror before she left for work.

'I am fine. Things could have been worse. I am going to have a great week.' Then she grinned at herself and stuck her thumbs up.

The phone was ringing when she entered the practice. Amy mouthed a 'hi' to Donna with a bright smile before heading to get ready. A few minutes later, she was examining a young Border Collie who had got its nose stuck in a fence.

The injury had occurred the day before. 'We back onto farmland, and there are sheep in the field. He's always wanting to be with them. I heard him squeal and saw him with his nose stuck in the wire.'

The wound looked sore, and the dog whimpered when Amy touched it.

'I don't think it needs stitches. I've applied an antiseptic cream and will give you some to take home and re-apply, but I'm going to put a collar on him so that he can't scratch it. It should heal nicely on its own.'

The owner looked as if she wanted to say more. 'I hope we did the right thing getting him. He's on the move all the time. He snaps at the children's heels and now the little one is frightened of him. He thinks he's a sheepdog.'

Because he is a sheepdog, thought Amy. He was probably bored and wanted to be doing something more demanding than being petted by children.

'Is he getting enough exercise?'

'My husband walks him after work every day. I don't have the time myself. I work from home and I let him out in the garden.'

Amy felt sorry for the dog, though he was clearly well-loved and treated.

'He's still young. He'll probably calm down. Some collies make perfectly good pets. They're not all cut out to be sheepdogs. But he will need more exercise and potentially some puppy-training classes.'

After saying goodbye, and washing her hands, Amy went into reception to see who her next patient was. A man marched in carrying a large bag.

'Good morning, Damian!' said Donna brightly. 'How was your holiday?'

'Great, thanks. Already feels like ages ago. I got back Friday, but it was a nice break. Looks like you've been having good weather here, too. I—'

He broke off. He and Amy were staring at each other. It had taken Amy a few seconds to realise that she recognised that voice, *and the pain in the arse it belonged to*. It was the interfering know-all from Saturday. *Oh no, not him, please! Please don't let him be my unseen colleague!* Just her flipping luck. She could feel her cheeks starting to flush.

'Oh, sorry, forgot you two hadn't met yet. Amy feels like part of the furniture already! Amy, Damian.' Donna pointed to each of them in turn.

'It's *you*. How's the ankle?' He didn't look particularly pleased to see her.

'You've already met each other?' Donna looked surprised.

Amy thought she would get in first. 'Yes, by the river on Saturday. I tripped over and twisted my ankle. This, um, Damian—' it felt awkward to say his name, but even weirder not to, 'came to my assistance.'

'I don't recall you wanting any,' said Damian, before walking straight past them both into the corridor leading to his consulting room.

Amy watched him go, then, embarrassed, picked an imaginary piece of fluff from her scrub top.

'We didn't get off to the best start,' she confided, clearing her throat.

Donna shook her head. 'That wasn't like Damian. But don't you worry. I think he's had a tough morning. He took the first off-site call. Old Charlie up on Hilltop Farm isn't the easiest customer. One of those types who thinks he knows it all. And he does know most of it, most of the time. But he wouldn't have called us if he could deal with it on his own, would he?'

***

'I hear you two already know each other. Splendid!' said Mark, as he and Damian walked into the kitchen together while Amy was having her lunch. She had brought a small salad in a Tupperware container from one of Lauren's well-stocked cupboards – she had never seen so many utensils in her life! – that she was eating with the last of Mary's quiches. Whether Mark actually knew the details of their encounter and was glossing over it, was hard to say. Damian nodded and Amy forced a smile. The two men joined her at the table.

'How are things going in Ivy Cottage, Amy? Are you settling in?' asked Mark.

'I love it there, thanks. You should have seen my London flat. No room to swing a cat.'

'Ooh, not sure if vets should talk about swinging cats in earshot of customers,' said Mark jovially. 'Though I believe it's a naval expression originally. I say, Damian, what have you got there? You runners are healthy sorts, aren't you!'

Damian was also eating salad. Amy saw couscous flecked with colourful pieces of pepper and vegetables. Something that must have taken time to prepare. She wondered if he had made it himself, or if he had a wife or girlfriend – *poor thing!* – who lovingly made it for him.

Donna stuck her head round the door. 'Mark, urgent call from Noddy. Can you get there? He asked specifically for you.'

Mark leapt up. 'I'll leave you two to get to know each other.'

'Want me to lend a hand?' offered Damian.

'No, I know what it's about. Stay put for now.'

They were both silent for a while after he had gone. Amy was very aware of a clock ticking on the wall, and the sound of her fork in the Tupperware pot.

'Feeling better on your feet?' It was Damian who spoke first.

'Absolutely fine.' That was a lie and they both knew it. She corrected herself slightly. 'A tiny bit sore, but I'm fine. Thanks.'

Silence again.

'There's a group of women in the village who run together. You might benefit from joining them.'

'Why's that?' Amy hadn't meant her reply to sound so confrontational. But she knew where this conversation was going; could feel the passive aggressive comment about her getting lost without a street atlas, or something similar, coming her way.

'For the company?' He lowered the fork that he had raised towards his mouth. Smirking slightly to himself, he added, 'Plus if you do have an accident, miles from anywhere, there's someone around to help.'

'Well, I'm not intending that to happen, thank you.'

'Surely no one's ever intending it to.'

She cleared her throat and averted her gaze. 'Well, you know what I mean. I'm usually very careful. I'm sure Saturday was a one-off.'

They both continued to eat.

'You're from London, right?'

'Yes, well, lived there for a few years. From Surrey originally.'

'Hmmm.'

Their eyes met over their forks. *Why is he smirking again*?

'Do people keep cows and sheep in London these days?'

'Some of them do.'

'But they weren't your regular customers?'

'Nooo. But—'

'You're going to find it very different here.'

'I'm *very* well aware of that. It's actually one of the reasons I've come.'

She had finished her lunch now. While Amy still had a mug of tea to drink, she had no desire to prolong her conversation with this condescending arsehole any longer. Was he deliberately trying to rile her? He was doing a good job, if he was. She went to the sink to wash the container.

He wasn't finished yet. 'Look, I can see you're one of these people who doesn't like to listen to anyone else. I had a taste of that on Saturday. But you'll need to—'

'I beg your pardon?' She spun to face him, arms folded. She wasn't going to listen to this any longer. 'You don't know anything about me. Please don't make assumptions, it's a waste of both of our time. How about we make this less difficult: you do your job over there and I'll do mine over here.'

Amy could hear her voice shaking as she returned to drying the container. She picked it up, along with her mug, and left the kitchen.

***

It was starting to feel more autumnal now. Those lingering days of summer were finally over. When Amy looked out of her bedroom window after sunrise, she saw cobwebs strung between the bushes, shimmering in the glow.

One morning, Amy had realised that most of the apples from the tree now lay on the ground, their skins pecked and withered. What a waste. She ought to have picked them when she arrived. Hadn't that gardener friend of Mary's offered to help her? She should have taken him up on the offer after all. Not that she needed more apples herself. After it had sat in the corner of her kitchen for a couple of weeks, Amy had taken the bag of apples from her parents' garden to Mary. She knew she had been rather abrupt with her at their last meeting. Mary wasn't in, and feeling slightly relieved, she left them on the doorstep with a note.

Hope you can use these! Amy x

The evenings were still light enough to squeeze in a run after work, but Amy knew she needed to rest her ankle for a few more days. It was important that it healed as soon as possible, so as not to provide Damian with any more ammunition. He had caught her limping once past his consulting room door, and made a snarky comment. Even going for a walk was not a good idea when she had been on her feet all day.

She loved the window seats in her kitchen and living room. Because the houses on her side of the street were set higher up from the road and the main pavement, and as the windows were small and thickly leaded, she could sit and look outside without it being obvious to pedestrians that they were being watched.

One evening, as she was about to sit down, she saw the backs of two people, a man and a child, going past on the pavement below. She thought – from his height and the jacket he wore – that the man was Damian. The child, who looked about five or six and had very dark hair, was skipping. The man-who-might-be-Damian prodded the boy on his shoulder and the pair of them appeared to be laughing. She was surprised to feel a smidge of tenderness at the scene, until she quickly talked herself out of it.

***

'There's been a dog attack up at Yew Tree Farm. I want you both there, and sharpish. Doesn't sound as if they'll all make it.' Mark's face was grim.

Amy and Damian had managed to keep out of each other's way for the rest of the week. They had sometimes passed each other in the corridor, or ended up in the kitchen at the same time, but longer encounters could be avoided.

'We'll take my car,' said Damian.

When Amy looked at him, he reasoned with her, 'It's an old Land Rover. It's used to muddy farmyards.'

This she could accept, until he added, 'You're not in the city anymore, I know that Fiat 500 has to be yours.'

God, he's annoying.

***

Damian's car smelt of dogs, a smell she wasn't unused to, but in a confined space it wasn't so pleasant. It wasn't particularly clean either. An empty crisp packet and drink can sat on the floor, while a messily-packed gym bag lay on the passenger seat. It made her wonder if he ever had any passengers. Surely a wife or girlfriend wouldn't put up with it in that state? Or perhaps the rubbish belonged to the child she had seen with him – if it had indeed been Damian she spotted.

'Just shove it all into the back,' he said. The back seat was littered with all sorts of detritus too. Underneath it all was a rug, covered in dog hairs.

'Sorry about the whiff. Car was Dad's.' No further explanation.

Damian knew where he was going. He turned left out of the practice. Amy hadn't been that way yet. A sign announced two villages a few miles further on, but before reaching either, he turned into a narrow road that wound up into the hills. The land was wooded on one side, but on the other, Amy saw a fast-moving stream tumbling off the top of an escarpment scoring a steep valley in the land.

Damian drove a bit too quickly for Amy's liking, but he clearly knew the road well. It was a bumpy ride. Amy could feel the metal beneath the covering on her seat digging into her thighs. Damian didn't speak. Even without looking at him, Amy could sense that his expression was stony. *He really doesn't like me*, she thought. *Feeling's mutual, I guess.*

'Where are we going exactly?'

'Yew Tree Farm. Up the dale.' He said it briskly.

'Is that the address?' asked Amy. She said it teasingly, to lighten the atmosphere. 'Everyone talks about "up the dale" or "down the dale" and I must confess, I'm not quite sure how to pin that on the map.'

'Huh.' He clearly didn't think it deserved an answer, much less a laugh. They arrived at an entrance to a farmstead and Damian stopped the car. Amy felt his head turn towards her, and realised she was expected to open the gate. She jumped out. It was a wide metal gate with a heavy bar that fitted into a notch on the gate post. She pulled the bar, but it didn't budge. She pulled harder. Was she doing it properly? Feeling stupid, and knowing they were in a hurry, she turned to look at Damian, shrugging, and mouthing, 'Sorry! Can you help?' but someone else had appeared. A woman on the other side of the gate, tall and thin with a long brown ponytail, wearing knee-length boots and a mud-spattered jacket, yanked the bar and it slid back easily. She gave Amy a brief nod, whether in greeting or sympathy Amy wasn't sure, and held open the gate as Damian drove through it. She pointed to the field on the other side of the steading as he drove past them. Damian didn't wait for Amy, but carried on driving in the direction she indicated.

'Terrible thing,' said the woman, as she and Amy walked towards the field. 'Some walkers with dogs. At least a couple, I'd say. As if there aren't enough signs up to tell them not to be letting dogs off the leash here. They'd disappeared before we arrived but I think someone from farm yonder might have got some photos.'

'How bad is it?'

The woman grimaced. 'Hard to say which came off the worst – the ones with the facial injuries or the ones bitten on their legs and bodies. One poor girl has had her cheek ripped to shreds. I think we might lose her. But they often surprise us, you know, they're tougher than you think. Keith has already given antibiotics to the worst off, but we need to know what you think about the others.' She glanced at Amy. 'New here?'

Amy felt the weight of the situation: time to prove herself.

'Yes.' They were at the field now.

'Thought I hadn't seen you.'

Most of the other sheep were on their feet, but rather than happily feeding, they stood in clusters beside the food and water troughs, looking dirty and distressed. Chunks of bloody wool lay on the ground. There was a meaty smell in the air that churned Amy's stomach.

'They didn't touch the tup,' continued the woman. 'He probably scared them off.' Amy noticed the ram standing protectively beside a group of his ewes. He was huge.

Her husband said, 'If I got my hands on these animals I don't know what I'd do with them, but I'd string their owners up, that's for sure.'

'Some people shouldn't have dogs.' Damian was bent low, examining the face of one of the ewes. Amy thought it was probably the one the woman had told her about. He looked up, and she saw him frown and shake his head. 'I think we're going to have to let this one go.'

The farmer looked at his wife in dismay. She held his gaze without speaking.

Amy crouched down beside Damian to see for herself, putting a comforting hand on the ewe's trembling body. Although her legs and torso appeared to be unscathed, her face was a mess of blood and torn flesh. She was taking rapid shallow breaths, but as the pain relief Damian had given her started to act, she began to breathe more slowly.

'I don't know …' Amy began uncertainly, 'but if we keep her inside for a few days, help her with feeding, she might be OK.' She said it with a questioning tone, but she gave the farmer and his wife a hopeful smile.

'And how is she going to eat?' Damian more or less snapped the question at her. 'No one has the time to spoon feed her, they've got a farm to run, Amy.'

'I just think that with a few stitches she might heal quite quickly. It's perhaps not as bad as it first appears. And she looks fairly robust otherwise.'

The farmer and his wife both looked at her, then back at Damian. It was as if they were watching a tennis match, the ball bouncing from one player to the other. They were waiting for him to speak now.

He exhaled noisily. It sounded as if he was trying to steady his temper. 'I know it's hard for you both – and for you, Amy, with it being your first job on a farm – but I know a sheep who's lost the will to live when I see one.'

'Your first job, eh? You newly qualified?' It was the farmer who spoke.

'No.' *Why did Damian have to bring that up? The dick.* 'I've been working for a few years, mainly with small animals but not exclusively. I do however have experience on a farm. *Thank you.*' She glared at Damian.

The couple looked back at her tormentor.

Amy stood up. It was getting silly. And there were other animals to examine.

'I'll take a look at the others.' She wasn't sure that she was strong enough to stand up to all three of them if they were questioning her abilities to assess the animals. Moreover, she knew that she and Damian couldn't fight in front of the farmer. It was unprofessional.

'Nah,' the farmer said suddenly. 'You do what you can to this one – had her a long time, I have. I'm rather attached to the old girl. If there's a chance, I'll take it. If she's still in a bad way tomorrow, we might have to think again.'

A few minutes later, Amy was in the barn with the farmer, sewing up the torn skin on the ewe's face, while Damian and the farmer's wife ministered a sugar water drench and vitamins to the less seriously injured sheep in the field.

'She looks like the bride of Frankenstein,' said Amy, once she had finished.

'She certainly won't win any beauty contests,' the farmer joked back. 'But she's a good mother, this one. Knows what she's doing. Hopefully she's got another few years in her yet. Thank you for not giving up on her.'

To their pleasure, the ewe managed to drink some water unaided.

They left her to rest and returned to help the others.

'How's the patient?' the farmer's wife asked as they approached.

'I think she's going to pull through,' said the farmer. He caught Amy's eye, and tilted his head in the direction of Damian, who was checking some sheep at the other end of the field, avoiding looking in Amy's direction. 'He's not happy, is he? Don't think he likes the new kid on the block knowing more than he does.' He winked.

'Oh, I think he genuinely thought he was doing what was best.' Amy heard herself defending Damian, though she didn't know why.

'I'm only kidding, lass. He's a good one. Anyway, we've done a grand job between us, haven't we? It's been good to meet you, miss. I'll hope to see you in better circumstances next time, ey?'

The drive back to Grassdale began, like the outward journey, in silence. Damian sat in the driver's seat as rigid as a corpse. Amy thought she could feel waves of animosity radiating from him as he drove.

'Are they common? Dog attacks, I mean.' The silence was deafening. She'd had to say something.

'More common than they should be.'

'Awful. I've never seen one before.'

'That much was obvious.'

'Sorry? What do you mean?'

He sighed, gripping the wheel tighter. 'I mean we're not in the city anymore. Things out here are tough. Farmers aren't a sentimental lot, like your typical dog and cat owners in Kensington, pampering their little darlings. They make life and death decisions all the time, even without us. That poor ewe was on her way out and it would have been kinder to put her to sleep. Or did you just want to make me look like a brute?'

Amy could feel her heart rate quickening.

'Are you suggesting,' she said, as calmly as she could, 'that I was playing a game of one-upmanship and not putting the welfare of the animal first? I simply thought the wound looked worse than it was and that she had a good chance of pulling through. I would never have subjected her to treatment otherwise.'

Damian didn't answer.

She carried on. 'When I said I hadn't seen a dog attack before, I meant on a sheep. It's true, we didn't see many farm animals at my inner-city practice, but I do know what dogs are capable of. I had to put down a cat once that had been ravaged by the beloved family pet. It was a far uglier sight than that ewe.'

She remembered another incident, one even more shocking, that had made newspaper headlines. 'Have you ever had to put down a dog that attacked a person? I have, unfortunately. A dog that had always been good-natured suddenly decided to attack the three-year-old child of its owner.' Fortunately, the child's injuries hadn't been too severe, but that had only been because of the swift intervention of the child's father. 'That's one of the jobs I had to carry out at my lovely little *Kensington* practice.'

Her heart was pounding in her chest. She couldn't stand being patronised any longer, and turned her head away from Damian, discouraging any further response from him. She felt the car slowing down. She wondered briefly if Damian was going to ask her to get out, but saw that the reason they had almost come to a standstill was because a farmer was steering his sheep down the narrow road in front of them. There was nothing they could do but crawl along until the flock reached the field they were moving to. Still fired up with adrenaline from fighting her corner, Amy couldn't keep herself from speaking.

'You don't see traffic like this in Kensington, either. Not that I lived in Kensington. Or even bloody worked near there. Archway, *actually*.'

They tailed the group slowly along the road. A Border Collie busily herded the stragglers. One sheep inexplicably decided to turn round and go back the way it came. The dog nosed it back into line in seconds. When the sheep had followed each other through a gate into a nearby field, the woman closing the gate gave the car a nod.

'Open your window, will you?' Damian said to Amy. It was stiff and heavy, not like the automatic windows in her Fiat 500.

He leant slightly across her in order to speak to the woman.

'There's been a dog attack at Yew Tree. Some nasty cases. Keep your eyes open.'

'Lost any?'

'Fortunately not.'

The woman nodded, and muttered something under her breath.

They completed the rest of the journey in silence. When they reached Grassdale, Damian got out of the car first and went into the practice ahead of Amy, not bothering to lock the car. She thought it unlikely, however, that anyone would want to steal such a battered, smelly old vehicle.

She took her bag from the car. A couple of people were waiting in reception with animals in baskets. She had a thorough wash then went back to see Donna to find out who her next appointment was with.

'Grab something to eat while you can,' said Donna. 'The girls are looking after these two.' The 'girls' was how Donna always referred to Fran and Sophie.

While she was boiling the kettle, Mark came into the kitchen.

'Amy, could I have a word in my office please? Now.'

Mark's office was upstairs. Amy hadn't been up there before. This was where Mark's living quarters were, as well as the nerve centre of the operation. The room was small, piled with boxes. In the middle of them all, sat a desk with an old-fashioned computer on it, with a revolving chair tucked under. A small, rather battered sofa faced the desk. Mark asked her to sit down and, as she did, Damian came into the room behind her. He stood by the door, his arms folded.

'I won't beat about the bush. I hear you two aren't getting along, and you know that just won't do.' Mark was closing his eyes again as he spoke. Amy wondered if he was aware that he did it. 'And Amy,' he continued, 'Damian tells me that you questioned his judgment in front of our customers. I don't need to tell you that this isn't acceptable.'

Amy edged forward on the sofa cushion. 'I'm sorry, Mark, but that's not really what happened. I was merely stating an opinion. And when it concerns an animal's life, I felt I had to air it.'

Inside, she was thinking, *what a snitch*. Did Damian really have to tell the boss?

'And you disagreed?' Mark was looking at Damian now, his eyes flickering.

'I most certainly did. You know what sensitive creatures sheep are. The poor thing was deeply distressed, as she would be with half of her face chewed off.'

'That was hardly the case.'

'Near enough.'

Mark held up both of his hands. 'You're clearly not going to agree on this one and I don't really want to hear more. I'm going to speak to Keith and check that he's happy with the outcome, but I want you two to sort this out yourselves and not bring it into work with you. We're a happy family here.'

Amy couldn't help feeling that this was all her fault, as the new girl.

She didn't see Damian again until the end of the day. He didn't have lunch in the kitchen, and he was called out on another farm job that afternoon. But when she left work, not long after five, he was getting out of the Land Rover. She hesitated, then approached him. She might as well make amends now. But Damian spoke first.

'I don't know what your problem is, but you'd do well to remember that I've lived here all my life – bar a few years in Edinburgh.'

Amy looked at him in disbelief.

'And I don't take too kindly to someone who's never set foot on a farm telling me what to do on her first week in the job,' he continued.

'What?' Amy was seething at this point. 'Who's the city boy now? You absolute hypocrite! I've already told you that neither of those facts are true. Are you going to keep repeating them, like a child?' She shook her head. 'I might also add that I have a first-class degree from the top vet school in the country. I also finished top of my year I'll have you know. So there you are.' She felt sick, and light-headed. She'd never boasted about that before – not once, not to anyone – but there was a time and a place for everything.

Damian threw back his head and laughed. 'Oh, you think your big professional qualifications mean something here! You need more than a top degree and your – what was it? – Sir Leonard so-and-so award to hack it in these parts.'

She hadn't mentioned the Sir Leonard Blackwell award to anyone, though of course it was on her CV. Had he been checking up on her? Why had he been doing that?

'Well, I think an outsider's eye is quite a good thing sometimes, and presumably it's why Mark hired me. I don't turn up to a job with any pre-conceived notions.' Her hands were trembling, and she stuffed them into the pockets of her jacket. 'And now, I really want to go home.'

She marched out of the car park, and round the corner. God, what an arrogant, condescending moron? He had the most enormous chip on his shoulder, that was for sure. It must be weighing him down. (*Good one, Amy, why didn't you think of that earlier?*)

Outside the store, John was closing up, taking in the large sandwich board.

'How's it going?'

'I've had better days.'

He pulled a sympathetic face.

She flapped a hand to show that it didn't matter. 'Oh, it happens. And this place more than makes up for it.'

'It's even more magical here in the winter. We have it to ourselves a bit more. We still get visitors, and the café does well all year round, but we won't have as many walkers until next spring. Oh, you will let me know if there's anything you'd like me to order, won't you? I appreciate your custom, and I don't want you being deprived of your … I don't know … goji berries and tahini!' He grinned.

Amy grinned back. 'I haven't had a craving for them yet, but I'll let you know when I do.'

She felt better already.

9

Amy and Damian had kept a wide berth of each other since that day at Yew Tree Farm, and Mark, thankfully, had thought better of sending them out together again. A few days after the dog attack, Mark informed her that Keith, the farmer, had rung to say that the sheep whose face she had stitched was doing well, and would be back with the others soon. She wondered if he had also told Damian, and what his reaction might have been.

Apart from her unpleasant colleague, Amy felt she had made the right decision about moving to Grassdale. Although she still arrived home tired after a day at work, the cottage restored her in a way the London flat had never been able to. As she slipped off her boots and thick socks, she felt the cool flagstones under her stocking feet.

Her mind now slipped into a different gear, one that she hadn't known existed in her London life. She felt protected by those thick, centuries-old walls. She could sense the history of the people who occupied these rooms before her. There was something satisfying about the thought that people who had lived on and worked the land had been born and died within these walls for hundreds of years, long before Lauren's grandparents. It didn't take her long to shake off any lingering stresses of the day like drops of water.

It was too dark to run in the evening now, but she made up for it at the weekend. Her ankle was fully healed, thank goodness, with no lasting effects. Even if she hadn't enjoyed her job or liked her new home as much as she did, the running would have kept her in Grassdale. It took just a few minutes to be out of the village and onto the moors.

She had started to incorporate hill-running into her routine. Her new favourite run carried her up the hill to Ram's Seat, the rocky outcrop that overlooked the village. She would start the ascent with small, light steps on the gentle lower slopes, threading her way around the gorse thickets. As the slope grew steeper, she slowed down and took long strides, her hands on her thighs, breathing fiercely, but confident that there was no one around to hear. She had occasionally seen a walker, or someone with a dog, but as the year wore on, those encounters became rare.

She might break into another run to haul herself to the top, from where, slightly breathless, she looked down at Grassdale, a smile of satisfaction teasing her lips as she saw how perfectly it fitted into the pillowy hills around it. She could see part of the road to Crowdale before it disappeared within the curves and bluffs of the hills, and in the other direction, the road that she and Damian had taken that day to Yew Tree Farm, the farm itself hidden behind another hill.

Here on the peak, a broad plateau spread out before her: this high ground was Grassdale Moor. She could run for several miles, the wind in her hair and the ground soft and giving beneath her feet.

Amy still watched the birds and the squirrels in the garden, but usually from the conservatory window. A bush growing beside the wall that separated hers from Mary's garden was covered in bright orange berries that were proving popular with the birds. She wondered what it would be like in the spring, her favourite season. The patch of garden her London flat had looked out on to hadn't seemed to change much from one season to the next, or perhaps she had just failed to notice. Perhaps she would have a little tea party when summer came, and invite Mary and her new friend Sarah from the bookshop. The bookshop had become her favourite place in the village. It was usually closed by the time she finished work, but she often popped in at the weekend. It was open on Sunday too.

'It's our busiest day for tourists,' said Sarah, who owned the store. 'There's still walkers around, the hardier ones, but you'd be amazed at the number of older folk who still go out for an "afternoon run" on a Sunday – and I don't mean our type of running!' Sarah was a runner too.

Amy remembered her grandparents doing just that: driving to a favourite village in the New Forest or the South Downs. Taking a gentle stroll, looking inside the church, followed by the obligatory visit to a teashop. The Snug also did a roaring trade at the weekend. If too many people were waiting for a table, Sarah often directed them to the community café in the store, which was open till five.

'Looking for anything in particular?' she asked Amy one day.

'Just browsing. You know I could spend all day in a bookshop!'

'Oh, me too!' Sarah added, with a giggle, 'I mean, I do anyway, of course, but I even find myself drawn towards them on my days off! Talk about a busman's holiday!'

Amy read mainly novels. They were her form of escapism. She had recently discovered an imprint that republished forgotten books by female writers of the twentieth century. She was amazed at how timeless some of them were; how even one hundred years ago, women were endeavouring to bring greater meaning to their lives – how their struggles with the opposite sex, their parents, their children, their sexuality, were still so recognisable today. Other times, when work was all-consuming, she would devour thrillers, one after the other, often figuring out who the criminal was long before the big reveal, but absorbed in the book nonetheless.

A young woman with a long black plait and a solemn face, who Amy hadn't seen before, was quietly stacking shelves. Amy noticed that when Sarah spoke to her, she did so slowly, carefully enunciating each word. She wondered where the woman came from and how she had ended up in Grassdale. It was nice to feel she wasn't the only outsider in the village.

Amy needed something special that day. Mary had invited her for a meal in the pub on her birthday, and she wondered if she might find a small gift for her. It would be impossible to choose a book for her; she had no idea of Mary's reading tastes, and felt that she didn't know her well enough to hazard a guess. But perhaps she would find something in the stationery section. As a stationery junky herself, she was soon swooning over notebooks, pens and writing paper. After what felt like ages, she chose a small notebook with sunflowers on the front and a pen to match. Surely everyone could find a use for a notebook and pen, even if it was just to write a shopping list.

'You know there's a group of us who run together, don't you?' Sarah said to her as she paid. She pointed to a sign in the window. 'Saturday mornings. I can't always make it, but I try to if I can. We stop for a couple of months in the winter, but only December and January. After that we start gearing up for the Easter Monday race.' She grinned. 'That can get quite competitive at times.'

That must be the group Damian had mentioned.

'Thank you for the invitation. I do occasionally work on a Saturday though.' Amy didn't have the heart to tell Sarah that she preferred to run on her own.

***

It was always busy at work, but in a different way from the practice in London. There, with such a large team of vets, she had rarely seen the same customer or animal twice. It had felt very impersonal at times. Here, she was already getting to know some of the regulars. The Major – everyone called him that, so she assumed that was indeed his title – often came in with his cat, Elsie. Sometimes she thought he just wanted someone to talk to. Elsie had some unusual hobbies, apparently. She had recently started watching football on television, according to the Major.

'I swear she follows the ball with her eyes. She's mesmerised by it,' he said. The Major was tall, though slightly stooped, and he always wore a shabby tweed jacket with a shirt and tie. Amy was becoming very fond of him.

An elderly woman who lived in one of the tiny cottages had an old parrot called Peanut who was refusing his food. Amy went to see her in her home as the woman said it would be too stressful for Peanut to come to the practice. The bird was lethargic, but his breathing was unlaboured. Amy suggested some soft, easily digestible food, with added vitamins, but suspected he might be simply nearing the end of his life. To her surprise – and delight – the bird had rallied, and his owner now telephoned every day to give Amy an update on Peanut's health.

'You've been marvellous, dear. I can't thank you enough. He's all I have now, since my husband died.' Amy felt her heart squeeze. It was days like these that confirmed she was in the right place.

***

One Sunday afternoon, there was a knock at the door and a young woman was standing there.

'Hi, Amy! I'm Lauren. I was just passing, so if it's a bad time, just say.'

'Lauren! We meet at last! I was just about to make a cup of tea, please come in.'

She was glad that she had done her cleaning and tidying the day before. It mattered to her that Lauren saw how well she was looking after her grandparents' old home.

As she stepped inside, and stood in the hallway, Lauren touched her arm. 'Oh, Amy, it's so nice to see Ivy Cottage lived in again. It means such a lot to me, this place.'

'I'm guessing you were very close to your grandparents?'

'You bet! My parents split up when I was very young, Mum worked long hours, so I practically lived here. I can't tell you the hours I spent with Nana showing me how to make bread, or pastry, or sponge cakes.' They were in the kitchen now, as Amy put the kettle on. 'She used to say it looked like an explosion in a flour factory when I'd finished! I don't know how I made so much mess. I'm just as bad today.'

'Milk and sugar?'

'Just milk please. Grandad was always very patient with me too. When Nana did her sewing – I had no interest in that, I didn't have the patience – I used to help him in the garden. He gave me my own patch to tend. Mind, he preferred to have his nose in a book – as you've probably guessed.'

'I've seen your nana's handiwork all over Ivy Cottage, Lauren. What a talent she had!' said Amy.

When the tea was ready, Lauren asked if they could sit in the conservatory. 'If it's not too cold for you, Amy. It does get a bit chilly in the winter months.'

Amy told her she never tired of spending time there, looking at the garden.

'The birds and the squirrels have been an absolute joy!'

'You know about the Squirrel Lady, right?'

Amy said that she didn't.

'You'd be interested, as a vet. She has a sanctuary for injured red squirrels. They're classed as endangered, you know. If you see any grey ones you need to report it. Her name is Linda, but everyone calls her the Squirrel Lady.'

They sat with their tea, then Amy remembered some biscuits that Mary had brought her, and went to fetch them.

'I recognise these!' exclaimed Lauren.

'Drat! I can't pass them off as my own!'

They both laughed.

'Isn't she just a whirlwind?' said Lauren. 'I bet she's taken you under her wing.'

'I think she'd like to.'

Lauren looked surprised.

Thinking of everything Mary had done – or tried to do – for her so far, Amy felt mean.

'I think I just found her a bit, well, overwhelming. None of my neighbours came near me in London. We all get a bit nervous there if someone gets too close. We're like, "What do you want from me? Back away!"' She held up her hands, palms facing forward, as a barrier.

Lauren laughed.

'But she's been very kind.'

'She'd do anything for anyone,' said Lauren. 'She co-ordinates the food bank in Crowdale, updates the village website, she did all the shopping for the old folk when she came back to Grassdale in lockdown. I think,' her voice dropped to a whisper then, as if someone else might be listening, 'that was when her marriage fell apart. She came up to look after her parents and he – the bastard – found someone else.'

'Oh, that's awful.'

'I know. I think she was very low for a while. No one saw her much. We thought she was going to go back down south, but then she decided to stay, and she's really thrown herself into things since then. Nana and Grandad adored her. I felt so much happier knowing that she was next door. She was a lifesaver, really.'

Amy felt guilty for having less than charitable thoughts about her neighbour.

'She's actually invited me to the pub for her birthday next Friday.'

'To the Fox? Oh, smashing! They do great food there.'

They chatted for a bit longer, then Lauren said she must go. Her husband was with Aidan at a children's event at the bookshop, and if it wasn't over yet, it soon would be.

'Remember, if there's anything you need, just ring.'

10

Amy spent some time getting ready for the pub on the night of Mary's birthday. She hadn't been out socially since arriving in Grassdale a couple of months earlier. She had a bath, and lay in it until she got bored. Penny always read in the bath, but Amy couldn't bear the thought of turning pages with damp fingers. She wondered what her friend would be up to this weekend; probably a hot new date, she'd have to text her later.

She was unsure what to wear. Surely a meal in a pub didn't necessitate dressing up too much, but if it was a foodie place, the restaurant part could be quite posh. All the same, a pub was a pub, so she opted for smart but not too smart. She put on slightly flared jeans that were her mainstay for social events, working well with both summery and warmer tops. Tonight she paired them with a loose-fitting pale blue shirt and rolled the sleeves back to put on some silver jewellery.

For work, she always wore her hair in a ponytail or pinned up, so tonight she decided to leave it loose. It was getting very long, she thought, as she combed it; she'd have to find a hairdresser and get it trimmed soon. Or perhaps she could wait till Christmas and use the one in her parents' village. She was going to stay with them for a few days over the festive period. Her feelings on the matter were mixed. There was a lot to tell her parents, and they would be interested – to a certain extent – until her father returned to his work and her mother switched the conversation to her own interests as per usual, or the holidays she was planning.

There would be a drinks party on Christmas Eve with some of their closest neighbours. That would probably be the most enjoyable part of the holiday, as Amy had known some of these people all her life, and one of the couples, much older than her parents, thought of her as a surrogate granddaughter.

Christmas Day would be pleasant enough, with her mother's delicious lunch, an afternoon walk, turkey sandwiches on their return. But by Boxing Day she would probably be itching to get away. The annual lecture from her father on the year ahead and what Amy 'should be focusing on' was bound to arise by then, in addition to some very much unwarranted relationship advice from her mother.

Mary had said seven-thirty, so Amy was there on the dot. She didn't particularly enjoy walking into pubs on her own, and had rather hoped she would meet Mary on the short walk down the road, but it was not to be. It was pitch black walking down the pavement, and Amy was pleased she was wearing boots rather than shoes with a flimsy heel, as she felt she would have done the other ankle in on the cobbles otherwise.

Even as she drew closer, only a few dots of yellowish light on the thickly leaded windows, along with the sight of a couple of smokers sitting at the patio table on the green in front, hinted that the pub was open. She thought she recognised one of the smokers as a farmer who had brought his sheepdog in recently. She smiled briefly, but although he nodded back, she was pretty sure he didn't recognise her. The door opened, some people poured out, and she heard laughter and voices from inside. The last person held the door for her, and she stepped inside.

The pub was a very old building, with exposed thick stone walls and a stone floor. Wooden beams ran across the ceiling. But the interior looked as if it had been newly refurbished, with smart tables and chairs. A huge fireplace with an enormous hearth – big enough to hold a small table and two chairs – was at one end. Amy remembered someone telling her that the place had a facelift after Covid, and that it now attracted a far broader clientele. They had recently brought in a new chef too. The smell of cooking was making Amy hungry. She had been working that day, and hadn't eaten since grabbing a very quick sandwich several hours earlier. Though she disliked eating between meals, she was starting to wish she'd tucked into a snack before coming out.

The place was packed. Amy walked along the narrow passageway at the side of the bar that led to the dining area to see if Mary was there, but there was no sign of her. There was no room to wait, and the tables all appeared to be occupied, so she went back into the bar.

Feeling slightly awkward, she scanned the room in case Mary was already there. The clientele seemed to consist of all ages and both sexes. Seeing the camaraderie on display, and hearing the animated voices and laughter, she was struck by the thought that though she was happy in Grassdale, she didn't actually have a close friend here. Not a *real* friend like Penny.

A sudden pang of loneliness hit her in the gut. But then she saw something that made her feel worse. In the corner, with a group of men – two older, the rest in their twenties or thirties – was a face she knew only too well.

Damian was leaning across the table talking, his face radiating a sort of happiness she hadn't seen on him before. He always seemed very serious at work; she thought she had heard him laugh maybe only once or twice. He stopped speaking, thumped his hand on the table, and the rest of his party burst out laughing, while the older man beside him – his father, perhaps? – patted him on the back. Trust him to be holding court.

Bloody Damian, the know-it-all. As he glanced up, their eyes met. He still seemed rather pleased with himself, and his eyes were creased with his smile. The glint in his eye however changed to – what? – amusement? Surprise?

He held her gaze for a couple of seconds, and all Amy could think in that time was, *this isn't my place. I don't belong here. This is his kingdom. These are his people.* He gave her a small nod of acknowledgement now, but she turned away and headed for the door. She'd make her apologies to Mary, tell her she had come over all peculiar. Then someone behind her called her name.

She turned and saw Sarah, the bookshop owner, sitting with another woman.

'You look lost!'

'No, I, er, was just leaving.'

'You can't! It's Friday night! Have a drink with us. This is Jenny, my sister. Jenny – Amy. Love the hair, by the way. Almost didn't recognise you.'

Amy said hello to them both but reiterated that she was about to go.

'Well have a quick chat first.' Sarah pulled up a stool from another table and, reluctantly, Amy took it. At least she had her back to Damian. She couldn't bear the thought of seeing him, so settled there, every time she looked up. But she was sure she could pick out his voice, even above all the others.

Jenny told her that she ran a guesthouse up the road in one of the Georgian houses and this was her quiet time of year. The guesthouse was currently closed while they redecorated some of the bedrooms. For the last couple of years, she and her husband had gone away for Christmas, but this year they were opening and trying something new.

'We're calling it "A Dickensian Christmas". We're having carol singers and parlour games, and there'll be a ban on phones in public areas. It's all about being together, and connected. We're already fully booked, so I hope the rooms are ready in time!'

'And they're having a little party a week before Christmas to celebrate the reopening,' added Sarah. 'I've booked her an actor who's going to read a Charles Dickens ghost story.'

'You must come, Amy.'

'W-e-e-ll …'

'You're such a good customer! My treat,' said Sarah.

'It sounds lovely, thank you.' She could hardly make up an excuse, especially as she didn't know yet what day it was. She added, 'Perhaps you'll have snow as well. That would be really Christmassy!'

'As long as everyone can get here, it can snow as much as it likes,' said Jenny.

'What's that about snow? I can't stand the stuff.' Mary had come in unnoticed by them all, and was standing behind Amy. She put a hand on Amy's shoulder. 'So sorry to be late, honey. I had the vicar round, talking about the Christmas fair, and I just could not get rid of him. I thought he'd taken root in my armchair.'

Amy and her companions laughed.

Under her jacket, Mary wore a linen shift dress in a striking reddish-purple.

'I don't think I've ever seen you in a dress, Mary,' said Sarah.

'It almost went to the refugee charity but I thought I'd give it a reprieve. Well, much as I hate to drag you away, m'dear, I think we should go in now. I don't want to lose our table.'

'You're eating? Lucky you,' said Sarah, flashing Amy a surprised look.

'I'd invite you both to join us, but doubt they could fit anyone else in,' said Mary.

'No no no, already eaten. Lovely smell wafting out of there though.'

'Enjoy your meal! Lovely to meet you, Amy.'

Amy refused to give in to the temptation to look at Damian again. She held her head high as a young woman in a smart black uniform showed them to a small table in the corner. *Maybe I could belong here after all.*

'They've certainly tarted this place up,' whispered Mary.

Amy hadn't been sure if anyone else was going when she accepted the invitation, but it seemed it was just the two of them. Something occurred to her. 'Happy birthday! Your present's at the cottage. I thought there was no point in bringing it here.'

'Amy! You weren't meant to buy me a present!' Mary's eyes widened as she picked up the handwritten paper menu. 'At my age, I don't do presents anymore. But thank you – in advance.'

'Well, I hope you like it. It's only small.' Amy studied her menu.

'I recommend the pies. They're freshly made in the kitchen.'

Game pie, curried parsnip and sweet potato pie, steak and ale pie. Even pork, stuffing and apple sauce pie, a meal in itself. Amy wasn't sure if she had ever eaten game before, but it felt like the place to try it.

'Oh, you won't regret it,' Mary assured her. 'Funny, though, I had you down as a veggie.'

Amy laughed. 'Not all Londoners are, you know. Mind, I was for a while.'

'Sussed you out!'

After they had ordered, Mary said, 'I haven't seen much of you lately. Mark must be working you too hard.'

Amy felt guilty, knowing that a couple of times, when she'd seen Mary around her cottage, she'd slowed down so as not to end up in a long conversation with her.

'It's busy, but nothing like London. The workload was crazy there and you weren't always thanked for it. I once worked two days non-stop, was on call for some of it but it was still hectic.'

'Crumbs! I thought I was a workaholic when I was younger, but nothing like that. I worked in TV production for years. Then I trained as a teacher in my forties, worked in a tough East End school. The things I saw there …' She shuddered and shook her head. 'You couldn't make it up. But I always enjoyed it. Then I came home and realised it was time for a change. I still like to keep myself busy, though.'

'I think that's an understatement, Mary!'

Their drinks arrived – a hearty red for Mary and a grassy New Zealand white for Amy.

'Cheers! And happy birthday!' They clinked glasses.

Amy's wine tasted like a summer's day. After taking a couple of sips, she had already forgotten about seeing Damian. She had another mouthful then put her glass down. *I'd better not knock too much back until my food arrives*, she thought. Wine went to her head quickly and, annoyingly, made her face flush.

'Tell me more about the village. You must have seen a lot of change over the years?'

Mary's eyes lit up. 'Dead right. It's different from when I grew up, but not really in a bad way. I mean, you're sure to hear some of the old folk moaning about not knowing anyone anymore, too many holidaymakers and cars parked inconsiderately. But tourism is our main business here, so we have to welcome visitors. Plus, they usually spend a lot in the store, and in here too. Fortunately, we don't tend to get the rowdy crowd. There was a large place in Crowdale that kept getting bookings for stag or hen weekends. Nightmare for the neighbours. We're still mainly owner-occupied here, thank heavens, not like in some other villages.' She counted on her fingers. 'Maybe half a dozen holiday places? We lost the primary school around twelve years ago, which was a blow, but I'd say we're quite well-served otherwise.'

Mary was easy company – and such a mine of information. Amy wondered now why she hadn't made more of an effort to socialise since she'd been here. Sophie from work had invited her to a party one night, when her mother was watching the younger children for the weekend, but she had felt shy about a gathering where she only knew the hostess, so had politely made her apologies.

'Having the store is wonderful – and a Post Office too. Most villages our size have lost theirs, or they get a van once a week if they're lucky. You do use it, don't you? It was up for sale a few years ago, and we thought we might lose it, but John and Andy arrived and it's gone great guns ever since. Val looks as if she's a hundred and two, but she's really on the ball. She's like the bionic woman – new hips, new knees. Good job you've only got two of everything, I say to her.'

Amy felt her cheeks glowing in the warm room. Her mind drifted for a few seconds. She felt happy and relaxed. She was facing the rest of the room, and couldn't help glancing over Mary's shoulder every now and then at the other diners. Couples, family groups, groups of friends. People talking, but not too loudly. Unlike in the public bar, she didn't recognise anyone. She suspected that as the pub had a reputation for good food, its clientele were coming from further afield. She wondered if she might bring her parents here when they came to stay. They'd been planning to do that ever since she arrived but had not yet managed to fix a date.

'Suits you.'

'Sorry?' She was back in the moment with a start.

'Your hair hanging loose. You usually have it tied back. Natural colour?'

Amy laughed. Mary wasn't one to beat about the bush. 'Oh yes, it was redder when I was younger.'

'Lucky you. I've always been a bit of a mouse. Dye it now. I go to a man in Crowdale though there is a girl here who'll come to your house. I've heard she's pretty good, but when you find a hairdresser you like …'

Their food had arrived, and even Mary was quiet for a few seconds as she contemplated the plate in front of her. Amy uttered a small gasp.

'Quite a size!'

A quarter wedge of pie sat on each plate, the crust thick and golden. Mary had chosen to have chips with hers, while Amy's was accompanied by a pile of mashed potato flecked with garlic. There was a large bowl of vegetables to share.

The pastry was buttery and crumbly, and the meat melted in her mouth. It was rich and full of flavour, but not too strong. She had made a good choice.

As they were eating, Mary told Amy more about some of the villagers.

'We've even got a family of asylum seekers on the council estate.'

The council estate was set back from the main road on the approach from Crowdale. Amy had driven right past the entrance without realising on the day she arrived in Grassdale, too focused on her destination to notice.

'They're from Iran. I'm helping the mother with her English, and Sarah has her lending a hand in the shop. The boy is at school, so he's almost fluent now.'

Amy remembered the attractive woman she had seen in the bookshop.

'The lady with the long plait?'

'That's her. She's called Fahimeh. The boy is Arad.'

Amy put down her knife and fork and looked at Mary. 'How do you have time for all this, Mary?'

Mary finished her mouthful and smirked. 'Keeps me out of mischief.'

After finishing her pie, Amy didn't think she could possibly eat another thing, but Mary asked for the dessert menu.

'I only have a birthday once a year.'

When Mary insisted that Amy keep her company, she chose a lemon sorbet that came with an almond biscuit, while Mary had a bowl of homemade coffee ice cream.

'If you find coffee ice cream on the menu, you have to have it,' said Mary.

Everyone else had left the restaurant by the time they finished. 'Coffee at mine?' said Mary. But it sounded more of an order than a query.

'I really think I should pay for this,' said Amy, when Mary asked for the bill, but Mary refused to entertain the idea. 'I invited you. And I'm glad I did.'

Amy would have happily gone straight home to bed, but that felt churlish when Mary had been so kind. But before going next door, she popped to Ivy Cottage to collect her gift. Then, as Mary had left her front door open, she let herself into her neighbour's house with a polite knock.

'Room on your right! Go and sit down!' called a voice from the back of the house, and she found herself in the living room. It was a long, narrow, rather dark room, with a low ceiling. A slightly sooty smell hung in the air. The décor was more old-fashioned than that of Ivy Cottage, with heavy fire irons hanging on a stand in the hearth, while a cabinet with open shelves was crammed with china ornaments, including owls of all shapes and sizes. The fire wasn't lit, but Mary had plugged in a small electric heater.

Mary came in carrying a tray. 'I haven't done much since I've had the place to myself. It's not as flash as yours.' She set the tray on a wooden trunk serving as a table. 'I can't bring myself to do anything too drastic. I've even still got Dad's wellies by the back porch. Just can't seem to get rid of them.'

Amy didn't know if it was the large glass of wine from earlier, but the thought of a pair of old wellies, whose owner was long gone, and the sight of the row of owls – surely collected so lovingly over the years – made her eyes fill with tears. Fortunately, Mary was too busy pouring from the cafetière to notice.

'I didn't think I'd like living on my own,' said Mary. 'I surprised myself to find that I did. What about you? Have you always been single?'

She put Amy's mug of coffee on a small table beside her chair.

Amy hadn't thought of Jake much lately, but the turn in conversation brought his face before her eyes.

'My last relationship ended in December of last year. I was mad about him in the honeymoon phase, we did so much together – running, sightseeing around the city, weekends away. He had a lot of friends and there was always something going on – he'd plan it all.'

Amy paused, gathering her thoughts. 'Everything always had to be how *he* wanted it, you know? Then the running became weirdly competitive, and I felt like my interests were being pushed aside for his. I started to feel as if I couldn't breathe. He wanted us to move in together. He was practically living with me anyway, but he still had his own place. And I panicked. I started to make lots of excuses about not being able to do things anymore. I even put myself forward to be on call when I didn't really need to. I suppose I was trying to ease things off by taking the coward's route. He got the hint in the end. But then, when he did go …' Her voice tailed off. She had never spoken this honestly about it all, not even to Penny. She felt her voice wavering.

'Oh, honey.' Mary pulled a sympathetic face and passed her a tissue.

She blew her nose. 'Sorry. Anyway, I missed him terribly when he went. I thought a few times about getting in touch and seeing if we could come to some sort of compromise, but I think I knew, deep down, that things weren't right. It's nice to be with someone, but …' She shrugged. 'It doesn't have to mean letting them take over, does it?'

'He sounds a bit controlling.'

She hesitated. 'Yes, I can see that in retrospect. He started resenting my job too. He knew my work meant a lot to me, and he'd seemed proud of me at first. My being a vet was always one of the first things he told his friends when he introduced me to them.'

'Bad sign.'

'Yeah. And then he started saying I thought more of my work than I did him. Which, in the end, I probably did. It was the one thing that remained mine, does that make sense? I just, well I don't think you should be with someone for the sake of it. It's not fair to either person.'

'You probably made the right call. Jealousy and resentment are such destructive things.'

'I'm glad I did – most of the time, anyway. But now my mother thinks I'll be "on the shelf" – her words – for the rest of my life. She can't understand what I'm doing here in the "back of beyond" – again her words not mine, Mary!' She forced a laugh.

'There are worse things than being single,' said Mary. 'But somehow I doubt you'll be single for long.' She added mysteriously, 'Village life is full of surprises – far more than city life. You'll see.'

11

'If we're lucky, we'll not have a bad winter this year,' said the farmer to Amy. She had spent most of the morning on Rowan Farm. His prize sheepdog, Tess, had given birth to a litter of eight pups six weeks ago, and Amy had come to vaccinate them, as well as examine one of his cows, who wasn't eating.

'Are they usually bad here?'

'Down where you are, the main problem is flooding. The river often comes up and over the road. Up here, we never used to be able to count on going anywhere in December or January because of the threat of snow. It's not what it was though. Climate change, eh?'

Amy wondered how her little car would cope if the weather worsened. On bright cold mornings, when the sun was too low to melt the frost on some of the roads, she had to take each twist and turn as cautiously as a learner driver. She knew her car would never cope in snow.

The puppies were the most adorable things she had seen for a long time. Even as a vet, accustomed to seeing cute animals every day of her life, she didn't think her heart would ever cease to melt when she witnessed a litter of puppies. Although they had a pen in a corner of the large kitchen, where their mother lay enjoying a rare moment of peace, they were currently enjoying the run of the whole room. Tess was a pretty red and white collie, most of her head and body a reddish brown, but with white legs and a white muzzle.

Her pups were mainly black and white, but there was one that stood out from the others.

'Look at the beautiful colour of this one!' Amy exclaimed.

'We call that a lilac. It's pretty rare. She's got a home to go to already. Most of them have.'

'It'll be a wrench to see them go. Always is,' said the farmer's wife, as she made coffee for Amy and laid a plate of chocolate brownies on the table.

'You're too skinny. Fill up on these.'

'Tempted yourself, vet?' teased the farmer. 'I'm talking about the pups,' he added, as Amy eyed the thick squares of brownie, while preparing to vaccinate another puppy.

'I'd love to, if my job allowed it. It wouldn't be fair, though. I'm out all day. Besides, they're working dogs, aren't they.'

'Yeah, you wouldn't think it, would you?' said his wife, laughing as she scooped up a bundle of fur that was wrapping itself around her leg, and eyeing three others that were zipping around after a ball on the stone floor.

'Some of them will be happy enough as pets,' said the farmer. 'You get an idea, even at this stage, about which ones might make a good sheepdog. See that one with the black spot on its nose? He's already rounding up the others. He's going to a farmer in Lancashire. I had him down as a contender right from the start, and when the guy got here, he spotted him straightaway. I've got another one going to the Borders and one up to Inverness.'

He registered Amy's surprise. 'The sire is a prize-winner too, like my girl. There's been a lot of interest. Of course it doesn't mean that they're all as sharp as tacks.' The sound of whimpering came from the boot room, which adjoined the kitchen, and a pup appeared with its head stuck inside a wellington boot. Everybody laughed.

'If there's trouble to be had, it's this one who finds it,' said the farmer's wife, putting down the pup she was holding to help the afflicted one.

With the last of the pups vaccinated, Amy sat down to drink her coffee and try one of the brownies.

'We got snowed in pretty bad a few years ago,' said the farmer, returning to his favourite subject. He stuck a thumb in the air as he saw Amy's dreamy expression after her first mouthful of cake. 'Good, eh? As I was going to say, Hettie couldn't get out for two weeks. It's the situation of her place – the snow just drifts there like you've never seen. As soon as we could get up the road, I went to see how she was doing, but I had to turn back. But she was grand. Hettie always copes.'

'Hettie? I don't think I've met her yet.'

'No?' The farmer's wife chuckled. 'I thought everyone knew Hettie.'

'A character, then?'

'I'll say. She's quite an age now. She'd left school by the time I started, so she's a good few years older than me. Never married. Did most of the work on her parents' farm. He was a lazy bugger, old Robinson was. Even when Hettie was a lass, she was doing a man's job when she wasn't at school. By the time she was in her mid teens she was one of the best shearers in the county. She made quite a bit of money doing that every summer.'

The name Hettie conjured images of an old-fashioned grandma, small and rounded, like one in an early twentieth-century children's story, perhaps who spent her days baking or sewing – rather as Lauren's grandmother had done. But now Amy pictured a weather-beaten woman wearing an old jacket and boots, her face brown and lined, a dog at her heels.

The farmer took up the story. 'Her dad died of the drink when he wasn't that old. Her mother was a weak woman, but she became a different person after he'd gone. Started appearing in the village, at the Women's Institute, things like that. Dorothy didn't drive, so Hettie had to ferry her around, as well as doing everything else. She passed on a few years ago so Hettie's on her own.'

'And probably a lot happier,' his wife chipped in.

'You'll meet her sooner or later, I'm sure.'

***

Amy had answered the door twice at the weekend to local organisations – the Women's Institute being one of them.

'We wanted to tell you what we're about these days, in case you'd like to join. We're a mixed bunch, aren't we, Sylvia?' said the younger of the pair. She wore an expensive-looking tailored coat, a large Mulberry bag over her shoulder. The other woman was also smart, but more casually dressed.

'We have all sorts of interesting speakers,' she continued. 'Last week we had someone telling us about her recent cycling trip round India – she was fascinating, wasn't she, Sylvia? And this week we're learning all about cactuses – or should it be cacti?'

'Both are acceptable,' said Amy, immediately feeling like a nerd.

'We have such a laugh together,' said Sylvia.

'A barrelful!' said the younger woman.

Amy had politely told them she was rather too busy to join their group. She noticed the older woman looking past her into the hallway.

'I hear Lauren's done a lot to the house since her grandparents' day. I bet it's like a show home now!'

Amy knew they were angling for an invitation. Well, if they expected her to ferry them in and pop the kettle on then they had another thing coming. Nosy lot. They could take their cacti and stick them … *never mind*.

She relished her time at home, and rarely felt lonely. There was always something to do. When she wasn't at work, or running, there were books to read, whether for work or pleasure. And she felt a duty to keep Ivy Cottage clean and tidy. It was a big place for one person and she usually spent a couple of hours on a Saturday doing her housework. She always scoured the bathroom from top to bottom, and quickly ran over the rest of the house with a duster. She cleaned the kitchen frequently, wiping the hob meticulously every time she used a saucepan.

The other caller that weekend had been a smartly dressed man telling her about the different organisations that met in the village hall. He was the chair of the hall committee, he'd said, and he wanted her to know that the building was available for everyone to book if they needed it. He handed Amy a leaflet detailing the regular events held there: yoga on a Monday, French conversation with Francine on a Tuesday, book club every other Wednesday and community cinema on the week that the book club wasn't taking place, Women's Institute on a Thursday evening.

'I'm also church warden,' he told her, 'and a ringer, along with Mark Jeffreys.' Ah yes, she might have seen his photo when she'd googled Grassdale all those months ago, when the thought of living here had barely been a consideration. 'We do tell everyone, there's no age limit on ringing – providing you can manage the steps to the tower. We're always trying to recruit younger members.' And his eyes had twinkled.

Amy used the same excuse she had used for the Women's Institute callers. She liked it here, she really did, but she wished people would leave her alone sometimes. That Hettie character probably had it right – she wouldn't get many people knocking on her door, by the sound of it. Surely she could be part of the village without belonging to every organisation going?

***

Amy veered off the road and began the ascent to Ram's Seat. The ground was spongy now after the dryness of the summer months, and her feet sank into sopping patches of heather. The slope became steeper and slippery in places. She had to be careful where she trod. The ground was littered with rocks and stones and some holes that might have been dug by animals. She slowed to a walk as she scrambled up a barefaced slope, then broke into a trot again as she neared the summit, the momentum helping to propel her. It was relatively flat on top, so she picked up speed again, following a rough track north. There were dips and rises, but she could move more freely now. It was like running on top of the world!

The day was cold, and the air stung her face, but the rest of her body was warm in its layers. She wore a hat and gloves, and carried a waterproof jacket, a drink and some emergency snacks in a small backpack. A guide she had read recommended always having a map and compass too, and even a bivi bag, but that seemed excessive with Grassdale or one of the other villages often visible below her. She had no patience with people who got into difficulty in wild terrain because they were either poorly equipped, not fit enough in the first place or caught out by bad weather. She'd kicked herself for weeks after tripping on the overgrowth when she moved here. *She'd not make that mistake again.* You prepared beforehand, you assessed your capabilities, you checked the weather. It could change quickly in these parts, she knew that, so all the more reason for good planning.

She was pleased with her new fell-running shoes. She felt the satisfaction of a child savouring a new toy. They fit perfectly and were pretty too: pink, with a yellow cushioned sole and purple studs. (She could hear Penny's voice in her ear, 'Is it fitness or is it fashion?' which made her smile. But so what? There was nothing wrong with wanting to look good at the same time!) The shoes had arrived the day before. A man she had never seen, wearing a tatty denim jacket and a thick black woolly hat, had appeared on her doorstep holding a package. She had left instructions for it to be left round the back of the house if she wasn't in, so was surprised when the man said, 'I caught the delivery guy and said I'd take it for you.'

'And he just handed it over?' Amy wanted to say, but didn't.

'I'm Tizz, by the way – three doors down. I thought it was time we met.'

The name Tizz sounded familiar.

'I'm semi-retired but I do odd jobs. Basic plumbing, carpentry. I put a new door on the cupboard in the bathroom before you moved in. If there's anything else you need doing?' He looked at her, questioningly.

'Not at the moment, but thank you.' Amy took the parcel.

'New hobby?' he queried, looking at the label on the package.

'Erm, not exactly. Sorry, I really must go back in, I've … left a pan on.' It was a lie, but she wasn't really in the mood for a conversation. She was too eager to open the parcel!

'Won't keep you then. Pleased to have made your acquaintance.'

Amy thought he looked disappointed, nevertheless, at not being invited in.

She passed a plantation of conifers. A small deer skipped out from amongst the trees and then swiftly jumped back in again when it saw her. All around her, the land rose and fell, steeply in some places, more gently in others. Fields were laced with drystone walls, or bounded by trees on the lower slopes. Shepherds' tracks snaked up to the higher ground, purple with heather. She was overlooking Crowdale now. She stopped for a while to catch her breath and look at the view.

Though far larger than Grassdale, Crowdale looked small from this height. It was hard to believe that she had recently lost her way in its narrow streets. The village had a wide selection of independent shops, including several specialist food stores – a butcher, a fishmonger, a bakery, a sweet shop specialising in fudge (which she had a weakness for) – a craft shop with a window crammed with wools and yarns of every colour imaginable, and one or two selling outdoor clothing and equipment, though she hadn't been able to find the fell shoes she wanted there.

Beyond Crowdale, a flash of blue in the distance was the southern end of the reservoir.

Amy decided it was time to turn back. She didn't want to risk getting a blister in her new shoes. Just as she was thinking that she hadn't seen a single other living soul, she noticed movement about fifty metres down the slope. There was another runner, heading back in the direction of Grassdale. He took long strides and had a bounding gait. She watched him until he disappeared from view. Amy knew from his build and dark hair that it was Damian. Although they had been civil to each other when an encounter was unavoidable, they had kept out of each other's way at work as much as they could. Amy was sure that on at least one occasion, Damian had left the kitchen as soon as he saw her enter. None of the others had commented and she hoped they hadn't noticed.

Looking down at her fitness watch, she waited a couple of minutes. Amy didn't want to risk bumping into him today and only started running again when she felt that he was well ahead of her. Even though he was on a lower route, there was still the possibility that their paths would cross when they got closer to the village.

Back in Grassdale, Sunday-afternoon tourists were heading back to their cars. Amy saw that several of them clutched paper bags from the bookshop, and felt happy on Sarah's behalf. Nearing the top of Lower Street, she saw the stooped but agile frame of the Major striding towards her.

'Dying to get home! I've been on my feet all afternoon.' He added, by way of explanation, 'My stint at the community café.'

Amy commiserated.

'Oh, but it keeps me active. Besides, the mind gives up before the body. That's what I tell myself anyway.'

She was going to ask after Elsie, but he was already several metres past her, waving goodbye over his shoulder.

Suddenly, she felt a huge swelling of love for him and for everyone else in Grassdale.

12

Amy had designated the smallest of the three bedrooms for storage. True to its name, the box room contained just that. They were piled upon one another, some full, others empty. One of the boxes contained a set of china that she had brought from her London flat. In the end, the plain white Ikea crockery that was in the kitchen at Ivy Cottage was perfect for her requirements, so the china remained here. The delicate set had been given to Amy by her mother, and had belonged to her great-grandmother. It had a pretty design with a gold rim, pink and blue carnations around the edge, and the same flowers in a ring at the centre. She hadn't used it in London either, but was sure she would need it one day.

Her winter clothes were in the box room too. She would need some of the extra layers now. She found jumpers, a couple of pairs of boots and her smart winter coat. She had already invested in a second-hand waxed jacket from the charity shop in Crowdale that was perfect for call-outs to farms. In fact, she was starting to grow quite attached to it, even when she wasn't working.

A few rogue items had found their way into the second bedroom, but she collected and moved them into the box room. Amy needed to prepare the guest room as her parents were coming to stay, and had made up the two single beds. She had wondered at first if she ought to give them her room, but decided there was no need. The guest room was very pretty. Like her own, the roof sloped towards the low window and overlooked the garden. It had heavy, flowered curtains, a thick puce-coloured carpet, and cream walls. Knowing her mother would appreciate the gesture, she put a vase of flowers on the small table by the window.

She was slightly anxious about the visit, and whether everything would live up to her parents' expectations. *Probably not.* She wasn't entirely sure what her parents would want to do while they were with her. In all honesty, a part of her resented the thought of losing her precious weekend to entertaining, which she knew was selfish of her. She certainly wouldn't be able to go for a run. The easiest thing would be to go along with her parents' wishes – which really meant her mother's – and then everything would be fine.

They were driving up on Friday evening, after spending a couple of days with friends in Lincoln.

'Are you sure you have room for us, darling?' her mother had asked at least three times during phone calls in the weeks leading up to it. 'We're happy to book into a hotel, if it's easier.'

It would indeed be easier, thought Amy, but assured her mother that she had plenty of room. She was making beef Wellington. She had bought ready-to-roll puff pastry, but was proud to have made the rest of the dish herself.

Her mother sent messages to update her throughout their journey.

'An hour and a half to go!'

'An hour away now!'

'See you in thirty minutes – pop the kettle on!'

'Just left Crowdale. Daddy ended up in a cul-de-sac! But we'll see you soon!'

Amy sat patiently by the window; she knew her father was not one to be late. The headlights of the Audi shone through a chink in the curtains at almost exactly six-thirty, the time they had said they would arrive. She rushed out to greet them and help with their bags, feeling a sudden lurch of nervousness and love. The first thing she noticed was that her mother, whose auburn hair had faded to a silvery-grey in recent years, had dyed it a deep shade of red. Her father looked the same as ever – tall, still lean, with the piercing blue eyes that Amy shared.

'I'll bring everything in,' said her father, even before saying hello. 'Get your mother into the warmth please, Amy. It's freezing out here.'

It was true that the air was bitingly cold. The stars looked huge in the clear sky. There was going to be a heavy frost that night.

'It's a bit dark, Dad. Let me just run in and open the curtains so that you can see better.'

'Don't fuss. I've got it.'

A minute later, her parents and their luggage were inside. Her mother held her tightly for a couple of seconds, and her father kissed her promptly on the cheek with a small pat on the back.

'My, oh my! What a pretty place,' her mother said.

'Come in and sit down. This is the living room. I'll show you to your room in a bit. What are you drinking? I've got your favourite gin, Dad.'

'That's my girl!'

She had lit the fire as soon as she got in from work. The room looked cosy and inviting. Her mother followed her into the kitchen while her father flopped into the large armchair.

'Why don't *we* have an open fire, dear?' he called out.

Judith raised her eyes at Amy. 'Guess who would be cleaning it every day?' she called back.

She studied the kitchen. 'Let's have a look … Ooh, a granite top, very swish! I must say, I didn't think it would be so modern!'

'I told you it was, Mum! You didn't expect me to be boiling a kettle on an open fire, did you?'

'No, but I didn't think it would be as fancy as *this*.' She was running her hand over the polished work surface. '*Very* upmarket.'

Amy poured the gins – a generous measure for each of her parents, a smidgen for herself.

'Something smells tasty. What is it?'

'You'll see,' teased Amy.

Her mother peeped around the dining room door as they carried the drinks back to the living room. Amy had moved her laptop and all her papers from the table, which she had already set for three with a candle in the middle.

'Your daughter is spoiling us,' she said to her husband as she sat down on the sofa, patting the seat beside her. Amy, who had been about to take her favourite spot on the window seat, obliged.

'About time, too,' he joked.

Amy asked after the friends they had been staying with – the woman was her godmother, though she rarely saw her these days. She heard about their children, one of whom had children of her own already.

'But no hurry there,' said her mother, patting Amy's hand. 'I'm too young to be a grandmother.'

Her husband gave an amused grunt in response.

After a few minutes, Amy excused herself.

'Do you need some help, dear?'

'Just stay where you are and relax.'

'Are you sure? Amy, if you just let me—'

'Woman, do as your daughter tells you,' interrupted her father, raising his eyes at Amy. 'We're her guests this time.'

Twenty minutes later, the three of them were sitting at the dining room table. Amy had lit the candle. In its flickering light, their faces looked spooky one moment, angelic the next.

'Homemade beef Wellington with organic beef from Barry's Farm, and help yourselves to vegetables. Most of them come from the local area as well. I do most of my shopping at the store opposite.'

They were all silent for a few minutes as they ate. Her parents made appreciative noises.

'And how's the job going?' asked her father after a while.

Amy told him how much she was enjoying it. She spoke about her boss, about semi-retired Simon, about the three women who worked there. She didn't mention Damian; speaking of him was bound to leave a sour taste in her mouth and she was rather enjoying her dinner. In reality, she felt she had nothing nice to say about him. He had recently made a cup of tea for everyone except for her on one of the rare occasions when the whole team were in the kitchen together. To be fair, she hadn't been in the room when he had offered, but she had still felt slighted when the drinks appeared in front of everyone else. To admit to not getting on with a colleague seemed an admission of failure. Easier not to mention him at all.

'A pity we can't meet them,' said her father.

'Maybe on another visit,' said Amy.

The whole evening couldn't have gone better, Amy mused, as she prepared for bed later. She had switched the electric heater on in the spare bedroom before they went upstairs, which her parents appreciated. They seemed interested in everything, and delighted with the cottage, which brought Amy a sense of accomplishment. Their approval had always been a necessity in her life. Her mother had commented that it must feel like being on a permanent holiday. Amy agreed it was, except for going to work every day! But as she enjoyed her job so much, she knew she was very fortunate.

They woke up to rain, and as the forecast was poor for the rest of the day, the walk Amy had originally planned in the gardens of a country house was ruled out. In the morning, they made the most of a break in the weather to look around Grassdale. As they were about to leave the house, her mother suddenly released a startled yelp.

'Amy Ashton, what *are* you wearing?'

Amy looked down. Almost without thinking, she had thrown on the beaten waxed jacket.

'Don't you like it? It was a bargain.'

'I should think it was! It doesn't look very clean.'

It was true that it had become a bit spattered in places – with mud, definitely, but possibly something else as well – but it was perfect for a day like today.

'If you think—'

'I'm taking it off.' Amy went to find something else to put on. Sometimes it was easier to let her mother win.

They turned left first to explore Upper Street. Amy pointed out the practice as they passed it at the junction. Both her parents admired the large, handsome Georgian houses in this part of the village. Her mother spotted the antiques shop, as she knew she would. Amy hadn't yet been inside it, the items on display in the window never really took her fancy, but today she followed her parents inside.

It wasn't long before her mother was engaged in conversation with the owner, while her father rummaged through a box of military paraphernalia, one of his interests. Amy, standing near the window, flicked through an old copy of *Picture Post*. Every now and then, she was distracted by passers-by. She knew several of the locals by sight and could usually pick out who was a tourist and who wasn't. Even today, a miserable morning in November, a couple clad in waterproofs and hiking boots yomped past, ready for a day on the moors.

On the other side of the road, a small boy with his hood up went by on a bicycle, followed by a man who called something out to him. Crikey – was that Damian? Of course it was – although she hated to admit it, she knew that profile well, even down to the way he walked. Turning to listen to Damian's shouts, the boy pulled down his hood and Amy realised it was the same dark-haired child she had seen with him several weeks earlier.

She'd never imagined Damian with a child – certainly, no one had ever mentioned it – but then again why would they? There was no reason why he shouldn't be a father. Perhaps, she mused, it was a sensitive subject. Based on the fact she'd only seen them together twice, it could be that he only saw the child on certain weekends.

Amy watched them pass, confident of not being seen. She knew that Damian lived at the top end of the village, in the direction they were headed. Hopefully they would be indoors by the time she and her parents continued on their wander.

The family eventually left the antiques shop, and after ambling down to the other end of the village, stopping briefly in the store to pick up a couple of newspapers, her father wanted to see the church.

'I don't suppose it'll be open, Dad.'

'Of course it will. Churches are always open.'

She thought she had proved him wrong, but the door was simply stiff and heavy. The nave was a hive of activity.

A man and woman were on their hands and knees, polishing the wooden floor, while others were in the pews, dusters in their hands. One very elderly woman was sitting on a chair, writing in a heavy ledger that lay on her lap. They all looked up simultaneously at the noise of the church doors slamming. Amy recognised the only man amongst them as Charles Brady, the churchwarden and bellringer who had called at Ivy Cottage to tell her about the village hall.

'Ahh, Amy! We're on the cleaning rota,' he explained, as he clambered to his feet to greet the party. He was younger than most of the women, but seemed delighted to have an excuse to get off the floor and show them round the interior of the ancient building.

While the man clearly relished having an audience, he had a rather dry delivery. Amy thought that even her father might be regretting this move.

'Most of the building dates from the eighteenth century, but we believe there has been a place of worship on this site for five hundred years. The windows, however, are Victorian. If you look very closely at the figure in the background of this one …' Amy felt her eyes glaze over. Her father was managing to feign interest, her mother less so. She wondered how long their little tour would last.

'Some of our ladies are responsible for our kneelers.'

'Lovely design,' murmured her mother.

Seeing a similarity with the cushions in the cottage, Amy realised that Lauren's grandma must have made some of them, but not wanting to prolong the conversation, she decided not to mention it.

One subject seamlessly followed another. 'We will be in Advent soon so the time has come to … A Victorian parson used to ask his wife to send him a signal to indicate when he had been preaching for too long …'

Perhaps yours should do the same, thought Amy, as he carried on, his voice almost soothing in its monotony.

'We like to think we are a modern church. We have a group for everyone, even young women like yourself.'

Amy realised the others were all looking at her.

'This one's too busy for groups,' said her father, laughing, and fortunately the man just nodded and carried on with his soliloquy.

'I really think we ought to be making a move,' her mother said, as they heard about plans to instal a toilet in the church. 'We've taken up far too much of your time and we do have to be somewhere.' She caught Amy's eye in a conspiratorial fashion.

It was still another ten minutes before they managed to leave.

'Knows his stuff,' said Amy's father, as they walked back towards the lychgate.

'Oh, Tim, you rather landed us in that!'

'He is rather a chatterbox, Dad.'

'Still, nice to see people enthused about their subjects,' said her father.

Amy's mother had stopped to read some of the gravestones. Most of those close to the church were very old, the stone worn down and moss-covered, many of the words indecipherable.

'Look at this one, Tim. A father who outlived his wife and all *eight* children.'

'Rather like the Brontë family,' said Amy, who had visited Haworth Parsonage the previous weekend. She had always loved the Brontës, and was currently reading Agnes Grey by the lesser-known Anne, a book from Lauren's grandad's collection. Although it had been too late in the day to begin a long walk, she had ventured into the field behind the parsonage and seen the Brontë stone for Anne, one of four engraved stones commemorating the literacy legacy of the sisters, stark and solemn under the gloomy sky. The engraved words had brought tears to her eyes – she even had to stifle a sob. There was no one else around, but she wiped her eyes furiously in case someone appeared.

***

It was time for lunch when they got back to Ivy Cottage. After they had eaten, the rain started hammering down again. Her parents confessed that they would be happy to spend the afternoon curled up in the living room, reading the papers.

'Also, I didn't sleep particularly well last night,' said her mother. 'So a rest before this evening will be nice.'

Noting Amy's look of concern, she added, 'Just being somewhere new. I'll probably sleep like a log tonight.'

Amy had booked a table at an Italian restaurant in Crowdale with good reviews. She had decided against the Fox and Ferret, much as she had enjoyed her meal there with Mary, not particularly wanting to bump into people she knew, *especially* Damian.

Amy made a pot of tea. Her father was deep in *The Telegraph*.

'Put your feet up, Mum.' She fetched her the footstool.

'Thank you, darling.'

Her mother made herself comfortable. Amy sat in the window seat, flicking through the weekend magazine, surprised by the peace.

'You're not too bored here, are you, darling?'

No chance to read with her mother around.

'It does seem awfully quiet.'

Amy realised she had been waiting for a question of this nature ever since their arrival the night before.

'No, Mum, I don't have time to get bored.'

'It's pretty here, of course. I mean I absolutely adore this cottage, but how much better if it was in, I don't know, York, perhaps – now *there's* a beautiful city. There'd be more to do on a rainy afternoon, for a start.'

Folding up her magazine, Amy said, 'Mum, I think it was you who chose not to go out. There's plenty to do if you want to. And I've got my running.'

'You're still doing that?'

'You know I am. You've seen some of those lovely photos I've taken.'

'I just worry you might be …' she circled her hand, searching for the word, 'stagnating? I haven't seen many young people around.'

'There are plenty of young people! It's just a … gloomy day, that's all.'

'And I can't imagine you have much in common with these farmers you've been talking about.'

'Mum, give it a rest. Do you want me to fetch your book from the bedroom?'

'What your mother means— ' Her father had glanced up from the paper, 'is that with your qualifications, you could work anywhere. There'll be places crying out for someone with a degree like yours. And the award, as well. It marks you out.'

That bloomin' award! Amy sometimes wished she'd never won it. It would always be an instrument for her parents to leverage when they thought she was failing to make the most of her opportunities. She felt a pinch of irritation. Were they actually thinking of her desires, as opposed to their own? Did they, in fact, think of how it looked for *them* when they brought it up, rather than her? Did they dislike admitting to their friends that their 'brilliant daughter' was working in a village in the Yorkshire Dales rather than in one of the country's 'top' practices? Had she become a let-down to them, a failure in their eyes?

'I thought you both wanted me to be happy.' She felt her voice wavering. 'Isn't that enough – for me to work in a job I enjoy, be renumerated for it and have free time to pursue my other interests? I think I'm luckier than most of the people I know in that regard.'

They exchanged a worried look. 'Of course that's what we want, darling! It's what every parent wants for their child. But there's a difference between being happy and being fulfilled. You've always been so … ambitious in the past. It's hard for us to see you wasting some of those opportunities you've had.'

'Well I'm *sorry* that *you're* finding it *so* hard.'

Amy felt her face flushing. Her parents looked at each other and she saw her father give a little shake of his head to her mother before he picked his paper back up. Her mother flashed a forced smile. 'Yes I'd love my book, darling.'

She was seething when she went upstairs. Sitting on one of the beds in her parents' room, Amy watched the rain splashing on the window, taking slow, deep breaths. Her father's pyjamas were folded neatly on the pillow. Her mother's perfume lingered in the air. Could she ever please them? She'd always tried to do everything in accordance to their wishes. Even down to that stupid award. It seemed as though even that had become some kind of badge of honour for them to wear. Her thoughts continued to spiral and she felt more and more het up until a magpie started to squawk from the apple tree.

'Don't you start!' she growled, but managed to smile as the bird had reminded her of where she was. Amy drew another deep breath, picked up her mother's book and headed back downstairs.

***

The atmosphere remained strained for the rest of the afternoon, but Amy was determined that they were going to enjoy their evening. She would offer to pay for the meal, insisting it was her treat, but she knew her father wouldn't hear of it. It was a familiar pattern. They had always been generous, and she did appreciate it. She had shown this mainly by pushing herself at school, particularly when she was at Blake's. (It was not unheard of for her mother to slip into the conversation how expensive her education was, whenever she felt that Amy was disappointing her in some way.) When her GCSEs grew closer, she had stopped her after-school badminton club that she loved so much in order to make more study time, and turned down weekend invitations. Her parents had actually become a little worried about her then, but she didn't want them to be able to say she had done anything other than her very best.

The restaurant was bigger inside than it appeared from the street. It had two separate dining rooms, one at the front and one at the back, both of them small and intimate. The first thing Amy's father said was, 'Well this takes me back!' He sounded both pleased and amused. The restaurant had red and white-checked tablecloths on most of the tables, apart from those in the booths, which had smooth Formica tops. Every table was decorated with a wicker-covered chianti bottle containing a candle. The walls were coated in rough plaster, and decorated with what appeared to be fishing nets and photographs in wooden frames of Italian family gatherings. A handsome young man with slicked-back hair greeted them and showed them to one of the booths.

'Welcome to the famous Mario's,' he said, and Amy's mother raised her eyes at Amy. Amy had to force herself not to laugh. 'Mario is my grandfather, and he opened this restaurant in 1969. We are the oldest restaurant not just in Crowdale but in this part of the Dales.'

'I hope the food's up to scratch,' Amy panicked quietly after he had left them with the menus. Her mother could be quite particular when eating out.

'It sounds delicious!' her father said, 'and this crowd surely speaks for itself.' The place was packed, and a group of people who had walked in after them was soon turned away.

'I think it's perfectly charming,' said her mother, surveying their surroundings. 'And I know what I'm having already. Penne primavera. No starter.'

'And you both know what I'm having,' said Amy's father, snapping the heavy leather-bound menu shut.

'The steak,' Amy and her mother said in unison.

'You got it. And what are you ladies drinking?'

Her father was driving but allowed himself one glass of red wine. He ordered a bottle of Sauvignon Blanc for Amy and her mother, even though they both insisted they would have only one glass each. 'You can take the bottle home,' he said.

The tense atmosphere of earlier evaporated. Amy never loved her parents more than when they were like this.

Relaxed, happy, ready to laugh. They always seemed easier company when they were on neutral ground.

'I used to go to a restaurant like this when I was at school,' said Judith. 'We used to eye up all the Italian waiters. I had a real soft spot for one called Paco. He had long, dark hair and wore very tight jeans.'

'Isn't that a Spanish name?' said Amy.

'I'm starting to get worried about all these details you remember,' said Tim.

'Sounds as if you've still got the hots for him, Mum.' Amy elbowed her.

Her mother scolded her, and carried on. 'One night a group of the waiters asked us all to go to a nightclub with them.'

'And you were how old, Mum?'

'Oh, this was a bit later. Eighteen, I think. When Paco appeared, he was wearing a white leather jacket with tassels on it and a pair of cowboy boots. I went right off him there and then.'

'Poor Paco. I bet he's devastated to this day,' said her father.

'Probably not. He spent most of the night dancing with my friend Alison. I went home early. I realised I preferred to idolise them from afar.'

'Mum, you're such a dark horse!'

'Isn't she just! I didn't know any of this either.'

The food arrived while they were all chuckling. It smelt delicious. Amy had ordered a pizza with olives and anchovies, a side salad and garlic bread.

While they ate, it was her father's turn to regale them all with some of his teenage escapades. 'Did I ever tell you about the time I went hitchhiking in Italy with my friend Adrian? This chap stopped to pick us up, then after about half an hour he came to a complete halt. He said there was something wrong with the engine, and asked if we could push the car. We both got out, like a couple of muppets, and off he drove with all our things in the back.'

'Dad, no! Did you get them back?'

'Not a chance. We went to the police, of course, and they knew all about it. Turned out he'd done it several times.'

'I wonder if anyone hitchhikes these days?' mused her mother idly.

All three of them cleared their plates.

'Anyone tempted by a pudding?' asked Amy's father.

Both women said they couldn't possibly. Amy suggested coffee back at Ivy Cottage instead. She was almost starting to feel sorry that her parents were leaving the next day.

As she and her father fondly bickered over who would pay the bill – an argument he would inevitably win – she became aware of a presence at her shoulder, and was startled when a rather sheepish-sounding voice said, 'Amy? I had no idea you were here.'

She looked up and saw Damian, some people hovering behind him. He must have come out of the other dining room, which she'd had her back to all night, and was now passing their table on his way to the exit.

Stunned into silence, Amy's mother spoke up for her daughter instead. 'Well aren't you going to introduce us, Amy?' Her voice had gone fluttery, as if she was inhabiting her teenage self dreaming of Paco.

'Sorry, yes. Mum, Dad, this is Damian.'

'Pleased to meet you. I'm Tim and this is Judith,' said her father, thrusting out his right hand and indicating his wife beside him.

'And these are my parents,' said Damian, as the people he was with stepped out from behind him. Amy recognised the man from the night she had spotted Damian in the pub, on Mary's birthday. Just the three of them. No sign of the boy from earlier in the day. Or the boy's mother, whoever she was.

'Don't want to disturb your meal,' said Damian's father, shaking hands vigorously with them all. He was a large man, taller than his son, with a thick head of dark hair, a heavy jowl and black bushy eyebrows. Amy thought that despite his friendliness, his natural expression was rather stern.

'You're not disturbing us at all,' said Amy's mother. 'We've just finished. Did you enjoy your meal?'

'Very much,' said Damian's mother. She was tall too, with a smiley face.

'And how do you two know each other?'

God, her mother was so persistent. Amy could almost see her antennae twitching, as she desperately tried to ascertain the relationship between them.

'We work together,' said Amy. 'We're at the same practice, that is.'

'Splendid!' Damian's father rubbed his hands together. She noticed a look of surprised pleasure on her mother's face. She could read her like a book at times. Her mother eyed Damian even more keenly, then Amy.

'We're up for the weekend,' said her father, addressing Damian's father. 'Visiting our daughter's new home.' He regarded Amy with what seemed to be pride.

'How do you find it here? We're very proud of the Dales.'

'A beautiful part of the world,' said Amy's mother, rather too quickly. 'But unfortunately the weather hasn't been too kind to us.'

'Yes, too bad about the rain,' Damian's father continued. Amy noticed that his mother didn't say much.

'You're from these parts?'

'I'm a Dalesman. Clare's from Durham.'

'Best place in the world,' said his mother. 'I thought I was going to the back of beyond when I came here.'

Everyone laughed.

'Sometimes the back of beyond is what everyone needs,' said Amy's father.

Oh, you hypocrite, thought Amy. She wished they'd stop being so chummy. It was embarrassing. She saw the waiter hovering with the bill.

'Sorry, we're in the way,' said Damian, spotting the waiter. 'It was lovely to meet you, Mr and Mrs Ashton, and I'll see you on Monday, Amy.'

After they had all said their goodbyes, Damian's party left.

Amy deliberately didn't look at her mother, as her father grabbed the bill.

'My treat, dear. You've been such an amazing hostess this weekend.'

'Thank you, Dad. I do appreciate it. It was a lovely meal.'

'And a great choice by you.'

It wasn't until they were in the car that her mother had the chance to say what she had clearly been itching to.

'I don't remember you telling us about Damian.'

'Didn't I?'

'No, I distinctly remember the names of the two older gentlemen, Mark and Simon. Fancy you not mentioning that there was someone your age there too. And what a charming young man! Such nice parents too.'

'Give it a rest, Mum.'

'I'm not saying anything except what a nice family they seemed! I am allowed to say that, aren't I?'

After a while, she prodded further. 'There was no sign of a girlfriend, was there?'

'Mum! Enough!'

Her mother sighed. 'I'm just saying. Sometimes we don't see what's right under our noses.'

'He's actually a total knob. So please don't have us married off.'

Her mother was silent after that.

'Hope I don't meet another car on this road, Amy. Perhaps we should have taken yours.' Her father could usually be relied on to change the subject when things got too awkward.

Her parents left just before lunch the next day. They had a long drive ahead of them, and though Amy was all set to feed them, they insisted they needed to be on their way.

Mary had come round that morning, ostensibly as she was expecting a delivery and wanted to let Amy know that she might not be at home, but Amy suspected she had seen her parents' car and was curious.

'Oh, you two could be sisters!' she called, as she caught sight of Amy's mother in the hallway.

'Thanks, Mary. I really wanted to be told I looked sixty,' Amy joked.

'Rude girl!' said her mother, poking her daughter in the ribs as she came up to say hello. 'I'm nowhere near sixty,' she said to Mary.

'It's true, you're very alike,' said Mary, touching her own face and hair to show where she thought the similarities lay. Inevitably, she ended up coming in for ten minutes, was introduced to Amy's father too, and regaled them both with stories of old characters from the village.

'Quite a livewire,' said her mother, once she left. 'Exhausting, though.'

'She's great, actually. And such a good neighbour. She'd do anything for anyone.'

How times had changed! Amy realised how fond she had grown of Mary. Just knowing she was next door gave her a warm feeling inside.

Ivy Cottage felt quiet after her parents had left. Although Amy felt relieved to have the cottage back to herself, she was also aware of a nagging feeling she couldn't quite put her finger on.

They could get on so well at times, but why did they have to irritate her so much the rest of it? She shouldn't have been surprised that the second her mother set eyes on Damian she had him marked out as a possible 'beau'. So maddening!

But they only want the best for me, she thought, feeling suddenly very guilty. She wished she could have them back for just a few minutes, to apologise for being so touchy at times. She resolved to make up for it when she visited at Christmas.

13

Since discovering the run up Ram's Seat and onto Grassdale Moor, Amy had tended to stick to that route. The views felt slightly different every run, depending on the time of day and the weather: sometimes the grey skies gave the landscape an ominous look; other times, the fields and villages shone with a golden radiance.

One Saturday, Amy decided to try a different route. Instead of turning right out of Ivy Cottage, she headed for the crossroads then turned left again onto the road. It wasn't a busy road. Whenever she had used it to visit neighbouring farms or villages, she rarely encountered traffic other than farm vehicles or cyclists. The cyclists always looked serious, hunched over their handlebars, their faces grim as they tackled the often steep inclines.

Being of a cautious nature – and the road being narrow – she stopped and pushed herself into the hedgerow whenever she heard a vehicle approach, allowing them to pass before resuming her run.

Just before reaching the road that led to Yew Tree Farm, the scene of the dog attack that had deepened the friction between her and Damian, she took a turning on the other side of the road. She had seen on the map that this track led to a scattering of remote properties before turning into a footpath which skirted the base of a small hill. By continuing on the route and cutting through the dale behind it, she could then follow the river back to Grassdale. At least, that was her plan.

It was a crisp day in early December. There had been a light falling of snow overnight. Most of it had disappeared from Grassdale by the time Amy had left home, but away from the village it still lay in patches along the side of the road and had collected in small piles on some of the stones in the drystone walls. The plants that grew in these walls displayed intricate icy patterns on their leaves. The fields and the hills appeared dusted in icing sugar, a yellow and white mosaic.

After a couple of hundred metres, she came to a pair of pebble-dashed semi-detached houses. A child played on a swing in the garden of one of them and a dog started barking upon her approach. She was silently thankful as she heard the child shout out for it to be quiet. The track rose as it cut between two hills. High above her, a bird of prey soared and she could see a white pattern on the underside of its wings.

Despite the cold, it was a beautiful day. Amy wore three layers for running in the winter, but had warmed up enough to shed the top layer. She did however wear a woolly hat and gloves, something she had rarely done in London, even on the coldest days. Her nose and cheeks felt raw but she felt invigorated by the icy air. It was wonderful to be outdoors.

It had been a busy week at work. Veterinary nurse Fran had been on holiday, then Donna had caught a bug, meaning there was no one to man reception. They had all taken their turn when they could. Neither she nor Damian had mentioned the encounter in the Italian restaurant with their parents, continuing to say as little to each other as they needed to (Amy did wonder if the rest of the team were starting to notice the frosty atmosphere between them).

Her mother had asked after her colleagues – 'and that very nice young man' – in a recent text message, and Amy had simply responded that everyone was fine. 'Will there be a work Christmas party?' she had persisted. Amy had no idea. The idea of the six of them – seven if you counted Simon – going out and getting drunk together, which had been the form at her previous work dos, seemed faintly ridiculous. They were all so very different, and though she liked most of them very much, she couldn't really imagine hanging out with them all at once.

But then as if by magic, the day after the exchange with her mother, Donna had announced that they were to have a Secret Santa swap on the last day they were all together before the practice closed for a festive break. They would also have champagne and mince pies before heading their separate ways. She had asked them all to pick a name out of a hat – actually a paper bag from the store next door – and to buy a present worth approximately ten pounds for the person they selected. Amy felt a deep dread within that she would pick Damian, but managed to pick Simon instead. When she thought about it later, Damian would have probably been easier after all, as she barely knew Simon.

The path wound past some dilapidated farm buildings and continued upwards. Sheep were grazing, seemingly unperturbed by the snow. She was walking now rather than running, partly due to the steep incline, partly to appreciate the scenery. Occasionally, she had a glimpse of grey farm buildings high above her. They kept appearing, then vanishing again. She almost jumped out of her skin when, from nowhere, something gently butted her from behind. She turned and saw a goat was the culprit. It was a small creature, less than two feet tall, mainly black but with white patches on its back and around one eye. Its horns were small and fairly straight rather than curved.

'Hello, what do you want?'

The creature seemed friendly, and nuzzled Amy's legs. It was very clean and looked well cared for. It appeared more like somebody's pet than a wild goat. So what was it doing out here on its own?

'What shall I do with you, then?'

The goat bleated and rubbed its nose on her thigh.

'Are you lost?'

Perhaps it belonged to people in one of the houses she had passed. Perhaps it belonged to one of the farms. She looked around helplessly, but no other building was in sight. She could hardly take it with her. There was nothing she could do other than stop at the next building she came to and hope that whoever was there knew where it came from.

The snow-speckled footpath wasn't so easy to see now. Heading in what felt instinctively like the right direction, she was relieved to see the grey farm appear again, this time much closer. There were no other signs of habitation. The temperature seemed to have dropped suddenly, and the cold air made her nose run. She stopped to blow it, and noticed that the goat, which had found something to occupy its interest, was back at her heels again like a faithful puppy.

'Hey, you! I wish I knew where you lived.'

The goat was a female, Amy noted as she stopped to pet her. Did her stomach feel a bit bloated? The goat didn't show any sign of discomfort as she touched her, but was her rumen a bit tight? She stood back and studied the goat for signs of enlargement. Maybe not, but it was worth mentioning her concern to its owner if she ever found them. Bloat, if not treated, could be very serious. She felt again, and as she was talking to the goat she became aware of a noise, the first mechanical sound she had heard since she left the main road. A quad bike was driving over the moors towards her.

The driver threw her a large wave. As it neared, the figure shouted something but Amy couldn't quite catch what they were saying.

She paused and waited for the bike to reach her. It had a small trailer on the back in which a sheepdog was sitting. Amy saw a woman wearing a thick headband – the sort that also covered her ears – with a sheep design on it. A short, frizzy, greyish-brown ponytail stuck out of the top. The woman was also wearing an oversized pair of sunglasses, in which Amy now saw herself reflected in the low amber light. Little of her face was visible so it was hard to tell the woman's age. The driver pushed up her sunglasses so that they sat on the headband, revealing a rosy complexion.

'What are you doing with my goat?' she said rather abruptly, while looking Amy up and down.

'I, er, she followed me. I was worried she was lost. And I—'

'You don't need to be Einstein to see that.'

The woman dismounted the bike. She was stocky but nimble, a few inches shorter than Amy. The goat trotted up to her and the woman broke into a smile. Amy saw a large gap between her two front teeth.

'Aww, what are you like? Trouble, that's what you are.'

She scooped the little creature up and lowered her into the trailer, tying her up securely.

In a friendlier tone, she said, 'I think I'm going to start calling her Houdini. She can get out of anything. That's the second time this week she's done this.'

Amy, remembering her concern, said, 'I thought it might be worth saying that I did detect a bit of tightness in her rumen. I wondered if it was worth checking for bloat.' She added, 'She looks very healthy otherwise.'

The woman cast her a queer look.

'I'm a vet.' Amy validated her previous statement.

'A vet? Ah, you're not the new one at Mark's place, are you?'

'In Grassdale? Yes, that's me. I'm Amy.'

'Hettie,' said the woman.

'Oh, I've heard people talk about you,' said Amy, adding quickly, in case it had sounded rude, 'All good things, of course!'

'Tscch! You'll hear all sorts about me. Most of them true. Listen, time's ticking and it'll be dark before you know it. Why not come up for a brew and then I'll run you home? I'll get this one back and check her over, and see you in the house. It's the farmhouse yonder. If you take that path through the field and follow your eyes, it'll take you straight there.' She gave Amy a rather disdainful look, 'What are you doing out here anyway in your next-to-nothings? You must be nithered.'

While they were talking, the temperature had dropped further and the winter sun sunk even lower. Half of it had disappeared behind the hills. Amy still had a few miles to go. She could wear her top layer if she needed to, so was unlikely to freeze, but she knew that compared to Hettie, she looked skimpily dressed.

She found herself agreeing.

Hettie turned the quad bike round. 'Unless you fancy hopping in with Josephine, I'll see you up there.'

When Amy reached the farm, she was confronted with several doors, unsure which one led to the house and which to outbuildings. Fortunately, Hettie appeared from one of the sheds, so she followed her across the yard and through a door on the side of the house. They were in a sort of boot room, where Hettie sat on a wooden bench to take off her heavy shoes. They looked like a man's footwear. Amy removed her fell-running shoes and followed Hettie inside. Her feet left damp patches on the stone floor.

As in her own cottage, the walls were very thick – probably thicker – and in the dim light, under low ceilings, the effect was rather like entering a cave. It felt almost as cold inside the house as it did outside. Hettie led the way down a long corridor into the kitchen, where, as soon as she opened the door, several dogs came bounding up: two more collies, a black Labrador, and a springer spaniel. Hettie shouted at them to stay down, and they all obeyed, but the Labrador stayed close to Amy. The kitchen was warmer than the hallway had been though still not exactly cosy.

'Put the wood in the gap will you, duck?' Hettie said to Amy. She moved a kettle from one ring to another on the Aga. 'Sit yourself down. Warm up. Tea won't be long.'

She laid a plate of biscuits on the table. They were shop-bought, unlike Mary's offerings. As if reading Amy's mind, Hettie said, 'Never seems much point in baking just for one. Besides, you can't beat a custard cream.'

She muttered to herself as she found mugs and rinsed out a teapot, occasionally issuing a command to the dogs. A large black cat came out of another door, stopped to rub its head against Amy's leg, then carried on, its tail in the air. 'That's Eliza. She's the boss round here,' said Hettie, as the cat went to lie on a bed that was instantly vacated by one of the collies.

Although the kitchen appeared old-fashioned in its décor, it did have a modern dishwasher, which was gushing away in the corner.

'I assume you don't take sugar. No one does these days.'
'No thanks.'
Finally, the tea made, Hettie sat down beside Amy.

'Well, well, well. I didn't think I'd meet you for the first time like this. Good job you came along, otherwise I don't know how far Josephine would have wandered. She's a nuisance that one is, but she's a darling too. And a good milker. Oh, thanks for the bloat warning. She seems fine at the moment, but I'll keep an eye on her.' She poured the tea.

'Do you mind if I—' Amy gestured to her socks, which were sodden. Hettie shook her head in bemusement and indicated that she should hang them on the rail in front of the Aga.

'Do you really get pleasure from that lark? You'll not be able to do it soon, though. Ground'll be far too boggy. Here, let me get you a towel. Warm those toes up.' She chuckled as she went to fetch a towel from a drawer.

Amy thanked her, and dried her feet. The floor had made them even colder than her damp socks had.

'Do you live up here on your own?' she asked, and immediately wished that she hadn't.

'If I had a penny for every time someone asked me that!'

'Sorry.'

'Oh, don't apologise. It's natural to be curious, I suppose. Anyway, I'm hardly on my own with all this lot.' She looked at the dogs, all of them now lying at her feet, apart from the Labrador, which lay by Amy's chair. (She wondered if she could stick her feet underneath him to warm them further.) 'I manage very well on me own, thank you.'

'Oh I'm single too,' offered Amy in solidarity.

Hettie raised an eyebrow but didn't say anything. They both sipped their tea. Amy could feel the hot drink trickling down her throat and slowly warming her. She glanced around the farmhouse kitchen. It wasn't quite as large as some of the ones she had visited, but it was a big room nonetheless. An old-fashioned pulley hung from the ceiling, and Amy saw large thermal layers and a heavy pair of corduroy trousers draped over it before she looked away. She could see through another door into a small room dominated by a vast sink. She had visions of Hettie doing her weekly wash in it, pounding away at her clothes like a Victorian washerwoman.

Hettie seemed comfortable with the silence, but Amy felt she had to say something. 'I hear you were a champion shearer,' she blurted out.

Hettie put down her mug and chuckled. 'I don't know about champion! But that was a long time ago.'

'You don't do it anymore?'

'Oh, I'm still capable. I do some of my own, just to keep my hand in. But it's a young person's game. These days I have a lad from New Zealand to do mine. Drinks coffee all day and beer all night but they don't come much better.' She gazed at Amy, nursing her mug in both hands. 'Mark says you're settling in grand.'

So people spoke about her too. Though she knew that news travelled fast in a little place like Grassdale, it still occasionally took her by surprise.

'He told me he'd had a brilliant application from someone in London,' she continued. 'I said he should have his head examined if he thought a Londoner would stick it out here.' She regarded her with a quizzical look.

'I was ready for a change,' said Amy. 'I'm really—'

Hettie interrupted her. 'A change? That's what they all want these days. No one ever sticks at anything. Always looking for better things round the corner.' She sighed.

Amy wasn't sure if Hettie was criticising her or simply making a general observation about modern life. Defending herself seemed silly, so she smiled and said, 'I guess we're lucky that we have more choices today. My mother always felt she could have done more with her life. Instead she poured all her dreams and expectations into me.'

She had never voiced those feelings before, and was surprised how the thought came out of her mouth, fully formed.

'That right? Tscch.' Hettie shook her head but didn't appear too surprised by what Amy had told her. 'I never had much of a choice about anything myself, and no one's more contented than I am.'

Amy wasn't sure what to respond. To say how wonderful that was sounded trite, or even worse, sarcastic, so she stared into her mug and drank some more tea.

Every time she looked across at Hettie, the other woman was eyeing her. She had the sense that Hettie was sizing her up. She thought that she had probably found her wanting.

'You've been very kind. I suppose I had better leave you in peace and get back.'

'Finish your tea, duck, and I'll get the chariot ready.'

A few minutes later they were walking across the farmyard to a spot where two cars were parked – a battered pickup and a modern Volvo. She opened the Volvo with her key fob. It was almost totally dark now, the first stars appearing above them. They bounced over a rough, potholed track.

'Hold on to your hat.'

After about a mile, the track joined a minor road which, a few minutes later, connected with the road at the bottom of Grassdale, near the bridge. 'You're up here, aren't you?' said Hettie, turning into Lower Street.

'Yes, the last house on the left before the junction.'

'Knew the old couple there. He was a great friend of my father.'

'They sounded like wonderful people.'

Hettie didn't feel the need to reply. As they passed the pub, Amy could see light spilling through the thick glass. It looked cosy and inviting, the way glimpses through other people's windows sometimes were. She almost wished she was meeting someone there later rather than spending the evening on her own.

Hettie tooted at a pedestrian as she drove past.

'Good old Tizz,' she said, as he lifted an arm in reply. 'Our celebrity author.'

Amy remembered a poster for a book event: *that* was when she had first come across the name of the neighbour who delivered her parcel a few weeks earlier. Unsure if Hettie was being genuine or sarcastic, she decided not to risk a reply.

Hettie pulled up in front of Ivy Cottage.

'Thank you so much for the lift.' She was suddenly desperate to get inside and have a piping hot bath. She had left the cottage several hours earlier on a sunny afternoon, dressed for a light run, and now it was dark and below freezing. She felt foolish beside Hettie, who seemed almost mountainous in her bulky jacket.

'I'll see you around.' Hettie waved briefly before driving away.

14

Christmas was less than three weeks away. Determined to buy locally, Amy visited the bookshop to see if she could pick up any gifts there. She didn't have many people to buy for other than her parents. She remembered a time, at school, when she and her group of friends took great delight in shopping for each other. Little notelets decorated with cute animals when they were eleven, cheap jewellery the next year, Avon cosmetics the year after. She supposed she should buy something for Mary, who was always so kind. She hadn't seen much of her recently, actually. She wasn't sure if that was down to her or Mary. Admittedly, work had been busy, and given the signs about donations for Christmas hampers for the food bank, and a poster about the church Christmas fair, she supposed Mary had been busy too.

The bookshop window looked beautiful. One side of it was devoted to new books – the latest bestsellers in cosy crime, romance and thrillers; a cookbook by a celebrity chef; TV's newest guru offering top tips to improve your life, starting by clearing out your attic. On the other side, on a set of rustic shelves strung with fairy lights and with pictures of Victorian Christmas scenes behind them, were a selection of books from the second-hand section of the store.

Inside, the shop was very busy, and Sarah had a queue of customers at the counter. Amy waved but she was clearly too preoccupied to notice her. She crossed to the room that housed the second-hand section. You never knew what gems you might find there. An Edwardian edition of *A Child's Garden of Verses* by Robert Louis Stevenson stood on the shelves, its cover turned outwards. She picked it up and read some of the poems inside. Her eyes stung a little as she remembered her mother reading them to her when she was very young. Judith would love it, and it was beautifully illustrated too, as was a handsome copy of *Peter Pan*.

As she browsed, she noticed the striking dark-haired woman she now knew to be Fahimeh, thanks to Mary, tidying the shelves. Sarah had told her that Fahimeh was a volunteer in the shop as she did not yet have her official papers, but that she was a hard worker nonetheless. Fahimeh was interrupted by a customer who asked her where she could find the crime section. She stopped what she was doing and escorted the woman straight to it. When she returned to her original spot, Amy caught her eye and they exchanged bashful smiles.

Amy's father was fairly easy to choose for. He never read fiction, preferring both popular and heavyweight biographies, which he interspersed with his medical reading. She looked at several, before spotting a new book about The Beatles. Ah, that was perfect! He was a huge fan.

As the queue was still long, Amy went next to the local interest section, where she saw the book whose title had made her smile: *Postmen of the Dales*. She read the blurb, learning that Tizz had been born in Hebden Bridge but lived in Grassdale all his adult life. His book was about the challenges faced by postmen and women in this sometimes inaccessible part of the country. Amy saw that he had written several other books: *How to be a Dalesman*, *My Dales Christmas*, and *A History of Grassdale*. She wondered if one of these titles might work for the Secret Santa gift she had to buy. Simon was a local man so would hopefully appreciate one. She read the back of each one several times, before telling herself that it was all a bit of fun anyway. Reasoning that Simon might already know all he needed to know about the history of Grassdale, she chose Tizz's latest, about the postmen, featuring a cover illustration of a postman stuck up to his waist in snow, while an angry-looking woman on a doorstep queried, 'Why are you so late today?'

'Beautiful cover, isn't it?' said Sarah of the Robert Louis Stevenson book when Amy reached the counter. The rush had died down. 'I bought a wonderful collection of Victorian and Edwardian books from a recent estate sale. That was one of them.'

'I love it! You're very busy today.'

'Everyone's realising how close Christmas is!'

'Your decorations are lovely. Mark won't allow any until the week before Christmas.'

'Oh, he's an old grouch!' said Sarah affectionately. 'I hope he's going to let you put a tree up!'

As Amy bundled the books into her tote bag, preparing to leave, Sarah said, 'Jen's round the corner with some of our running crowd.' She pointed through the archway that led to The Snug. 'They're just on the left. Why don't you go and say hello?'

'Oh, I, er— ' Amy felt a little shy. Supposing Sarah's sister didn't recognise her? But as if sensing it, Sarah stepped out from behind the counter.

'Could you hold the fort for just a second, Fahimeh,' she said to her assistant, and steered Amy round the corner into The Snug. She clearly wasn't taking no for an answer this time!

Amy had pictured a big crowd, but there were only three women sitting there. She recognised Jenny, who introduced her to the other two, Chloe and Grace. Sarah glanced back into the shop, and said that she'd sit with them for a few minutes while it wasn't as busy. Jenny told Amy that they met up every now and then over the winter, when they weren't running.

'Let me get us both a tea,' said Sarah. 'Any other orders?' She went to the counter, leaving Amy at the table. 'Cake?' she called over. 'I recommend the Dundee cake.'

'No thanks.'

'How do you know each other?' Chloe asked, looking from Amy to Jenny.

'Amy's the new vet here, lives just over the road.'

'Ah, Mark Jeffrey's place? You work with Damian?'

Amy nodded.

'He's an old family friend. My parents and his are thick as thieves.'

'Poor Damian,' said Grace to Chloe. 'How is he these days?'

Amy gave them both a questioning look.

'Must be a good sign if you don't know. He had a serious girlfriend until a year or so ago. They trained together in Edinburgh, and he somehow talked her into coming here. She was a Londoner though. A bit …' She wrinkled her nose in distaste.

'Chloe! Amy's a Londoner,' said Jenny, poking her friend, and mouthing 'Sorry!' at Amy.

'Oh, it's fine,' said Amy.

'No offence, but this one gave Londoners a bad name. Nothing was good enough for her. They spent most of their weekends jetting off to Leeds or London because she said there was nothing to do here.'

'And then one weekend she didn't come back,' said Grace.

'How awful.' Amy hoped she sounded sincere.

'What was her name again, Chloe? Crystal?'

Chloe chuckled. 'Coral. Not quite as precious.'

'Pretty name,' said Amy, absentmindedly. She had another question on her mind. 'Did they have a child together?'

'Blimey, no! I don't think Coral was the child type.'

'What makes you ask that?' Grace looked curious.

Sarah had reemerged with a tray containing the teas, along with a plate containing a huge slab of cake and two forks.

'You have to try it, I insist.'

'I've seen him with a boy a couple of times,' Amy continued. 'I thought maybe he had weekend custody or something.'

Grace and Chloe both looked puzzled.

'Maybe a nephew?' suggested Jenny, glancing at each of her friends.

'What are you all on about?' Sarah made smacking noises with her lips as she urged Amy to try the cake. 'Go on! It's amazing!'

Amy relented.

'Amy thinks Damian has a child!' Grace said with a laugh.

Sarah made a little choking sound and put her hand in front of her mouth. She pointed a finger in the air to indicate that she would speak when she had finished eating. 'I know exactly who you're talking about, and the boy's mother is a few feet away from us. Hah! You can see how rumours start!'

Amy was more confused than ever. So he did have a child? She didn't know why, but the idea of it niggled at her slightly.

'What? He had a … with someone here?' Jenny looked incredulous.

'He's not his child!' Sarah said impatiently. 'For God's sake.' She shook her head. 'It's Arad, the lovely Fahimeh's son. He takes him out every now and then. He even got hold of a bike for him. Such a sweetie.'

'And are he and Fahimeh …' Grace let the question tail off.

'No! She has a husband! Honestly, you lot! Now, Amy, you're going to have to finish this.' She put down her fork. 'I have to go. I can see the shop getting busy again.'

Sarah went back to serve her customers. The Dundee cake tasted moist and buttery, lighter than the dark fruit cake her mother made every Christmas. She thought about what she had just heard about Damian. Funny how people had a habit of surprising you. Not that she really knew him well enough to be surprised. And not that it mattered, anyway. Still … It was interesting, though, and for some reason she couldn't quite understand, it pleased her.

'How's the work going at the hotel, Jenny?' She had to change the subject. She wasn't sure what her expression was, but didn't want anyone deciphering it.

'It's going well, thanks. They're due to finish in a couple of days, then we just have time to give the place a thorough clean and get it ready for the party. Sarah's got your ticket. It should be a good night.'

***

Amy wrapped the gifts she had bought that evening. She hummed along to some Christmas music while she tied decorative ribbon. *God, I am so turning into my mother*, she thought. *I'll be listening to Carols from King's College Cambridge next and watching* It's a Wonderful Life! Actually, come to think of it, both ideas were rather appealing.

She recalled the conversation that afternoon about Damian. Perhaps she *had* misjudged him. Spending time with young Arad was such a kind thing to do. His heart was clearly in the right place. Maybe only she brought out the worst in him. He got on well with everyone else at the practice, as far as she could see. She had never heard anyone bad-mouth him. *Are we too alike?* She pondered, *does he see me as competition, being the only other vet of a similar age?* Perhaps the quip from the farmer about him not liking to be told what to do, or whatever it was he had said, was in fact true.

Then she remembered what Sarah's friends in The Snug had said about his ex. How she had hated the Dales so much she had gone back to the city. Back to London. Perhaps there was something about her presence that reminded Damian of Coral, rather in the way he had brought back memories of Jake to her? Perhaps they had both taken against each other for the wrong reasons? She almost felt sorry for him, until she remembered how touchy he had been; how condescending! All those snide remarks about her being a city vet and out of her depth in the country. He had spoken as if she worked in a dog-grooming parlour in Chelsea rather than a gritty urban veterinary practice in Archway. Riled up by the conflicting thoughts, Amy sought out a way of regaining her lighter mood.

She had a bath and then went downstairs to watch a film. Her shopping trip had put her in a Christmassy frame of mind, and when she saw a recent adaptation of *A Christmas Carol* on one of the streaming services, she decided to give it a go. Amy poured a glass of wine and put her feet up before clicking play. But after twenty minutes, she was finding it hard to concentrate. The actor playing Scrooge was tall, with saturnine good looks that brought visions of Damian unbidden into her head. Feelings that could only be described as tenderness kept surfacing until she pushed them down again in a panic. All the same, she vowed to make an effort to be nicer to him; not that she had been unpleasant, she told herself, just a little cool. *Talk about Christmas cheer,* she thought. *I must be getting soft in my old age.*

15

Amy was surprised by how much she was looking forward to Christmas. In London, she typically barely had time to prepare before it arrived, and had been lucky to have two days off back to back. That didn't mean she hadn't loved the city in the run-up to Christmas, in all its frazzled chaos, when she did manage to find a spare couple of hours for a last-minute dash into the West End. The old-world charm of Liberty's on Regent Street; the police barking instructions into megaphones at the busy crossing at Oxford Circus, followed by a tidal wave of people surging over the road together; the Salvation Army band and carol singers outside Selfridge's. She had rather enjoyed the feeling of being swept along with them all until she escaped into the perfumed tranquillity of John Lewis.

Less pleasant were the loud, drunken parties staggering out of pubs and restaurants, getting in the way on the pavement, vomiting in doorways and generally being a nuisance. But they were a small price to pay. London always made her feel Christmassy in a way that her parents' small village didn't.

In Grassdale, coloured bulbs had been hung on the trees of the green on the main road. The Fox and Ferret displayed a Christmas tree in a huge beer barrel outside the front door, decorated with baubles and coloured lights. Many of the houses bore wreaths on their front doors, and twinkling lights could be glimpsed through their windows.

When Mark had deemed that the time was right, Donna had decorated the main waiting room, adding a small tree to the counter, safe from wagging tails and curious noses. Several of their customers sent cards, which she hung on strings around the walls.

Amy received a number of personal cards too, some of them sent to her home. Every day, when she returned from work, there would be a small pile of them on the mat. Most of her customers signed off with the names of their pets in their cards, which she always found amusing.

She received several cards from locals featuring the same village scene, bought in aid of the St John's bell fund. There was a beautiful one from Betty and Octavia the tortoise, thanking her for everything she did for them both. A couple of days later, there was yet another from Betty and Octavia. Then a third. Studying the identical cards, Amy recalled how the elderly lady had confused her pet with its predecessor, prompting the comment from her daughter about her mother's worsening memory.

Mary had designed her own card – how she found the time, Amy had no idea, but the painted holly motif was beautiful in its simplicity.

One old university friend had addressed her card: 'Amy Ashton, New Vet, Grassdale, Yorkshire.' She made a point of catching the postman when she saw him to thank him for delivering it.

The Dickensian evening in Jenny's hotel was held on the Friday evening of the week before Christmas. Amy wasn't entirely sure what to expect – was it a performance, a promotional event, or even just a jolly social gathering? She didn't particularly enjoy chit chat with strangers, but Sarah would be there, and Chloe and Grace, the two women she had met in the bookshop that afternoon, and potentially some other familiar faces. She wondered if it might interest Mary too; it would be nice to have someone with her for company. She knocked on her door a few days beforehand to see.

Mary took a while to open it. When she did, pieces of Sellotape were stuck to the back of her hand and all the way up her arm.

'Great timing – you can give me a hand!' was her greeting.

Amy hadn't intended to stay, but had little option other than to follow Mary into her living room. The fire was lit and the room looked brighter and cosier than it had on her last visit. The floor was covered with large boxes, some with their contents stacked in piles beside them, and rolls of wrapping paper.

'I'm getting ready for the old folks' Christmas party in the village hall. It's a bit of a tradition here. The couple who ran it for years moved away this year to be closer to their daughter – they were no spring chickens themselves – and we were going to call it a day but we hadn't counted on the reaction. Oh, my days! You'd have thought we were announcing the cancellation of Christmas itself! They were so disappointed. And we realised how much some of them rely on it.' She pulled a sad face at Amy. 'There are some lonely people around, you know. So, it's back to the grindstone! We've got a little team, and—'

'And you're doing most of it, it seems!'

'Oh, I wouldn't say that, but I'm sorting out the gifts. They all get something from under the tree. Ladies get theirs in this wrapping paper,' she brandished a roll decorated with sprigs of holly and robins, 'and the chaps get this one.' The other roll was bright blue, dotted with silver stars. 'So if you've got a moment, even just while we're talking, you could perhaps stick a bit of paper round these.' She added, 'I prefer to sit on the floor but you could go to the table if you want.'

The ladies' gifts were matching soaps and hand creams in pretty boxes, so easy to wrap.

'Are you expecting a lot?'

'About forty.'

'I didn't know there were that many old people in Grassdale!'

'Some come from the hamlets around here too.'

Amy set to work. It was a Sunday afternoon, and she had a few chores to do before the day was over, but it was pleasant in Mary's room, with the fire burning, and Mary's soothing chatter. She enjoyed the precision of wrapping gifts. She took great care with each one.

'Oh, blimey, yours are making mine look like a right dog's dinner!' quipped Mary.

She went to make tea, and came back with a plate of shortbread biscuits which Amy was set to refuse, until her host argued, 'It's a new recipe. My friends will be getting them for Christmas if they pass the test, so I need your verdict.'

'Which means I can't decline.' She was glad Mary had persuaded her, as they were delicious – rich and buttery.

'I heard you met Hettie,' Mary said as she settled herself back down. She was pulling out pages of newspaper from *The Telegraph*. 'This is for pass the parcel. They love it. I'm alternating newspaper with fancier paper. Not my paper of choice, by the way. The Major saves them for me. I'm more of a *Guardian* reader – when I get the time.'

'You know Hettie?'

'Of course I know Hettie! She's been around even longer than I have.'

'I thought she was a bit of a loner? You know, a wild woman of the hills!'

Mary laughed. 'Well, she's wild at times, she's a woman, and she lives in the hills … But a loner she's not.' The glasses typically worn on top of her head were perched on the bridge of her nose, so she could see what she was doing as she fastened Sellotape over a loose flap. Lowering the parcel to her lap, she peered over the top of them at Amy. 'Do you think I'm a loner?'

'You? Of course not!'

'Well, there you go. Not everyone who lives on their own is a loner. Hettie's like me – happy with her own company, but enjoys other people now and then. She'd go potty up there otherwise.'

It occurred to Amy that perhaps *she* was more of a loner than the two older women. Other than work, she spent most of her time by herself. She lived alone, she ran alone, she rarely socialised.

As if reading her thoughts, Mary said, 'There's plenty to do here if you make the effort, you know. You only need to look at the notice board in the store, or the posters in Sarah's window.'

Amy suddenly remembered the reason for her visit. 'Actually, Mary, that's partly why I popped in. I was wondering if you wanted to come to the Dickensian evening with me.'

Mary paused her wrapping. 'Sounds interesting. Where are we talking about?'

'The hotel Sarah's sister Jenny runs. Up the road?'

'Oh, Upper Street Guesthouse? I've seen the builders there. What's happening?'

'I don't know all the details, but there's going to be a Christmas ghost story, and there'll be some drink and nibbles I suppose.'

'When is it?'

'Friday night.'

'Drat!' Mary seemed genuinely disappointed. 'I can't do it, Amy. I'm at a friend's in Crowdale that night. What a shame. But thank you for thinking of me.'

'Ah well, never mind. I'm not too bothered about going really.'

'You've got to go. It sounds fun!'

'Yeah, well …' Amy tailed off. Jenny and Sarah would both be busy at the event, she supposed, and she barely knew Chloe and Grace – in fact, did she even know for sure that they were going? It would be fine while the reading was taking place, but standing around like a spare part before and after with a glass of mulled wine and a mince pie didn't really appeal.

'I'll see.'

'I assume you're away for Christmas? Those lovely parents of yours will be wanting to see you again.'

'Yes, I'm leaving on the twenty-third. I'm actually looking forward to it, though I'm sure I'll want to leave about five minutes after arrriving.'

Mary laughed. 'I was like that myself once upon a time. There was even a spell when I lived down south of skipping Christmas with the family for several years. I miss having them around now though, don't waste that time.'

***

Amy pulled on a pair of black trousers and a sparkly top. It was Christmas, after all. The darkness outside still had the capacity to shock her. Sometimes she missed the sparkle of a London night – spangled lights on the cobbles at Covent Garden, the Palace of Westminster reflected in the Thames – but there was compensation to be had looking up at the sky and seeing a densely studded ceiling of stars.

It took only a couple of minutes to walk from the cottage, over the crossroads and up the steep road to the guesthouse. The larger houses lay closer to the pavement, so the way was lit more clearly than it was on Lower Street. Feeling rather hesitant, she swallowed nervously as she arrived at the handsome black door of Upper Street Guesthouse, its brass fittings including a knocker in the shape of a lion's head. Amy almost expected the lion to start speaking to her, like the ghost of Jacob Marley to Scrooge in *A Christmas Carol*. Thinking it might be open, she gave the door a gentle shove but it was locked. She rapped on the lion's head gently, figuring that if no one answered she had an excuse to chicken out. *Sorry, Jenny, I did try, but no one let me in.*

When the door opened, she was assailed by the sound of laughter and voices – the cheery notes of people enjoying themselves.

'Sorry, Amy! Have you been there ages?' It was Jenny, wearing a knee-length black dress with a rhinestone belt. 'It's getting rowdy in here. Luckily someone said they thought they heard the door.'

She stepped inside and found herself in a large hallway. The lower part of the walls were wood-panelled, with a William Morris-style wallpaper on the upper portion. Ahead of her, lights were strung around the balustrades of a grand staircase.

'No coat? I suppose you don't need one being so close. Follow me, Sarah's around somewhere and I'm sure there must be someone else you know here.'

The corridor stretched back a long way, with rooms going off on both sides. A large group of people were gathered in the first of these, seated on one of the squishy sofas or standing in small groups, clutching their drinks. The room had two cream-coloured walls and two dark red ones which already felt Christmassy. The room next door, which Amy took to be the dining room, had been set out for a performance with rows of chairs, the tables either removed or pushed to the side.

'Jen, can I borrow you for a sec?' A man appeared at her elbow, and after Jen had quickly introduced Amy to Greg, her husband, she apologised to Amy and pointed her in the direction of the kitchen. 'You'll find Sarah there. Sorry! Back in a jiff!'

The kitchen was at the far end of the corridor, smaller in its proportions than the other generous-sized rooms. Amy saw Sarah there, wearing a butcher's apron, filling glasses from a large jug.

'Amy! So pleased you've made it! Mulled wine?' She handed her a glass. 'Sorry, all a bit hectic in here. One of Jen's young neighbours was going to be our waitress, but she's come down with something.'

The wine smelt delicious, full of cloves and cinnamon. Amy took a few sips before stopping. She would have to be careful not to knock it back. That was the trouble when you were nervous.

'How's business?' She could see Sarah was busy, but she didn't want to venture back into the hallway on her own, to be faced by people she either didn't know or recognised only vaguely. She had caught a glimpse of John from the store, with his partner Andy. Gregarious John was chatting to a group of people, while Andy, who was a lot quieter, stood silently beside him. Despite wanting to join the conversation, Amy feared she didn't really know either of them well enough, and she wasn't the sort of person who easily interrupted a flow. She wondered again what sort of party this actually was: a do for friends or more of a networking event? Perhaps she should be wearing a sticker saying 'Amy Ashton, veterinary surgeon'.

'Oh, business is ...' Sarah broke off, distracted by a cork that had split into two in the bottle she was opening. 'Pesky thing!' She started to rummage in a drawer of utensils. 'Oh blimey, the sausage rolls will be burning!'

'Let me.'

Happy to have something useful to do, Amy grabbed a pair of oven gloves and took the trays out of the oven. There were other delicacies in there too. Dainty vol au vents, onion bhajis, crispy little empanadas.

'Thanks, Amy! I haven't got enough pairs of hands. Jen really needs to be with her guests but it's all happening at once in here. If you could just stick them on those plates and perhaps, if you wouldn't mind awfully—' She pulled an apologetic face, 'you could pass them round? I would say to put them on a table but there are folk all over the place and they might not see them.'

Amy left her mulled wine in the kitchen and set off on her task, a plate in each hand. Sarah called after her, 'You can introduce yourself to everyone at the same time!'

Three women wearing black cocktail dresses were perched on chairs in the otherwise empty dining room. They were deep in conversation, their heads close together.

'Ooh, thank you, waitress!' said one of them. 'They've got you working then?' Amy realised that the person who had spoken was one of her colleagues.

'Sorry, Sophie, didn't recognise you for a second! Yes, I believe they're a bit short-handed.'

'You're doing a grand job,' said one of Sophie's friends. 'Ooh, these look tasty!'

'Is there anyone else from work here?' Amy asked.

'Haven't seen anyone,' said Sophie. She added conspiratorially, 'I don't think it's Mark's cup of tea though. Oh, this is Scarlett, my eldest.'

A pretty girl with long blonde hair wearing a silver sheath dress had entered the room. She scowled, and looked behind her.

'Mum! You didn't tell me it would be all old people here!'

'Scarlett, don't be so rude. Come and say hello to Amy, our new vet. As you can see, *she's* a youngster like you.'

The girl smiled apologetically.

'Hello, Scarlett. You've finished for the term now?'

'Yes and she wishes she was back,' said her mother, replying for her. '"It's so boring in Grassdale, Mum!"' she imitated.

Scarlett made as if to shove her mother, but thought better of it when she was holding a glass of mulled wine.

'Remind me what you're studying?'

'Criminology.'

'A new one on me.'

'They're all doing it now, Amy,' said Sophie. 'Latest fashion. In my day it was law.'

'Are you suggesting I'm just following the crowd, Mum?'

Amy left the mother and daughter gently bickering. She passed a couple of groups in the hallway, leaning against the wall. Someone had put his wine glass on the wooden shelf above one of the antique radiators, and she hoped it wouldn't leave a stain. She'd ask Jenny where the coasters were if she ever saw her again. She heard a woman with a rather shrill voice, announcing to someone, 'I run Fell View B&B over the road. We've had a lot of Americans this summer. I've got an Australian couple here over Christmas doing some family history research.'

The living room was full, with all the chairs taken and several people standing. She recognised the Major, sitting in an armchair in the corner. A woman on the edge of the sofa beside him was using her hands to demonstrate whatever she was telling him. Amy thought she saw his eyes starting to flutter closed. It was very warm in the room.

'Major! Can I interest you in a sausage roll, or another titbit?'

She lowered the tray between him and his companion. 'How's Elsie?'

He looked at her, blinking. 'I'm Amy – from the vet's practice?'

'Yes, my dear, of course. I hardly recognised you in your finery.'

The woman who was talking to him took a sausage roll and stared at Amy.

'I've got the antiques shop over the road. You came in with your parents not so long ago. If you need any gift ideas …'

Amy thanked her and carried on with her circuit of the room. The plates were soon empty and she had to weave her way back to the kitchen for a refill. Behind her in the hallway someone clapped their hands loudly.

'Ladies and gentlemen,' said Greg, 'if you'd like to take your seats. This evening's entertainment will begin shortly.' He cleared his throat. 'If anyone is of a nervous disposition, may I suggest they leave now.'

People laughed and someone else made a ghostly 'ooing' noise as they made their way into the dining room.

'Go in and get yourself a seat,' said Sarah to Amy after she had put down the empty plates. 'And thanks for your help. You've been a lifesaver.'

'What about you?'

'I'll be in shortly. Go on.'

'When you are all seated, ladies and gentlemen, Mr Charles Dickens will make his entrance.' Greg's voice was booming now.

Amy quickly took a seat on the back row, leaving the end one for Sarah in case she was able to join her. The lights were switched off. Sarah and Jenny whispered in the corridor, but everyone else was ready and waiting.

A black-clad figure swept past Amy and past the rows of seats to stand in front of them all. Illuminated by a single lantern on a table beside him, he wore a long dark jacket over a waistcoat, a cravat knotted at his neck, and sported a moustache and beard just like the novelist in one of the famous portraits of him.

'Ladies and gentlemen, what a pleasure it is to be with you all this evening! My name is Charles Dickens, and I am pleased to meet you all, and in particular, to welcome those of you who have not attended one of my readings before. I took the stagecoach to be with you all tonight, as last year, I had the misfortune to experience the railway crash in Staplehurst, an incident that haunts me to this day.'

In the warm dark room, Amy felt her eyes briefly close before she snapped them open. This afternoon, she had spent several hours in a freezing barn helping a pregnant heifer with a difficult birth. Her large calf was stuck, and no amount of pulling was doing the trick. The poor heifer was distressed and exhausted. Amy hadn't been much better. She had begun to worry about how much longer the calf could survive if she failed to deliver it soon. The farmer's gaze bore into Amy's back and she felt the weight of responsibility. His expression gave little away, but she knew that deep down, he was as distressed as she was.

She had almost given up hope when she felt something dislodge in the cow's pelvis. A moment later, the calf slipped out and landed in the straw. It was limp but breathing. The farmer dried it and rubbed it vigorously. It was wobbly and unable to stand, so Amy ministered some Calf Kick Start, an energy boost.

The farmer said he would take it into his kitchen to warm up and that they would monitor it there. There hadn't been much more Amy could do, but now she found herself thinking about the creature and whether it had pulled through. (She was also thinking what an undignified process giving birth was and wondering if she ever wanted to endure such an ordeal herself.)

She sat up straight, trying her best to stay present, and returned to the moment. Charles Dickens was still talking. She realised that the story was well underway and that she had missed the start. She must concentrate; this was what she was here for, after all. Someone sat down rather heavily on the seat beside her in a rush. 'Sorry!' whispered a man's voice. A late arrival. The man's right arm, in its coat, brushed against her bare left arm. Amy shifted slightly to the right to make more space. She smelt an aftershave that made her think of the forest – a woody, green smell. *Mmmm*.

It was rather nice to sit beside someone smelling so good, even though he was now wriggling out of his coat and causing her to lose her concentration once more. 'Sorry,' she heard again, as his arm knocked into her. He stood up briefly to make it easier to remove his coat and, perhaps intoxicated by the scent, Amy pulled at the arm to help.

At the same time, she looked up to see that familiar head and profile she'd been hell-bent on avoiding.

'Thank you,' he mouthed, turning towards her.

Did he have to turn up everywhere? She felt her heart pitter-patter. Damn him. She shifted a tiny bit further over. There was a spare seat on her right, but she could hardly move onto that. Instead, she tried to concentrate on the story. The audience jumped, then tittered. But she had lost the thread. The creepy atmosphere was ruined. All she was aware of was the bulk of the man beside her and his annoyingly nice smell. The actor's voice rose to a crescendo, and then lowered to a loud whisper. A sudden gasp from the audience and more nervous laughter. Before long, it was over. Everyone was clapping. Damian gave an appreciative whistle. Charles Dickens bowed and Jenny came forward to take centre stage and thanked him.

'Chris will be taking the role of Dick Whittington in the Crowdale pantomime, opening on the twenty-third!' Everyone clapped again. 'And now, ladies and gentlemen, coffee and Christmas cake will be served. Grab a comfy sofa, stay here, or float around wherever you wish. If anyone would like to see one of the newly refurbished rooms, please ask me or Greg and we'd be delighted to show you.'

Amy could feel Damian turn towards her. 'I'm sorry about my late entrance and disturbing the performance for you. I was stuck at Hilltop. Let me grab you a coffee?'

Before he could, Amy saw the flustered face of Sarah. 'Do you mind if I borrow you again?'

'Course not.' She stood up, both thankful for and slightly disappointed by the interruption. 'Sorry, they're short-handed here. I've been roped in.'

He swivelled round so that she could get out. 'Need me too?' he asked Sarah.

'You're fine, Damian. Could you help the Major into the other room for me? And sit with him for a bit. He's been cornered for most of the time by—' Here she whispered a name Amy couldn't catch, 'and I think he needs a break.'

Back in the kitchen, Sarah started to refill the coffee maker. 'Could you take the first tray round for me, please? Next lot won't be long. And I've got some decaf if anyone wants it. I'll put the cake on the tray and they can take a piece at the same time.'

Amy went back out with her wares. Everyone was talking about the performance. Charles Dickens himself was still in the dining room, a small crowd surrounding him, while he answered their eager questions.

'Wasn't he good?' said a woman to Amy.

'Amazing,' said Amy, wishing she had heard more of the story. She couldn't even really blame Damian, having started to zone out before his arrival.

Sophie's daughter was leaving. Jenny was walking up the grand staircase with a smartly dressed woman. Amy overheard a snippet of the conversation. 'We have eight bedrooms, with en suites. The bedding is all Hungarian goose down.'

Who knew that Hungarian geese were superior to others, she mused, with a smile. She went into the living room first, where Damian was sitting on the sofa beside the Major, who had sunk into it like a ragdoll.

'I'll probably never get out of this seat,' he said as Amy laughed.

Damian took a coffee for each of them, then some cake.

'Did you enjoy it, Amy?'

She couldn't remember when they had last spoken, at least not directly to one another. Had he even called her by her name before? If he had, it had surely been when he was annoyed with her.

'Yes, it was very good, wasn't it. Though I must admit, I was pretty tired, it's been quite a day. I almost nodded off a couple of times.'

Damian laughed. 'Me too. And there I was, about to ask you to tell me what happened.'

'Wrong person!'

He held her gaze for a few seconds longer before she moved on with her tray. *Was that butterflies in her stomach*? What was going on?

After people had finished their coffee, some began to slip away. Amy made herself useful by collecting cups and plates. Sarah had barely left the kitchen all night.

'It seems you got the worst end of the deal, Sarah. Your sister gets to chat and show her place off, and you're stuck in the kitchen!'

'I know, what a muggins! You've been amazing, Amy. I'll make it up to you.'

'Don't be silly, I don't want anything! I'm just glad it's gone well.'

'Yes, Jen seems pleased. There were some folk from the local tourist office here, and someone who blogs about the Dales. I think she's impressed them.'

'I should think so too. It's so beautiful in here. And I'm sure the rooms are too.'

'You'll have to have a look at one before you go.'

'Maybe another time. I think I'll head off in a minute, but thanks for a great evening. I'll just find the hostess.'

'You'll probably find she's back upstairs,' said Sarah, adding, 'so you might as well pop your head round one of the doors and take a peek.'

Amy walked up the grand staircase. A smell of paint lingered in the air. She could see an open door at the far end of the corridor, Jenny's voice drifting from inside the room. Not wanting to disturb her, she opened the door closest to her. The décor was simple but stylish. Grey muted walls, a plaid blind on the sash window that matched the cushions and the throw on the bed. A snowy scene of the Dales on the wall. Very tasteful.

She was about to leave when she remembered Jenny's comment about the Hungarian goose down. Smiling to herself, she squeezed one of the pillows. So soft, she wondered what it'd feel like to sleep in. Then, checking that the door was closed, she let her intrusive thoughts win. Slipping off her shoes, Amy perched on the edge of the bed, and before she could talk herself out of it, she giggled to herself and snuggled under the covers. She would see how it felt, for just a second. She sank into the mattress. It seemed to mould itself to her body. The duvet was thick and weighty, yet soft. Heaven. She closed her eyes.

'Ahem.'

Did she drift off for a second? Someone was standing beside her, clearing their throat. She snapped her eyes open.

'You know you can't just go round napping wherever you please. Plus, I think you'll find that's my side,' Damian quipped.

She sat up very quickly, a blush colouring her cheeks.

He gazed down at her with an amused expression.

'Jenny told me to look at a room before I left – but I didn't realise we were supposed to road-test the beds.'

'No, I, er, it looked so inviting, and … I can never say no to a Hungarian goose!' *Best to make a joke back to him.* She felt stupid, however, even as she ran her fingers over the surface of the duvet as if to explain herself.

'I'll take your word for it.'

Amy grabbed her shoes, racking her brains for something else to say.

'Has the Major left?' was the best she could come up with.

'I'm going to walk him home now. The poor old boy is exhausted – but not the only one by the look of things!'

As she led the way out of the room, Damian whispered over her shoulder, 'Don't worry, sleepyhead, I won't tell.'

Though still embarrassed, Amy found she was grinning to herself as she went to find Jenny to thank her for a lovely evening.

16

On Amy's last day in the practice before Christmas, they exchanged their Secret Santa gifts. Work had finished for the day, though Amy's last case had been a difficult one. A family in Crowdale had a beloved Labrador Retriever, now twelve years old, a good age for the breed. The dog had started to become less active some time ago, and slowly developed a limp that was becoming more acute. She had been diagnosed with dysplasia of the hips, a genetic condition the breed was susceptible to. This had been managed with anti-inflammatory drugs and hydrotherapy, but Bonnie was now getting worse.

'I don't think she's in pain,' said her owner, 'I mean, she still wants to have a walk, just not as far as she used to go. We had to carry her home last week, and that wasn't easy.' She wiped her eyes. 'It's so hard, because she's a member of the family. The children don't remember a time without her.'

Amy had agreed that Bonnie didn't appear to be in too much discomfort, and had suggested that the owners continue to monitor her condition. 'You know that Crowdale Practice offers emergency cover. Just in case.'

There was no need to clarify what 'just in case' meant. They both knew.

It was a sad way to begin her Christmas holiday, but it was all part of her job. She sighed after she had said goodbye to them, washed, took off her practice coat, and forced herself to smile as she joined the others for their little celebration. In the kitchen, Mark was pouring champagne into plastic flutes he had fished out of a cupboard, while Donna tipped crisps into bowls and arranged mince pies on a plate.

'Oh, almost forgot.' Amy went to the counter and picked up a paper bag. 'Mary made me these cheese straws, but I thought it would be nice to share them.'

Everyone was in a good mood, exchanging their plans for the break. Mark was spending Christmas Day locally, with friends, but putting his feet up for the rest of the time. Simon – who hadn't been working in the practice that day but arrived to join the festivities – would be visiting his daughter, who had recently had a baby. Donna was entertaining her parents, and Sophie had all her brood at home – 'no doubt expecting to be waited on'. Fran was going to stay with her boyfriend's family and Damian was spending the day with his parents.

After they had toasted each other, and Mark thanked them all for their hard work, Donna fetched the bag that held their Secret Santa gifts.

'No spilling the beans,' she ordered. 'Whoever has given what remains a secret.'

Mark received his gift first. He tore at the wrapping like a child. 'Someone who knows me well!' he declared, holding up a smart pen that looked as if it came from Sarah's shop. Mark was famous for always losing his biros. 'Thank you, whoever,' he added, grinning as he nodded at each of them.

Fran received a bubble bath and a shower cap in the shape of a fish – it even had frilly fins sticking out of the side. Sophie had a pair of fluffy ear muffs. Amy felt her face turn a little pink as Simon opened his parcel. The others had all seemed to receive very personalised gifts, and to be honest, she hardly knew Simon. Perhaps it would seem such an odd gift that everyone would know it came from her, the new girl. He opened it and she saw his face break into a broad smile. 'Oh, splendid! This will be my holiday reading. I've got all of Tizz's other books but haven't seen this one yet. It looks fascinating.'

He sounded as if he meant it too.

There was no accounting for taste, she thought, hoping her satisfied smile hadn't given the game away.

It was Damian's turn next. He was sitting at the table beside Amy. They hadn't spoken since the night at the Dickensian party, nor had there been the opportunity to do so. He opened his small square package slowly, keeping them all in suspense.

'Ta-dah!' He held out for everyone to admire a box containing a set of coasters of cartoon cats. Words beginning with C-A-T were illustrated with a cat in a humorous depiction of the word. Damian was a professed cat lover, and Amy had recently learnt that he lived alone with his very own feline friend, Arthur.

'Sorry, Amy, you've had to wait till the end. Let's hope it's worth it,' said Donna, as she scooped the final package from the bag. It was neatly wrapped in silver paper, and even had a small red bow stuck on the side of it. 'Ooh, posh!' Donna said.

'Favouritism!' declared Mark, who was topping up their glasses.

'Another careful opener,' said Donna. 'You'll be able to use the paper next year, Amy. Want me to fold it up and put it in this drawer?' She winked at the others.

There was a layer of bubble wrap after the paper. She opened it to reveal a pretty blue mug with white writing on the side that said, 'I'd rather be running', and a small bottle of bubble bath 'for achy joints' sitting inside the mug.

'Hah! Very appropriate! Thank you to whoever bought it for me.'

There was a murmur round the table from everyone else as she and Damian made eye contact for a brief second.

'Well, I think we've all done extremely well,' Mark interrupted their moment. 'Happy Christmas everyone!'

***

As she was driving home the next day, Amy couldn't help wondering if her gift was from Damian. Everyone knew she was a runner, of course, so it could have come from any of them, but she had a sneaking suspicion that it might have been him. Was the bubble bath alluding to her earlier accident perhaps? *No, I'm reading too much into it!*

It was the day before Christmas Eve and the roads were chock-a-block. She had barely left the village when she got stuck behind the little bus that trundled once a day from Grassdale and Crowdale to Hebden Bridge. There were no safe places in which to overtake until she reached Crowdale, when the bus turned into a side street. Then she ended up behind a tractor, though the driver did pull in and wave her past eventually. The A1 was very busy, the M25 a nightmare. Her nerves felt shattered by the time she drove up the wide driveway of her parents' house many hours later.

She would have liked to sit in the car for a minute, to compose herself, but even before she had turned off the engine, she saw a pool of light to her left indicating her parents standing on the doorstep, like a couple in the spotlight on a stage.

A few minutes later, the three of them were in the comfortable living room drinking generous gin and tonics. Amy gave a little grimace. Her father always made them too strong for her liking.

'It's lovely to have you home – and you look so well!' said her father.

Her mother tilted her head to the side and surveyed her more thoroughly. 'Oh, I don't know, Tim. I think she looks tired.'

'It's been a busy time,' admitted Amy. Aware that her mother might turn this throwaway comment into something negative about her life in Grassdale, she quickly redirected focus to her father. 'What about you, Dad? Still working as hard?'

'He never stops!' It was her mother who answered. 'I hardly see him. And he's off on a lecture tour to the States next year.'

'Ooh, you've kept that quiet! Can you go too, Mum?'

'She can come if she wants to,' said her father.

'Yes, and I'll be left on my own all day,' grumbled Judith.

Amy thought this sounded blissful – to be able to wander round galleries or museums or shops, not needing to worry about your companion's interests.

'You can do your own thing, Mum, and meet Dad for dinner at the end of the day.'

'She's not like you, Amy,' said her father, when her mother had popped out of the room to check on the meal. 'You're so independent. I think, between you and me,' he lowered his voice, 'she's a teeny bit envious of you living your life the way you do.'

Her mother had made her favourite fish pie for tea, with steamed broccoli and green beans. There was also apple crumble and custard for pudding.

'Mum, you shouldn't have gone to so much trouble, especially when you're entertaining tomorrow.'

'Oh, that's mainly drinks and nibbles. Besides, the crumble's been in the freezer since we picked the apples in the summer. What did you do with yours?'

'Oh, let me see …' Should she lie? Best not. 'I actually gave them to Mary, my neighbour.'

'Oh, the charming lady next door? How is she?'

'Same as ever. Even busier than me.'

***

Amy's old childhood bedroom still looked much the same as when she had been living at home. It had been redecorated, and there were no longer posters on the walls, but the furniture hadn't changed, her bookcase, with her childhood books, untouched. The desk – with its locked top drawer that contained old diaries – was in the same place, overlooking the garden. The hours she had spent at that desk, her head deep in textbooks or bent over essays, swotting for tests and exams! It sometimes felt as if most of her teenage memories centred around that item of furniture.

Had she missed out on other activities? She had eventually resumed the badminton classes, but stopped again when she began volunteering at a local animal sanctuary, which was important for her university application. On the social side, she sometimes met Penny and one or two other girls in Guildford on a Saturday afternoon, to trawl around the shops, trying on clothes and spraying themselves with perfume testers, but even these activities became less frequent as her work became more important. She had needed top grades to get into The Royal Veterinary College, her first choice, but couldn't she have had a bit more fun in the process?

The room gave her a feeling that unsettled her – sadness mixed with nostalgia.

The day of Christmas Eve was spent helping her mother get ready for the party she always threw – 'Not really a party, darling, just a gathering of friends' – as well as some preparations for dinner the next day. She peeled potatoes and carrots and washed sprouts. The food for the evening was a buffet consisting of a baked salmon, various homemade salads and some shop-bought titbits – 'to save a bit of time'. There was wine and fizz to drink, and a selection of soft drinks. Her mother went to change at about six o'clock, and came downstairs in a midnight blue dress with a mesh bodice that was decorated in tiny stars.

The guests started arriving at seven. First to knock on the door were the Clements from over the road, the couple Amy had known for most of her life. Victor Clement (Uncle Vic) was a retired bank manager, and his wife, Elizabeth (Aunty Liz), a retired school secretary. They both adored Amy and she had spent a lot of time with them when she was growing up.

'The country life is suiting you,' said Elizabeth, looking her up and down after they had both almost squeezed her to death. 'Still so slim, too.'

'It's all that running,' said her mother. 'There'll be nothing left of her soon.'

Amy started to tell them about life in Grassdale before excusing herself to say hello to other guests. A couple of her father's colleagues were there, and three of her mother's book group friends with their husbands. Some of them knew each other well, others recognised each other from the previous year's party and resumed conversations from then.

Amy spoke to each couple, often answering the same questions, as she moved between the kitchen and the living room, helping her mother to serve drinks.

'The buffet will be ready in five minutes,' her mother declared.

Her role tonight was reminding her of her stint as a waitress at Jenny's Dickensian evening. The memory made her smile. She had a warm feeling about that night, even if she had almost dozed off during the performance. She felt that she had seen a different side to Damian. She recalled his care and attention to the Major after the show. And she remembered how closely he had sat beside her – *had he really needed to be that close?* – and how he had held her glance when she served him coffee. Oh, and that cheeky comment when he found her in bed! Had he been flirting with her?

'Any nice chaps in this village of yours?' one of her father's colleagues suddenly asked her as they waited their turn at the buffet.

'We met a most charming man – and his parents too,' said her mother, who was eavesdropping. 'And he works with Amy. What was his name, again, dear?'

Amy knew it was very unlikely that her mother had forgotten. 'Damian.'

'Yes, Damian. How is he?'

'He's very well.'

Her mother turned to Amy's questioner. 'She thinks I'm a silly airhead for caring about these things, but it is important, isn't it, and especially at that age. I was already married when I was twenty-seven.'

'Different generation,' said the man.

'They think they've got all the time in the world.' The man's wife had been listening too. 'And that's why they're all having IVF and whatnot these days. There is a reason Mother Nature gave us the bodies she gave us.'

Her mother touched her friend's arm. 'I've just been reading about a sixty-year-old having a child.'

'Sixty! Who would have the energy?!'

They had forgotten Amy now as they rolled their eyes and wondered what the world was coming to. She carried her food over to speak with Uncle Vic and Aunty Liz again.

***

Christmas Day was as pleasant as always, with its routines that hadn't changed since Amy's childhood. Judith knocked on her door at eight-thirty to wish her a merry Christmas, and to say it was time for them to go downstairs and see if Santa Claus had been. The three of them trooped down the stairs together. Amy remembered the childish excitement of her younger years, the anticipation of what might be waiting for her. She was pleased to find that she still experienced an inkling of that wonder now.

Her father headed into the room first and switched on the tree lights. He always pretended that there had been no overnight visitor while Amy and her mother pretended to believe him. Then both her parents sat down to watch her open her stocking. It contained an apple and a satsuma, a bar of her favourite chocolate, a pair of novelty earrings in the shape of Christmas trees and a pack of biros. There was also a small wooden pot and a little hand-carved cat: 'I found them in the antiques shop in your village!'

They saved their presents for each other until after lunch. Amy had put her presents for her parents under the tree when she arrived.

Her father prepared breakfast: smoked salmon and scrambled eggs, with orange juice and coffee. The turkey went into the oven soon after they had finished eating.

Dinner was delicious, but seemed to disappear all too quickly. 'I bet you're glad you're not a vegetarian anymore,' quipped her father, as Amy served herself second helpings of the juicy leg meat. It was times like this that Amy missed all four of her late grandparents more than ever. If either set hadn't joined them on Christmas Day, being obliged to visit other grandchildren, they would have done so on Boxing Day instead. Three felt a funny number for Christmas Day. Two was intimate and special, but with three, it felt as if at least one other person was missing. Last year, that missing person had been Jake – the break-up had been recent, and Amy still felt raw from it when she'd sat at the table. But this year, she realised she no longer wished he was sitting beside her. Maybe she wished someone else was, instead.

They opened their presents to each other after lunch, as they had their coffee and chocolates. First of all, Amy passed her mother a beautifully wrapped gift. She had packed the books together in one satisfyingly heavy package. Her mother gasped when she saw them. The *Peter Pan* was in excellent condition considering it was over a hundred years old. It was illustrated by Mabel Lucie Attwell, who Judith adored. She spent ages carefully turning the pages and marvelling at each of the illustrations, uttering little gasps of delight.

'Oh, look at their little faces! Look at Peter trying to be brave while Wendy stitches his shadow on! Was there ever such a magical story as Peter Pan!'

Amy, who had wished she could fly to Neverland on many occasions, was inclined to agree. Her mother loved the Robert Louis Stevenson poems too. 'It brings back so many memories. Thank you, darling, I'm thrilled with these.'

Her father professed pleasure too in his Beatles book. 'I'm just finishing an excellent biography of Martin Luther King, so a move to music will be a welcome contrast when I'm ready.'

There was also a joint gift for them both in the form of theatre vouchers for a West End show.

'And now for yours,' said her mother, insisting that Amy sit down while she fetched them.

Amy opened a box that contained a beautiful pair of gold stud earrings, each one in the shape of a tiny bird.

'You've been talking a lot about the birds in your garden when we've caught up on the phone. I think they're swallows. You can wear them at work, can't you? They won't dangle.'

Next, there was a pretty dark pink sweater. 'It'll keep you warm in those northern climes.'

Another soft, but far heavier package also felt like clothing. Amy preferred to buy her own clothes, but she knew that when her mother had a bee in her bonnet, there wasn't much anyone could do. Something told her this present would be a response to her pre-loved charity-shop find. She opened the thick glossy paper carefully and peeped inside. It contained a dark navy waxed jacket with deep interior and exterior pockets and a soft tartan lining. Amy knew how expensive it must have been.

'It's lovely, Mum, Dad, thank you.' She kissed them both.

'That should keep you warm and dry on some of your outdoor jobs,' said her father.

'And far better than that eyesore you were wearing when we saw you.'

Honestly, her mother was so predictable!

***

Penny had been unsure of her Christmas plans when Amy had spoken to her earlier, but on Christmas night, as Amy and her parents were watching a film together, Amy saw a message pop up on her phone. 'It's crazy here but I could pop round for coffee tomorrow if you're free?'

'Please do!' Amy texted back. 'Any time!'

Her friend appeared on the doorstep just after ten the next day.

'I haven't seen you for ages!' Penny said as she hugged her friend.

'I know, it's bad. Was it as long ago as last Christmas?'

'No, we had lunch in London in January. But still, far too long.'

As she was taking Penny's coat, her mother appeared and offered her an equally effusive welcome. 'Darling Penny! You never change!'

'Nor do you, Mrs A!'

'Oh I'm not sure about that. But come through, come through – say hello to Tim before he shuts himself away and then I'll bring your coffee in.'

'You don't need to wait on us, Mum.'

'Nonsense. You girls have got so much to catch up on.'

A few minutes later, Amy and Penny sat facing each other in two of the armchairs. The lights twinkled on the tree. The room smelt of a Christmas pot pourri mix in a pretty bowl on the coffee table.

'Oh, Amy, you've still got that dancing reindeer!'

It was a mechanical toy that came out every year. The reindeer picked up its feet and moved from side to side to the tune of 'Jingle Bells'. Amy wound it up and they both watched it, giggling.

'Nothing ever lasts that long in Mum and Dad's house, especially with all the pesky grandchildren these days.'

'How are they all?'

'Oh, they're fine. Growing – in size and number.'

'How's work, Pen? I don't think I even asked about your job when we last spoke.'

'Not much change really. Teacher cum social worker cum childminder. Probably more of the latter two most days. But I do still love it. Most of the time, anyway. And what about you? How's life in Grassmoor?'

'Grassdale. Oh, I'm really settling in. Don't look so surprised!'

'You should see her, Penny.' Her mother interrupted as she walked into the room with a tray which she placed on the coffee table. 'She even dresses like a country bumpkin.' But she was beaming as she said it.

'Are you still running?' Penny asked her friend.

'Is the sky blue?' said Judith, in a resigned tone, plunging the lid of the cafetière.

'Hey, what about that chap who rescued you? Did you ever see him again?'

Amy noticed that her mother had looked up with interest. She felt a flush warming her cheeks. 'Yes – you wouldn't believe it, but he turned out to be my colleague. He'd been on leave when I started so we hadn't met. Quite embarrassing on the Monday morning.'

'No! Oh, that's hysterical!'

'I'm glad you think so. And then we had a disagreement at work, so it wasn't the best start. We made a point of keeping out of each other's way after that.'

She was aware of her mother's eyes fixed on her before Judith turned to Penny. 'Well I've never heard this story, Penny. Clearly not one for Mum's ears.'

'There wasn't much to say, Mum, but I told you that Damian was an idiot when we bumped into him in the restaurant.'

'Damian? I like it!' said Penny.

'That charming man? So you've been keeping more things from us about him? She's such a dark horse, Penny. I have to rely on people like you to find out what's going on in my own daughter's life.'

'I'll tell you what happened, Mum, if you're that keen to know. I fell over when I was running soon after I arrived.' She held up a cautioning hand. 'Don't say anything, I was careless I know. Anyway, he comes galloping up and makes me feel like an idiot.' Actually, that wasn't strictly true. He had wanted to help her, but she had spurned his offer because she was proud, and embarrassed, and, OK, a bit irritated by his manner. (And his resemblance to Jake.) How much easier it would have been if she had simply accepted his help. There would have been no awkwardness at work, and her ankle might have healed even quicker if she had allowed him to help her home.

'The age-old story of a knight in shining armour wanting to help a damsel in distress,' said her mother, while Amy raised her eyes and Penny chuckled. 'But then the poor chap happens to meet *my* daughter. Don't you just feel for him, Penny?'

They were all laughing now. Judith poured the coffee and Amy jumped up to pass a mug to her friend and share the plate of biscuits.

'What's your Christmas been like, Penny?' her mother asked.

'All I can say is, I was glad to escape. One niece wants me to play a video game with her, another wants me to be Darth Vader, the youngest boy wants to be read to all the time. Their parents are sitting around with their feet up making the most of having Aunty Pen in the house!'

'I always wanted a big family,' said her mother wistfully.

'Did you, Mum?' Amy was surprised.

'Oh yes, once upon a time. I pictured myself with a big brood of children. But your father wasn't keen, and I found motherhood harder than I'd expected.'

'Was I that awful as a baby?' She pulled a face at Penny, who pulled her teeth over her bottom lip in a look of exaggerated concern.

'You were difficult, especially for a novice like me. I didn't know anyone else with children, or if I did, I'd kept well away from them. But you used to cry and cry whenever I put you down. I'd take you out in your pram to lull you to sleep, but you never slept for more than half an hour at a time during the day, and when you woke up you started off again. Nights were a little better, but I do remember one in particular, when your father was on call and needed to grab all the sleep he could get, so I resorted to taking you for a drive just to shush you. I ended up on the M25 and once I'd joined, I just stayed on it, all the way round.'

'Blimey, Mum. I hoped I stopped crying after that.'

'You grew out of it in the end, and you were such a good girl after that so I suppose I was lucky in the long run.'

Judith glanced at the two younger women. 'You do forget most of the bad things.'

'It doesn't sound as if you did, Mum!'

All three of them laughed.

'Anyway, on to cheerier things, I'm going to leave you two to catch up properly while I make some sausage rolls. The book club ladies are coming round tomorrow night.'

Amy always felt better after talking to Penny. Her friend's sunny personality, her refusal to dwell on things for too long, her conviction that everything happened for a reason, always rubbed off on her. She discovered before Penny left that she was in a new relationship with a secondary-school teacher who taught history and politics. Amy felt happy for her friend, whose face seemed to soften when she talked about him. She left just before lunchtime. Amy went to see if her mother needed a hand.

'Turkey sandwiches are made. Go and see if your father's ready for lunch.'

Her father appeared to be gazing out of the window. His laptop was on the desk in front of him, several books open beside him. He held a pen aloft in his left hand, as he often did, even when he wasn't writing, as if it was helping to formulate his train of thought.

She rapped lightly on the door. 'Lunch, Dad? Or are you in the middle of something?'

He didn't reply at first, then, when she repeated the question, gave a little start. 'Sorry, dear, I was miles away.'

'Preparing for your talks?'

'Yes, and other things. Worrying about the lack of funding.' He smiled weakly at Amy over his glasses. 'The usual. Don't tell your mother.'

He was forbidden from talking about funding – or lack thereof – to Judith, who said that she couldn't bear to hear the word one more time.

'She probably won't be happy until you retire,' said Amy, adding quickly, 'but she knows how important it is to you as well. I mean, nothing is as important as saving lives.'

'I lost a patient just before Christmas. He wasn't much older than you. Had a wife, young family. It's people like him I'm thinking of.' He gazed off again.

'Oh, Dad, that's awful.'

'He didn't know he had anything wrong with his heart until a couple of months ago.'

'Blimey.' Amy put a hand on her own heart, both in sympathy and to check that it was still beating.

He refocused his attention on her. 'Sorry, darling. This is most definitely not the right conversation for Christmas! I think lunch beckons.'

On her drive back to Grassdale two days later, she thought about the conversation with her father. It was unusual for him to talk about work, and because it was a forbidden subject with her mother, she realised that she rarely asked him about it. She found herself wondering if she had done enough to get to know her father. They both dealt with illness, life and death in their respective fields. Perhaps she could have supported him better in the past? Perhaps he too needed to offload his problems from time to time? Or did he feel it was his duty to protect his wife and daughter from the harsher realities of his job?

As she thought about his patient, she felt as if she had received an unintentional lesson in living each day to the full – in not wasting time by holding grudges.

'I moved for the chance to grow as a person but I've still got work to do,' she told herself. 'I have to take further steps out of my comfort zone, get involved and do more for other people.'

She wondered how Mary's old people's Christmas party had gone. Perhaps, next year, she would offer to help too.

17

Still basking in the afterglow of Christmas with her parents, Amy realised it had been more enjoyable than she expected. As an only child, she was accustomed to spending time with older people; she had spent a lot of her childhood in the company of adults, who either made a fuss of her or ignored her. She was quite content to be ignored, happy to sit with a book or a puzzle, waiting for her parents – or in most cases, her mother – to finish their socialising. However, she was looking forward to returning to Grassdale in a way that took her by surprise. The thought of Ivy Cottage waiting for her made her heart give a little flip. She pictured Lower Street, in all its quaintness. She hoped the Christmas lights were still strung upon the trees on the green. Some of her parents' neighbours had taken down their trees and lights already. She pictured the store, with John and Val, waiting for her custom; she would be sure to pop into the bookshop the next day to see how Sarah was, and hear how Jenny's Christmas guests had enjoyed their old-fashioned games – as well as their ban on phones!

The roads were busy with post-Christmas traffic. She had left Surrey early, but with the short days of winter, it was dark even before she turned off the A1. Fortunately, it was a mild night for this time of year, with no frost. All the same, she drove carefully in her little car. 'Maybe you should be thinking about a different model – something that suits country roads better,' her father had suggested. But she had come to realise that the little Fiat was better in many ways, squeezing through gaps that bigger cars couldn't manage. She had still – *oops*! – managed to scratch it one day. Woody had come to the rescue, restoring the paintwork and charging a fraction of what a specialist company would have charged.

She had told Mary that she was coming home. Something about the thought of having a catch-up with her over a cuppa put a smile on her face. Mary had been keeping an eye on the cottage and picking up her post. She had also put the heating on, so when Amy walked into Ivy Cottage at about half past five, it felt warm and lived in. She wasn't surprised when, about an hour later, there was a knock on the door.

'I won't keep you because you'll probably be about to eat, but just wondering how your Christmas was?'

Amy thought back to the conversation she'd had with herself in the car, and invited Mary in. She asked how the old folks' party had gone, and heard how there had been a rather unseemly fight between two of the revellers over whose turn it was to open the last layer in pass the parcel, but fortunately the Major defused the situation.

'He was supposed to be a guest, but he's such a trooper, he ended up mucking in and serving meals too, as we were rather short-handed.'

Amy had brought back a shepherd's pie from her mother, that was now in the oven, and though she was really longing to eat it in front of the television, she asked Mary if she'd like to join her for dinner. Mary looked pleased at the invitation, but said that it was a friend's birthday. However, she asked Amy if she'd like to spend New Year's Eve with her. 'It can be a difficult night for us singletons, can't it?'

'Thanks,' said Amy, inwardly balking at the comment. 'I'll look forward to it.' And she realised that she meant it.

***

Damian wasn't at work the next day.

'He's picked up a bug over the holidays, poor lamb,' said Donna.

Amy felt strangely disappointed. She thought about how his name kept coming up in conversation while she was with her parents, then felt slightly embarrassed by the fact. She worried Donna would somehow know by looking at her – a ridiculous thought!

She was having a quick coffee between patients when Mark stuck his head round the kitchen door.

'Are you free, Amy? I wondered if you could see Arad? He's a friend of Damian's and he's rather disappointed that he's not here.'

Arad, the boy she had wrongly assumed to be Damian's son, had large brown eyes and very dark hair, cut in a slightly old-fashioned pageboy style. He was clutching a cardboard box. Amy recognised Fahimeh, his mother, from Sarah's shop. She wore a well-cut plum-coloured coat, a colour favoured by Mary. Amy couldn't help thinking that Mary might have passed it on to her. It was the sort of thing her neighbour would do.

'He found him in the garden,' said the boy's mother, a hand on his shoulder as they walked into Amy's consulting room.

Amy helped him to put the box on the table. It was very light, almost as if there was nothing in it.

'Can you tell me what's inside?'

She wasn't going to risk opening the box until she knew what she was going to find.

'A squirrel,' said the child. 'I think he fell out of a tree in the garden.' He stared at Amy with his big eyes. 'Or maybe other squirrels pushed him out.'

'We leave him at first,' said his mother, 'because that is what the internet tells us to do. We wait to see if he has mother. But he is there a long time and he does not move. It is cold, and we are afraid he dies.' She added, 'Arad says Damian will help, but Damian is not here.'

Amy carefully opened the box. She was wearing thick gloves. Sophie came in to help in case another pair of hands was required.

'You were clever to pick him up without being bitten. They have sharp teeth.'

It was worrying that the creature wasn't trying to escape. A cardboard box would usually prove unsuitable for a squirrel, which could rip it to sheds in no time. Amy gently picked him up. He showed little resistance. She examined him carefully, with the help of Sophie. There was no obvious sign of injury.

'He looks young. Squirrels usually have their second brood in August but I wonder if this one was born later for some reason. Perhaps something happened and he was in shock, and waiting for his mother.'

'Ah, we should not have taken him!' Fahimeh clasped her hands together.

Amy shook her head. 'No, it's not always so clear cut. Sometimes a parent abandons a child when something happens to it. It's not uncommon.' She looked at Arad. 'You've probably saved his life.'

Arad beamed at her and his mother. Fahimeh stroked her son's hair.

'You can help him?' asked Fahimeh.

It was Lauren who had told Amy about Linda, also known as the Squirrel Lady. Although Amy hadn't dealt with her on a professional level, they had been introduced to each other in the bookshop one Saturday afternoon.

'I know just the person to take care of him. If you can leave him with me while I see the rest of my customers, and give me time to make a phone call, we can take him together. In the meantime, we'll pop him in this comfortable little cage here.'

'Arad loves animals,' said Fahimeh. 'He would like a pet but I tell him we must wait until we have home of our own.'

When Amy looked at her questioningly, she added, 'They might move us. We move three times already – we were in Manchester before we are here. While we wait for official papers we go where they tell us.'

A few minutes after midday, Amy saw her last customer of the morning. She sent a text message to Fahimeh and, a few minutes later, she and her son were at the door of the practice. With the squirrel transferred to a solid carrier, the three of them headed down the road.

'This is a very special person,' Amy explained, 'who has a sanctuary for squirrels in her garden. But only—' she realised she was talking slowly, unsure how fluent they both were, 'for red squirrels. Do you know that we also have grey squirrels? Though the red squirrel is so rare these days, I had never seen one until I came here.'

'Really?' Fahimeh sounded surprised. 'So they are very special. You hear, Arad?'

'I know already,' he said. 'We talked about them at school. The grey squirrel is bigger and eats the food that the red ones want to eat. And they carry a disease that kills the red ones but not them.'

'You know a lot, Arad,' said Amy.

'I listen to the teacher. Some of the other children don't listen. They talk and are naughty when she speaks. She says to them, "Why are you not listening? Do you want to stand in front of the class and be the teacher?"' He looked most affronted.

'Tsccchh!' Fahimeh looked at Amy over the top of his head. 'This child! He is a chatterbox too. That's what you say, no? The teacher tells me he likes to talk.' She tapped Arad playfully on the head and said something to him in Farsi to which he replied in a gabble of his native language, interspersed with some English words.

'His English is brilliant, isn't it?' said Amy. 'How wonderful to be bilingual.'

'We speak Farsi at home, but he often wants to speak to us in English. Of course that is good for his father and me because he can teach us, but we do want to keep our native language alive, even if we cannot go back to our country.'

Amy thought she appeared sad. She would have liked to know more about their situation and where they had come from, but even if they hadn't already arrived at their destination, she felt it wasn't the sort of question she could ask her. She was conscious that Fahimeh's experiences might be too painful to relate.

Instead, all she said was, 'I'm so sorry, Fahimeh. I can only imagine how hard it must be sometimes.'

'Thank you.'

'But now,' she said, turning up a small narrow path to a cottage door, 'we have arrived.'

Linda greeted them at the door and led them through a narrow passageway into the kitchen at the back of the house, then through a door into the garden. It was hard to discern the size of the garden as the winding path was lined with small trees and bushes that obscured a view of the whole plot. Most of the trees, their branches now bare, had bird feeders hanging from them and bird houses attached to their trunks.

The squirrel enclosure was close to the house, constructed from wooden posts and thick mesh. It resembled a mini woodland inside, with twigs and branches, rope to play on, and plenty of hiding places.

'We released the mum and kittens I had just the other day, so the hotel is free right now. He can settle in peacefully.' Linda unlocked the door. 'Do you want to come inside with me?' she asked Arad.

The boy nodded. He had grown unusually quiet. The two of them entered the enclosure and shut the door behind them.

'We'll let him come out in his own time.'

The container had a door on its side, which Linda opened. 'He might want to wait until we've gone, but if we're very quiet …'

The little party stood there, hardly daring to breath. Thinking of how still the creature had been, Amy was surprised to see a head poke out of the opening, followed by a dainty body and bushy tail. It sniffed its way along the ground, moving cautiously, then stopped to pick up an acorn.

'He looks pretty healthy to me,' said Linda. 'But I'll keep a close eye on him. He'll probably be happier when we disappear. I have a camera in the house so we can look at him there.'

'A camera? We can watch him?' Arad was fascinated.

They all trooped back inside. Linda opened her laptop and clicked on one of the icons. There was the cage and the squirrel inside it, still nibbling the acorn.

Arad watched it, his eyes even wider.

Amy checked her watch. 'I really must get back to work, but—' she broke off, looking at her new Iranian friends.

'We must go too,' said Fahimeh. 'I am helping Sarah this afternoon and my husband is taking care of Arad. You have been very kind. Both of you.'

'If Arad wants to come back and see his friend, he's very welcome,' said Linda.

As they walked back up Lower Street together, Amy asked Fahimeh what her house was like and if there was anything she needed.

'Oh, we are very happy we have house. I do not complain,' said Fahimeh.

Amy persisted, asking her how well equipped her kitchen was.

Fahimeh laughed. 'They give us three of everything! We wash up a lot of dishes. I say to Arad, "We must not break a thing!"'

An idea had occurred to Amy. When she got home that evening, she found her great-grandmother's china in the boxroom. The set contained six of everything: dinner and tea plates, cups and saucers, soup bowls and dessert bowls, as well as a gravy jug, a cream jug and two tureens. How much better to give it to someone who needed it than have it growing dusty in here? Her mother would probably have a fit when she learnt that Amy had got rid of it, but at the end of the day, it was just a pretty set of china that wasn't being utilised. Even Mum might be able to admit, when she had got over the initial shock, that it was good for it to see the light of day again. She put it in the car and drove it straight round to Fahimeh's.

18

Amy barely saw Damian in the last days between Christmas and New Year. He remained off work for another day, after which their paths did not cross. She had planned in her head how she might casually drop into the conversation a comment about enjoying her Secret Santa bubble bath over the holidays, to see how he reacted – she felt sure it came from him, and equally certain that he must want her to know that – but the opportunity seemed to have passed her by.

Donna, Sophie and Fran were all full of their plans for New Year's Eve, an evening Amy had never particularly looked forward to, even when she had been with Jake. It felt obligatory to have a good, even wild time on New Year's Eve, so much so that, whatever happened, it was always going to be a let-down. She was glad to be popping next door to Mary's, armed with a bottle of champagne – actually a Yorkshire-brewed sparkling wine from the store that had cost an arm and a leg, which she was eager for them to sample.

Mary had cooked coq au vin – her speciality, she claimed – after which they had chatted in front of the fire, nursing their glasses. They toasted each other as Big Ben chimed midnight, and Amy wondered, for just a split second, what Damian was doing at that moment and who he might be with, before Mary interrupted her thoughts by announcing that if Amy didn't mind, she really needed to get to bed as she had to be up early to visit cousins in Leeds the next day. Amy didn't mind at all, and went home feeling a little tipsy, but happy.

***

The new year brought with it a spell of Arctic weather. The moors were baked hard with frost, and solid underfoot. Each blade of grass was threaded with silver. Though her cheeks stung with the cold when she was out, Amy loved the bright clear light and the way everything was picked out more vividly. The bare trees were crisply reflected in the flooded pasture at the bottom of Grassdale, near the bridge. Flocks of long-tailed tits or bluetits descended suddenly like swarms of locusts on trees and hedges, fluttering and twittering wildly as they looked for insects. Colourful pheasants waddled over the fields.

It was too slippery underfoot to run, so on the first Saturday after new year, a bright but bitter day, Amy decided to embark on a walk instead. Perhaps, in the process, she could scope out some new routes for her runs when the weather became more clement. She wore her hiking boots and several layers of clothing, topped with a waterproof jacket. She had yet to wear the jacket her parents had given her for Christmas; it was too heavy for a long walk and too smart for work. She supposed she would have to start to wear it in one day.

The ground glistened in the low winter sun. She set off along the road in the direction of Crowdale. She had driven along it plenty of times but rarely walked that way. She knew there was a path through the fields about a quarter of a mile up the road, through a five-bar gate, from where she had planned a route. She passed the small estate where Fahimeh and Arad lived. A handful of other houses were dotted at intervals along the road, slightly out of the village itself. The front garden of one of a row of three cottages was filled with gnomes of all shapes and sizes: one smoking a pipe, one fishing, one – oh surely not! – bending over and showing a bare backside. It made her smile, but she couldn't help wondering what the neighbours thought of it. A bit further along was a flash-looking new-build with floor-to-ceiling windows and a roof terrace. It had been built to merge into the landscape, with its bleached grey-green wooden cladding and a living roof. It was certainly eye-catching, though lacked the charm of its neighbours.

Amy reached the five-bar gate. It didn't seem to want to open. Try as she might, she couldn't get it to budge more than a few inches, and resorted to squeezing through a tiny gap, leaving a scuff on her jacket. The path she was taking was well-defined, though slippery with patches of frost and black ice. After a while it came to a fork, one track leading further west onto the moors, the other looking as if it might eventually veer back towards the road.

Amy chose the first one. It was still early in the afternoon, the sun still bright, and she was keen to go as far as she could before turning back. She passed a ruined barn. It had clearly been deemed unsafe as there was fencing round it. She had passed someone walking a dog on her way out of the village earlier, but here there was no one, and she felt more solitary than before, perhaps because she was venturing into the unknown. The track was becoming less clearly defined.

She reached another point where paths converged. There was a signpost, but the sign itself had been broken long ago. She stood there for a while, searching her surroundings. There was nothing to see other than hills and moorland, the snowy landscape making one view much like the other. Should she pick a direction and carry on? If she could find a feature to gather her bearings, then when she came back to this point she would know which way to turn. She noticed a small copse to her right; that would do it. She took the left fork. A couple of times, just to test herself, she broke into a run, but her heavy boots weighed her down.

The afternoon grew colder and the moors began to turn amber in the low sun, while the higher ground glowed a delicate pink. She snapped some photos on her phone. *I suppose I should turn back now*, she thought, *before it gets dark*. She turned round and began to retrace her steps. She was surprised how different the landscape appeared in this direction. *Did I really pass those trees?* she thought. *And surely I would have noticed that boulder at the side of the path?*

She carried on until she reached the confluence of paths where she had seen the copse. Except that now it seemed different … and where were the trees? She was at a different junction. Had she gone too far, or not far enough? Sure that she would have spotted the trees, she carried on. This was why you had to plot your route and remember markers when venturing on a solo walk. The sun had sunk behind the hills and it would be dark soon.

Finally she came to the junction – of course, the broken signpost. The relief was palpable. She started to walk more quickly. By the time she reached the ruined barn, it had become a hulking, spectre-filled mass. She tried not to look at it and was thankful that she had brought a torch or she might not have seen the path at all. When she laid eyes on the five-bar gate, she had never been so pleased to see anything in her life. Her face was frozen, her hands icy in her gloves, even her feet were cold, clad though they were in two thick pairs of socks and solid boots.

She also noticed that there was a stile, the kind with stone steps that jutted out from the wall, beside the gate that she had tried to open earlier. *What an idiot*, she thought; *I wasn't supposed to open the gate at all!* However, the frost-bitten steps were so slippery, it was safer to squeeze through the narrow opening again.

Amy began to walk back along the road just as her torch battery died. *And this, Amy, is why we leave with our headtorch and reflective bag too.* So much for all her sanctimonious thinking that *she*, Amy Ashton, was too well-prepared to ever get caught out herself.

She could feel a new frost forming and her foot skidded at one point. She had just crossed to the left in order to have a wider verge to walk along when she heard a car approaching from behind. She instinctively moved further into the hedgerow to let it past, hoping there was no ditch, and stopped in her tracks, fixing her eye on the vehicle until it had passed her. She shielded her eyes as the headlights appeared round the corner. It was being driven fairly quickly, and it pulled into the middle of the road to overtake her. Then it braked sharply and stopped, twenty metres ahead.

Still thinking of the spooky building, and having seen too many films in her youth about hitchhikers meeting grisly fates, Amy's heart was hammering as she considered walking towards it to get further up the road. She didn't recognise the car. Why had it stopped? There wasn't much room for her to pass it on the near side, but if she walked on the other side to see what the driver wanted, she risked being hit if another car suddenly appeared.

Then the passenger door opened and a voice from the driver's seat said, 'What on earth do you think you're doing walking on the wrong side of the road? I could hardly see you! Get in!'

She opened her mouth to say something, then shut it again. In the interior light of the car she saw that the driver was Damian. Annoyed to be spoken to like that, but grateful to have the chance to get off the road – she had felt more vulnerable than she had anticipated – she jumped inside.

Their paths had barely crossed since the work party. She had felt a little deflated when she had returned to work to find him absent. There had been some sort of mutual connection between them, she was sure, at the Dickensian party, and she would have liked to talk about the evening at some point – even though he would have been sure to embarrass her about the bed incident! – but it already seemed so long ago, and bringing it up now felt forced. She was even starting to wonder if the flirtatious part of their conversation that night had been in her imagination.

'You're practically invisible out there in your dark jacket. What are you playing at? These roads aren't meant for walking on at the best of times, but on a night like tonight – and facing the wrong way …'

He uttered a weary sigh as he peered through his rear-view and side mirrors, indicated, and set off again.

Amy didn't want a lecture, but she was so relieved to be in the car, which was warm and comfortable, unlike the Land Rover, that she decided to be more contrite.

'I didn't mean to be out so late. I mean, an hour ago it wasn't even dark. My bloody torch died and it was safer for me to walk that side of the road on the bend.' She pointed out to the tarmac with the useless torch.

He tutted, then said in a more conciliatory fashion, 'Well, good job I came along.'

'I didn't recognise the car. I thought you might be a mad axe murderer.'

No doggy smell this time, but Amy recognised the aroma of the nice aftershave he had worn at the guesthouse do. She found herself wondering where he had been, and who he had worn it for, as he was clearly on his way home now.

Damian laughed at her comment. 'Just me. Far more run-of-the-mill. The Land Rover is mainly for work. An old car of Dad's.'

'Thank you, anyway. I appreciate it.'

She saw his exaggerated nod of acknowledgement in the darkness.

Neither of them said anything for a few seconds, until they both spoke at once.

'I—'

'Did—'

They both laughed. 'You go first,' said Amy.

'I heard you met Arad.'

'Oh, isn't he adorable? Yes, we paid a visit to the Squirrel Lady together.'

'He told me all about it. He was so excited. He was on his way to see how his little protégé was doing when I last saw him.' Amy could hear affection softening his words.

'How did you get to know him? I gather you're good pals.'

'Chance encounter. He was waiting for the school bus one day with his mum when I was parking and we just got talking. The next time I saw him he invited me to his house for tea, right in front of Fahimeh. His poor mother didn't have much of a choice! She and Salman are a wonderful couple. They've had a tough time that family.'

'You've been good to him. He thinks highly of you.'

Damian chuckled. 'I don't know about that, but he's a bright kid. It's great to see him thriving.'

They were coming into Grassdale now.

'Well, where shall I drop you?'

'Home would be nice.' Then, in case he didn't know, she added, 'Oh, I live in Ivy Cottage, right on the end.'

'I know where you live.'

As they drove into the village, John was carrying the advertising board into the store.

'Drat! They're closing already. I was going to pop in. Never mind.' Amy was thinking aloud more than anything else.

'You need anything?' Damian pulled up in front of Ivy Cottage.

'Nothing I can't live without. I'll pull something out of the freezer.'

'You know, if you wanted, I could—'

'Oh, look!' Amy saw that the door to the shop was still open, and John was talking to someone outside. 'If I'm quick I'll catch him. Thank you, Damian, for the lift. Thanks so much! I'll see you Monday, right?'

She leapt out of the car and ran towards the store. It was only when she was packing away her items that she re-ran the conversation in her head and wondered what Damian had been about to say.

19

Octavia was back. The tortoise was 'off-colour', according to Betty, her owner. This time Betty came in without her daughter. She carried Octavia in a large flat-bottomed shopping bag, the reusable type sold by supermarkets. Amy was alarmed at first, but was relieved to see that the elderly woman had placed a firm piece of card at the bottom to make her pet more secure.

'Betty, how lovely to see you both again.'

'And you too, doctor. And you remember Octavia?'

'One of my favourite patients! How could I forget?'

Betty handed the bag to Amy before taking a seat and surveying the room, as if she was there for a social engagement rather than as a customer. Amy carefully placed the bag on the table and retrieved the treasured pet.

'The real problem, doctor,' Betty confided, 'is that I'm worried about what will happen to Octavia when I'm gone. I won't go on forever, in fact, when you reach my age, you sometimes wonder if you'll wake up the next morning.'

Amy lowered Octavia safely to the floor, where she began to explore, then sat down beside Betty.

'Betty, you seem fit as a fiddle to me!'

'Hmmm, looks are deceptive. Sometimes I feel as creaky as an old gate.'

Amy laughed.

'You've got a very caring daughter, Betty. I'm sure she'll give Octavia a good home if she ever needed one.' She squeezed the old lady's hand. She was surprised at how soft her skin was.

'I don't know, doctor. I don't think she cares for Octavia very much. Besides, she has a big family to take care of. I rather feel I'll be overburdening her.'

They sat there without speaking, both of them watching Octavia, until Betty said, 'Did you know, I got Octavia when I was a little girl? She's almost as old as I am.'

'Yes, I remember you telling me.'

She thought about the three Christmas cards she had received from Betty, and wondered how well the old lady was coping at home now that she had become so forgetful.

Betty looked sad. Amy gently squeezed her hand again. 'I think Octavia is looking very well today. And I don't want you to worry about the future. My mother sometimes says to me, "Yesterday is gone, tomorrow isn't here yet, we have only today".' It didn't actually sound anything like her mother, but she couldn't remember whose quote it was and she was trying to keep things simple. 'If Octavia ever needs a home, I'll be sure to find her one. You can count on me for that.'

'Oh, doctor, would you?' The old lady's eyes brimmed with tears. 'That would be a great weight off my mind. Did you hear that, Octavia? The lovely doctor will find a good home for you – if you should need one.' She said the last five words in a whisper, putting her finger to her lips as she glanced at Amy. 'Don't want to get her worried.'

***

A week after being rescued by her colleague, Amy had finished changing for a walk when she looked out of the kitchen window and saw Damian striding down Lower Street in his waterproof coat and hiking boots. She watched him until he disappeared from view. It was impossible to see which way he had turned when he reached the bottom of the road: whether left, over the bridge into Church Lane, or right and onto the moors to the south of the village, where one of the footpaths bypassed Hettie's farm.

She had been intending to walk to Bottom Farm and back, avoiding the boggy moorland. Did she want to bump into Damian? She wasn't sure. She didn't want him to think she'd followed him! That would be embarrassing. On the other hand, it might be pleasant to meet under less confrontational circumstances. She had the feeling that if the situation was right, they might even find other things to talk about. She could ask him about Arad's visit to see the squirrel, for a start.

She went outside, locked the door, and hesitated for a second, looking both up and down the road as there was often someone she would wave to. Before she had chance to set off, she heard her name called. It was Val from the store. She was standing on the other side of the road, gesticulating and trying to catch Amy's eye.

'Yoo-hoo! Can I borrow you?'

Amy crossed the road to see what she wanted.

'I know it's an awful cheek, duck, but as you don't look as if you're going anywhere important—' with that remark she eyed Amy's outfit in a way that made it clear she considered walking a frivolous pastime – 'is there a chance you could lend a hand in the café for half an hour? A couple of our volunteers are off sick and Sue and Edith are run off their feet. We've just had a coach party descend on us.'

'Err …' She could hardly make up an excuse. Val was right, she supposed. Whatever she was doing could wait for another time. Plus, she'd made a promise to herself to get more involved!

'I'd better get changed, won't be a sec.'

She was surprised to find herself less irritated by the request than she might have expected. She knew that she would not have got round to joining the café rota – her weekends were too precious – despite her best intentions. Being put on the spot like this was taking the decision out of her hands. She quickly changed into jeans, a T-shirt and a pair of deck shoes and dashed over the road to the store.

The store's community café was bigger than it appeared from the road, with ten tables in the room that overlooked the street while a smaller room, known as the garden room and with a view of a small courtyard, contained half a dozen. Every table was occupied, and while some customers were tucking into tea and cake, a queue was forming at the counter.

Two women were attempting to keep things running smoothly. The older of the pair was in the process of carrying a tray to the garden room. She shuffled rather than walked, the plates and cups jingling dangerously as she moved. Although she was making very slow progress, she looked determined. The other, younger woman, was more frantic as she moved from one job to another: filling a teapot one second, cutting cake another while accepting money from a customer's outstretched hand.

'Bless you!' she said, when Val took her through. 'I'm Sue – at least I think I am. My brain has gone a bit frazzled. I've no clean plates or cups after this lot, so if you wouldn't mind washing up for me.' She added more quietly, 'Edith is wonderful but she only moves at one speed – and she refuses to wash up. She fancies herself as a waitress and won't entertain the idea of doing anything else.'

Amy went into the tiny kitchen, where she quickly washed and dried half a dozen plates, cups and saucers. It was a decent start, and she took them back to a grateful Sue. She cleared a couple of tables while she was out there before going back to tackle more washing up. She worked quickly and methodically, finding satisfaction in the task. When the drainer was almost full of crockery, she quickly dried each piece and returned them to the counter.

Customers continued to pour in.

'You're keeping us busy today,' she heard Sue call over to one of the visitors.

'We're on a tour: Dales Holidays. This is such a pretty village!'

While at the sink, Amy heard raised voices and laughter that suggested familiarity. A few seconds later Hettie burst into the kitchen carrying a tray piled high with cups and saucers.

'I left the pick-up with Woody – she needs some new tyres – and I saw all the people streaming down the road. Struth! I wondered what was going on. When I got here, Val told me she was having to send folk down to The Snug. Thought I'd better lend a hand. I did try to take a tray from Edith but she almost bit my head off.' She dusted her hands. 'Right, I'll go and clear some more tables then I'll dry for you, duck.'

'I'm surprised you've got time, Hettie,' said Amy, when she returned laden with even more dirty crockery. Hettie had taken off her chunky outdoor jacket and wore a jumper with a bright orange zigzag design that looked as if it was homemade.

Hettie seemed taken aback by the remark. 'I like to do my bit, like everyone else. It's only right, isn't it? Good to see they got you on the rota. Some of the newcomers keep themselves to themselves, and that's their business. But what's the point in living in a village if you don't do your fair share every now and then? Besides, we all reap the benefits of this place.'

Amy, her fingers wrinkling in the water, didn't confess that she had been given little choice in the matter.

Hettie put a pile of plates into the bowl and nudged Amy at the same time. 'Stops me turning into a wild woman of the moors, if it's not too late.'

When she had finished her new load of washing up, Amy headed back into the café. A stout woman poked her head round the door to the street and announced in a loud voice that the coach for Dales Holidays was leaving in fifteen minutes. 'If you're not on board, we'll go without you.' It was hard to tell if she was joking or not.

Sue was busy loading up a tray for Edith, and thinking it appeared heavy – as well as trying to speed things up – Amy asked Sue which table she should take it to. It was a mistake. Amy felt Edith's bony shoulder nudging her out of the way as her hands moved quickly to the tray. 'That's my job, duck. You stick to yours.'

Sue offered Amy a sympathetic look. Once Edith had set off on another slow shuffle, she said to Amy, 'She's just a tad possessive about her job, take no offence, love.'

'I think we'll all need a cup ourselves when this lot have left,' said Hettie. Amy, who was gasping for one, nodded gratefully as she returned to the kitchen.

Half an hour later, with the coach party customers gone and only one table still occupied, Sue switched the sign on the door to 'Closed'.

'Well, you've had a telling-off from Edith so you're well and truly part of the village now,' she said to Amy, laughing. 'Don't worry – we've all had it. You keep us all in order, don't you?' she said to the older woman, who had sat down at a table in the corner where she was wolfing down a scone with far greater alacrity than her earlier demeanour had implied was possible.

'It was good to be able to help,' said Amy. 'I do get a bit bogged down with work and other stuff and, well …' She tailed off, wondering if the single-girl lifestyle was making her self-centred.

Hettie sat down beside Edith and patted the chair beside her for Amy. 'It's true. We all get consumed by our own problems, duck. Sometimes it's good to take a step outside. Puts things in perspective, I think.' She added with a wink, 'Mind, you shouldn't have done such a good job. Val will have you on the rota next weekend too.'

20

'I've got a rather strange case,' Mark announced to Amy and Damian in the kitchen one afternoon. Nurses Fran and Sophie were looking after customers whose pets had straightforward or minor issues to deal with. Fran was cutting a guinea pig's nails and Sophie was cutting the matted hair of a very fluffy ginger tom called Bear.

Amy had met Bear in her garden several times as he lived just a few doors away. He was a beautiful cat, who had an endearing way of gently headbutting her in greeting. All the same, she preferred not to encourage him as she was very fond of her visiting birds, who were understandably nervous when this large predator took to sunning himself on her lawn. Bear's owner had assured Amy that he had never caught a bird in his life, nor was he interested in hunting them. It was true that he seemed to have found a spot where he felt comfortable, and that a lot of the birds even ignored him.

Amy and Damian hadn't spoken much since he had rescued her from the dark road, though Amy thought she was starting to sense a thawing between them during their limited interactions. She sometimes had the impression he was about to speak to her, even if he didn't, or that he was trying to be helpful in ways that were probably indiscernible to the others. For example, making her a mug of coffee unprompted, helping remove the waste from her consulting room for her, or even having a pen ready when she'd misplaced the one she often kept in her bun for ease. They'd even accidentally held hands last time he'd passed something over; she felt a touch lightheaded after that experience.

But when Mark started discussing a veterinary matter, Amy couldn't help feeling that any good humour that had been engendered between them was surely about to evaporate. Damian would probably rather spend a day with his arm up a cow's backside in a freezing barn than listen to Amy's opinion about something, especially if it was at odds with his own view. Mark may not have realised it, but he was surely asking for trouble here – and just when everything was starting to go well.

'Tabitha is an English bulldog. Always been healthy.' Amy waited for Mark to close his eyes as he launched into his story, and he duly obliged. 'She's three years old, sociable, a real family pet. But she's been having seizures – at least that's what they seem to be. The first time it happened, her head dropped, she started to tremble and seemed to be in distress. It only lasted a matter of seconds, then she was fine, so Clive forgot about it. But it happened again a few weeks later, and this time he thought she might have been in pain. She was fine in between, eating and drinking normally. But he says when it happens it's very alarming. I told him to video it. I'm running some tests anyway, but nothing has shown up. I've told him to keep a diary too, to see if there are any patterns, but they haven't produced anything noteworthy.'

'Epilepsy? Brain tumour? It sounds as if she needs an MRI scan to provide the answer,' said Damian.

'Well, I'm leaning that way. But it's going to cost the customer a small fortune.'

'Definitely not just muscle tremors?' Amy guessed that Mark had probably ruled these out already, but she knew how alarming muscle tremors could look, and how they were sometimes mistaken for something far more serious. 'Idiopathic head tremors are common in bulldogs and boxers.'

Mark shook his head. 'It's what I thought originally, but it's starting to seem less likely.'

'And she's not unconscious during the seizures?' she asked.

He confirmed that she wasn't.

'It does sound neurological,' said Damian.

'The maddening thing for Clive is that Karen – that's his wife – doesn't know what he's talking about. She's yet to see it. Says he must be dreaming.' He let out a sigh. 'I must say, it's got me stumped.'

'I wonder ...' Amy began. Both men turned to her. 'I mean, it sounds an extreme example of it, and we'd need to know more about the family set-up to be sure, but could it perhaps be separation anxiety?'

They both studied her in silence.

She continued. 'At my London practice, we noticed it more often after Covid. People who'd always gone out to work started working from home. Their pets – well, it was mainly dogs, but we occasionally saw it in cats too – got used to them being around all the time. A lot of people bought pets for the first time in lockdown, too, so those animals only ever knew twenty-four-hour care and attention. So, when their owners did start going back to the office – or even just leaving the house again – their pets grew very anxious.'

'And they were having seizures?' Damian asked.

'Well, it wasn't exactly common; usually it was demonstrated by destructive behaviour, self-harm, or even just increased vocalisation. But I did have at least one case where the shivering or trembling was so bad that we thought it was something far more serious. It was pretty problematic, though, because the owner couldn't take her dog to work and couldn't work from home any longer, so there were no easy options. One day this poor dog was in a kind of trance-like state all day while its owner was out. Her partner witnessed it all. It was pretty disturbing for him.'

Mark and Damian were both staring at her intently now. It was hard to know what they were thinking.

'The next day, he rang his girlfriend at work and put her on speakerphone so that she could talk to the dog. That did the trick, but it was only temporary. Later, she started to record videos for him. The dog was always happy when he could see or hear her. I did give them some techniques for getting the dog used to being on its own, but it was a long, slow process.'

She shrugged. 'So perhaps that's Tabitha's problem too?'

'Sounds a bit far-fetched to me,' said Mark with a laugh. 'Londoners, eh? Their pets are as crazy as they are!'

But Damian looked serious. 'It all sounds perfectly plausible to me, Mark. Especially if your bloodwork tests aren't flagging anything. Worth finding out more from Clive. I think Amy may have hit the nail on the head.'

Amy, who had been starting to feel a little foolish, flashed him a grateful look. She wasn't used to Damian defending her like this. If anything, it was from him that she had half-expected a comment about pampered pets and their owners in the big city. Hadn't he said something like that to her before?

'Is it starting as soon as Karen leaves the house?' he asked Mark. 'He might not have put two and two together before.'

Mark breathed out noisily. His eyes flickered open and closed. 'I'll give Clive a ring and see what he says.'

Mark caught her after work a few nights later.

'That dog I was telling you about.'

'Tabitha?'

'That's the one. Well, would you credit it, I think you were spot on with your diagnosis. Clive's wife Karen recently got a new job that takes her away from home a few days a week. Clive looked back at that diary I told him to start keeping, and he started to see a pattern. To start with, it didn't happen when Karen left the house, because Tabitha expected her to be back. She was used to her popping out, and she was never the sort to wait by the door or cry at the window. But over time, when she realised that she wasn't coming back as soon as she used to, she started showing symptoms as soon as she went out the door.'

'I think it's more common than a lot of us have realised,' said Amy.

'And now we've got to work out what to do about it. I've told him that pheromones are a possibility, but we're going to try to avoid medication to start with. Try to get the dog used to being on her own a bit more. I don't know if he'll resort to what your London folk were doing, though. Karen spends a lot of her time on trains. Don't think she fancies talking to the dog within earshot of her fellow passengers.' He chuckled. 'Talk about barking mad, eh?'

***

One day, while popping quickly to the store, Amy was surprised by the sight of a police car and an RSPCA car parked on the other side of the road, a bit lower down from Ivy Cottage. She had barely seen a police car since moving to the Dales, and never in Grassdale itself. She wondered what was going on, but was distracted as soon as she was back at work.

She found out a couple of days later, over a glass of wine with Mary, when she was telling her neighbour about the anxious dog.

'I think Mark has the idea that London pets are all neurotic, as are their owners,' she said. 'Most of my customers were ordinary working folk.' She paused. 'Though I did have the odd eccentric character from time to time.'

'Are you thinking of anyone in particular?' asked Mary, seeing her smile to herself.

'I'm just remembering the customer who was kind of responsible for me coming here in the first place.'

Mary raised an enquiring eyebrow. 'Well, not totally responsible, but I'd had a bad day because of this woman and her guinea pig, and that was how I ended up browsing the internet for jobs. The poor thing had bumblefoot.'

'He had what?'

'Bumblefoot. It's an infection.'

Mary grimaced. 'Talking of poor things, did you hear about Colin's weasel? He rescued it when it was a baby. I can't remember the story exactly, but it became a pet. I don't know if you know Colin, a few doors down? He's an odd one. A bit of a loner. His parents died a few years ago – they were actually friends with my folks – and he's been bumbling along on his own ever since. We're all fond of him, though he tends to keep himself hidden away most of the time. Anyway, he was really attached to that animal.'

'Is he that slightly shabby chap, who looks as if his mother cuts his hair? He was the first person I met here! I had an accident getting my stuff out of the car and he appeared suddenly and helped me carry it all inside. Anyway, I didn't know he had a weasel. What happened?'

'He had a visit from the police, and the RSPCA took it away.'

Amy remembered the cars she had seen.

'But why the police?' She frowned. 'That sounds heavy-handed.'

'I don't think they were necessary in the end. But it was illegal, you see; apparently he needed a licence.' She shrugged. 'Maybe it was best for the creature in the long run, but no one disputed that it was being well cared for, and now Colin is distraught. I've been to see him myself, but not sure that it did much good.'

'That's really sad. Poor Colin.'

The women's faces were pink from the warmth of the fire and the wine.

Mary's eyes alighted on the book that lay on the coffee table. Amy was currently reading *Tess of the d'Urbervilles* by Thomas Hardy, her latest selection from Lauren's grandad's collection. She had decided to alternate a classic title with a contemporary book.

Mary pointed to it. 'I love Hardy but there's too much tragedy for me. After I read *Jude the Obscure*, I said, "Never again, Mr Hardy! You're destroying me!"'

'Yes, you're right, I'm probably due a happy-ever-after tale next.'

'And a happy-ever-after in real life too?'

'That would be nice, but I'm not sure I believe in them any more.'

21

One Saturday morning in February, while Amy was doing her chores, she heard the dull bang that signified someone was at her front door. It couldn't be Mary, as Mary would do so *several* times, each knock louder than the one before. To her surprise, Arad and Fahimeh were standing on her doorstep. Fahimeh offered a nervous smile and put a hand on Arad's shoulder.

'We hope we don't disturb you, but Arad, he is very—' She tailed off. 'I do not know the word but he is a boy who knows what he wants to do. He has something for you.'

'Do you want to come in?' asked Amy.

'No, no, we do not bother you.'

Arad held out a piece of paper. Amy saw a drawing of a squirrel, and although it wasn't the most accomplished piece of art, its bushy tail was unmistakable.

'That is the squirrel and that is where he sleeps and that is his tree and that is his food.' Arad pointed at everything in the picture in turn.

'He visits him at Linda's house. He took Damian with him this morning.'

'Ah.'

'At first she let me in the cage, but now I can't,' he said, sorrow glazing his big eyes.

'Oh?'

'She thinks it is best that he becomes – less tame?' said Fahimeh.

'Ah, yes, that's a very good thing. It means, Arad, that your squirrel might be able to live out in the wild with other squirrels again. To run around freely in all this lovely countryside. If he's too tame, and relies on people too much, he might not survive out there.'

'I know. I understand. But I'm still sad.'

Amy tried to pass him back the drawing. 'It's beautiful. You're very clever.'

'It's for you,' he said, pushing it towards her.

'We're very grateful for your help,' said Fahimeh. 'Damian tells Arad that he is very lucky to have seen you.'

'He did? That's kind.'

'He says you're the best one!' added Arad.

'Sshhh!' said his mother, smiling and nudging him. 'He does not want you to say that, remember?' She was laughing now, as the boy covered his mouth in exaggerated horror.

'That's kind, but everyone there is very good at their jobs. I'm actually the new girl. They're all more experienced than I am.'

Fahimeh smiled. 'Damian talks about you sometimes. I ask him if he has – how do I say it?' She put her right hand on her heart.

Bemused and a little embarrassed, Amy said, 'Oh, heavens, Fahimeh! I think you're getting carried away!'

***

Passing pregnant ewes on a walk round the reservoir, Amy realised that it wouldn't be long till lambing time. She had been to Hilltop Farm recently, where a ewe had given birth while she was there. She and Charlie, the farmer, had stood in the barn for a while, looking at the newborn twins with their mother.

'Not sure how she managed it, the sneaky old girl, but she got herself pregnant before all the others,' said Charlie.

'Must have been an immaculate conception,' said Amy, with a laugh.

'Well, I did wonder. The rest aren't due for another month. Thankfully she's an experienced mum and knew what to do, but we've brought them in for a bit of TLC.'

The young lambs were both a good size. They looked strong and confident as they fed greedily.

Amy knew that most farmers planned their lambing, their busiest time of year, to take place over a four-week period. Extra staff might need to be booked, as someone was required in the lambing shed day and night, so organisation was key.

It was Amy's first visit to the beauty spot and reservoir. It was one of those places people were always gushing about. 'You've got to go! It's so pretty!' said Donna. 'And there's a stately home next door with the most wonderful café.'

Amy thought that the moors around Grassdale would take some beating, but the main attraction for her that Sunday was the track that circled the edge of the reservoir, firm ground at a time when the moors were wet and boggy, and safer than walking on the road. There were actually two tracks, one for walkers and runners and another for cyclists, making it a popular destination.

The car park was busy. It was the starting point for several walks and trails, including a woodland walk on raised decking, cycle tracks, and trails into the hills, as well as the reservoir walk. People were putting on boots and waterproofs, or transporting small children into buggies. Despite the throng, Amy found herself on her own as she followed the path to the reservoir. The five-mile circuit was perfect for a run, though Amy had decided to walk today in order to better enjoy the unfamiliar surroundings. Although the lake was dark and slightly sinister-looking under the grey February sky, it always soothed her to be close to a large mass of water. The land rose gently around it on three sides. Along the top of one of the ridges, a row of oaks were evenly spaced like sentries.

Most people she passed said hello, though others were preoccupied by their conversations, or lost in their own thoughts. A cyclist rang his bell as he steamed by on the cycle track. She overtook a young couple with a child who was refusing to walk.

'We'll have ice cream after.'

'You can choose a film when we get home.'

'Just ten more steps, then I'll carry you.'

Kids. It was hard to imagine ever wanting them herself.

She had gone most of the way round when she heard heavy breathing and the slapping of footsteps behind her, then someone stopped alongside her.

'We meet again!'

It was Damian. *Of course it was Damian.* He seemed to make a habit of popping up when she least expected him.

'Hi.'

'Not running today?'

'I wouldn't have minded if I'd brought my shoes. I just came to check it out.'

'It's not a bad spot, but it can be busy. You can't move here in the summer. Mind, Grassdale gets pretty busy then too.'

He continued to walk in sync by her side.

'Don't let me slow you down,' said Amy.

'It's fine. I've done enough for now anyway. Listen, I usually have a cuppa before I head back. If we take the path here it leads us straight to Roseburn House. The café there is famous. It'll probably be busy, given it's a Sunday, but we could give it a try?'

Amy appreciated the olive branch and nodded in agreement. A path led through a small plantation and took them to the bottom of a driveway, at the end of which was a small Gothic revival house, with pointed arches and intricate chimneys.

'The holiday home of a prominent mill owner,' said Damian.

The café was located in the former orangery within its grounds, a beautiful building with tall windows dominating the south-facing side and a domed glass roof.

'Do you want to go and find us a seat? I'll get the drinks. Tea and something to eat?'

'Just tea please.'

Damian had been right. It was very busy. Sunday was obviously family day, and most tables seemed to contain at least two generations, with babies and small children all the way up to very elderly-looking grandparents. Amy pounced on a tiny table in the corner that had just been vacated, cups, saucers and plates still strewn all over. She tidied it as best she could, but didn't dare move them for fear of losing the table. Amy smiled in sympathy when the tired-looking waitress reached her.

'You're run off your feet!'

'Never seen it so busy!' said the woman.

She saw Damian scanning the room, unable to find her in the throng. She stood up and waved. When he caught sight of her, his face broke into a wide smile. As well as the tea, he had brought a large slice of coffee and walnut cake. 'I highly recommend this. Dare I say it, but it even beats my mother's.'

'Don't worry, I won't tell.'

'You'll try some, won't you. I got two forks.'

'Well I'd hate to deprive you. But maybe a little taste. Look at all that icing! There's more of it than cake!'

Damian laughed. 'The way it should be!'

Amy broke off a chunk of cake with her fork. It was crumbly and very sweet.

'Mmmm, scrumptious.'

Their eyes met for a few seconds longer than was necessary. She was the first to look away.

'Popular place. Is it always this busy?'

'Hmmm, yeah, I'd say so. At the weekend especially.'

Damian poured the tea from an old-fashioned brown pot.

'My grandma had a pot like this,' said Amy.

They were silent as they both took their first sips.

Damian helped himself to a mouthful of cake. 'Have some more.'

Amy declined. Actually, she wouldn't have minded more, but somehow, sharing it here with Damian, on this tiny table, felt like too intimate an act.

'Do you—'

'Have you—'

They both started speaking at the same time, then laughed, embarrassed.

'Have you always worked for Mark?' she asked him.

'No, didn't you know? I worked for one of the big practices nearby when I first qualified. I'm afraid I became disillusioned with it all pretty quickly.'

'Oh yes?'

'It was all money, money, money. I felt that the welfare of the animals was getting lost in the pursuit of profit. They started to bring in milestones. If I had a poor transaction value one month, I was told I had to increase it the next. If I didn't, they demanded to know why. It was on my mind all the time. I even started to question why I had wanted to be a vet in the first place. It took me a while to realise that it wasn't me, it was the operation.' He added, glumly, 'And no doubt there are many others like it.'

'Oh, Damian, that's awful.'

He appeared embarrassed at his frank disclosure. He gave his head a little shake. 'I did have a pretty bad spell, including some nights when I couldn't sleep. But thankfully I moved to Mark's place and all has been well since.'

'Did you know Mark before?'

'No, not really. We had met through work, but as he's a newcomer himself, it wasn't as if he was an old family friend.'

'A newcomer of twenty years,' laughed Amy.

'Yeah, well, it's a bit like that here, as you've probably found out for yourself.' He toyed with a piece of cake, before asking, 'Do you like it here? It's not exactly the Big Smoke, is it?'

'I love it. More than I expected, to be honest. The people are great.' She quipped, 'But who knows what they're saying about me!'

'I hear you've done your bit in the community café. That'll get you some brownie points.'

'Ahh, who told you that?'

'Word gets round in these parts,' he said, tapping the side of his nose.

Amy laughed. 'I forgot. The Grassdale bush telegraph. Nothing goes under the radar here. I probably could have had my London next-door neighbour turn up as a customer and they wouldn't have recognised me. Nor I them, I must admit.'

Damian poured more tea for them both.

Amy checked her watch. 'Sorry, but I'll have to go pretty soon. This is lovely, of course, but Sophie invited me over for drinks for her birthday this evening. I was planning to go early and show my face then make a hasty exit.' She said it with a nervous laugh, hoping she hadn't put her foot in it.

'Ah yes, it's her fortieth! Annoyingly, I can't make it. Family do.'

Damian cleared his throat, then put a hand on her arm across the table. 'Listen, Amy, I'm sorry we didn't get off to the best start. At work, I mean. I've been meaning to say this for ages, but it never seemed to be the right time.'

He removed his arm and carried on. 'Honestly, I was mortified when Mark got wind of our little disagreement over the sheep at Yew Tree. I mean, I know I was probably a bit miffed, but I would have calmed down and apologised for my behaviour eventually. Being hauled into his office like a pair of naughty schoolchildren was just horrendous!'

'Wait, so you didn't tell Mark all about it as soon as we got back? I thought …' It was a few months ago, and the memory had faded, but she was pretty sure that was what she had thought at the time.

'God, I'm not a snitch, Amy! Keith and Mark are good mates. I gather Mark gave him a call when we were on our way back and it came out then. He gave me a good grilling after that. It probably didn't help that I was still riled at the time.'

'I'm sorry too that it made things awkward between us. Let's not mention it again.'

'Agreed.'

They finished their drinks, left the orangery and headed back to the car park.

'If you're up for it – I mean, I know how precious weekends are – but next weekend, I could show you one of my favourite walks from Grassdale.'

'Next weekend … ummm, yes, I think that's OK.' *Who was she kidding*? She rarely had plans other than for a solo walk or a run.

'Either day suits me. We can decide nearer the time if you like.'

'And my turn to treat you to tea and cake after.'

'Sounds like a date,' said Damian, then added with an embarrassed laugh, 'I didn't mean …'

'I know what you meant. I'll put it in my diary when I get home.'

22

'There's a story of a man who lived in the hills, high on the Dales, who still thought there was a war on until the nineteen seventies. He used to come to the village for his supplies, but he never asked and no one thought to tell him,' said the Major to Amy.

She was helping him to carry his bags home after a visit to the store. John had offered to give him a hand, but Amy could see that he was really too busy to leave the shop.

'Surely he must have seen the news? Or heard it on the radio?'

'No television, and probably not a wireless either.' The Major shook his head. 'Poor chap can't have had many friends either.'

Amy thought it sounded rather far-fetched, but a lot of things stretched credibility here. Grassdale was proving to be as weird and wonderful as London had been, just in different ways. What was it that Mary had said to her? Something about village life being full of surprises?

They paused at the bridge to allow a car to cross. The Major waved at the driver.

'Poor Betty,' he said to Amy as the car passed them. 'That's her daughter Katherine, going to check up on her. She can't really cope in that big house anymore.'

He shook his head, then changed the subject, telling Amy he had bellringing practice later that day. He was still nimble, but Amy wondered how easy he found the steps to the church tower.

'We're planning a quarter peal for Easter Day, but it's proving tricky. We lost it the other night.'

'Lost it?'

'Darned nuisance, but it happens, especially as we've got some relatively inexperienced members.'

Seeing Amy's look of incomprehension, he carried on. 'Sometimes, if someone makes a mistake, it can lead all the others astray too – not a pretty sound – and we can't recover.'

Bellringing is clearly a lot more complicated than I realised, she thought to herself as she stifled a smile.

***

Damian was waiting outside the bookshop. Amy could see him as she sat lacing up her boots on the metal bench by her front door. The bench proved handy when she needed to put on or remove muddy footwear, but she drew the line at sitting watching the world go by, preferring to do that from the privacy of indoors.

Damian appeared to be reading the notices. There was a new flyer in the window, announcing the Easter Monday fell race, which was organised by the group Sarah and Jenny belonged to. After much cajoling, Amy had agreed to join them for a run one Saturday morning. She had enjoyed their company – they had, naturally, headed to The Snug afterwards – but they all ran more slowly than she did and she had found it a strain to alter her pace. Once again, she found herself realising how, truthfully, she preferred to run on her own.

Tall and undeniably handsome in an olive green waterproof jacket, Damian looked like a model for an outdoor wear catalogue. He grinned when he saw Amy.

'I wondered if you'd still fancy it. It's a bit nippy, isn't it?'

It had snowed overnight. A fine layer dusted the pavements of Grassdale, but it would be thicker on the moors.

'I'm well wrapped up.' Amy rubbed her gloved hands together and stamped her feet, as if to prove her point. 'When *does* it warm up in these parts, though?'

'How does August sound?'

'Nooo!'

'I'm going to show you a favourite place of mine. But not too far away, because I think we'll freeze otherwise.'

'Sounds good.'

They set off down Lower Street, a road as familiar to Amy now as Camden High Street had been. There was no approaching traffic so they crossed the humpback bridge onto Church Lane. The church bells were ringing.

'A wedding this afternoon, I wonder?' mused Damian.

'No, I don't think so; I believe that is the sound of bellringing practice.' Amy felt rather smug at possessing this insider knowledge. 'They might be practising their quarter peal.'

Damian glanced at her, surprised. 'I don't suppose they have an awful amount of weddings these days,' he mused. 'Not like the old days, eh?'

'I suppose not.'

Amy loved the way a snowfall always seemed to bring with it a stillness and silence; it had even felt like that in London, not that it happened often. It had rarely snowed when she was a child, but when it did, she felt the magic of it, much like the child in *The Snowman* animation, still a favourite book and film of hers. They carried on, neither of them speaking. She hoped that Damian wouldn't feel the need to fill in the silences with stilted conversation.

Damian indicated that they were to leave the road and cut over the moor. The snow was thicker on the hills, but easier to walk on than the slippery path. The snow was pristine apart from the tiny tracks left by birds and small mammals. Their boots made a crunching sound that satisfied Amy greatly.

'These are a rabbit's footprints, though, hmm, it might be a hare,' said Damian. 'This one is a fox.'

'How do you know?'

'My obsession as a boy. I was a little David Attenborough. I could identify lots of birds' calls as well.'

'Oh I'm hopeless. I think a blackbird is my limit. They always started such a racket in our garden at home when they were worried about something.'

'But they have a beautiful song too. Some people say it bears comparison to a nightingale's.'

'Really? I don't think I've ever heard a nightingale. I'd love to, though.'

They were climbing the hill now, but instead of heading north in the direction of Crowdale, they carried on east, straight over Grassdale Moor, down into a dip then up again where another expanse of moor glimmered in the snow.

'You been this way before?' he asked her.

'No, I don't think so. I always worry about leaving the routes I know, just in case I get lost.'

'It will be a surprise for you then.'

'Can't wait!' She felt his head turn towards her, and they grinned at each other. 'I wasn't being sarcastic!'

After walking for a few more minutes, she saw something sparkle in the sun. It was only when she was much closer that she could see what it was. About a dozen standing stones formed a rough circle ahead. They ranged in height from half a metre to more than twice as tall, spaced at roughly equal intervals. Though mainly free of snow, a dusting had settled on parts of them. One of them, thanks to its shape, now resembled a stout penguin.

'Wow! What are they?'

'Rather like the other stone circles in this country, no one really knows for sure. Some of the stones have been destroyed, and they think some may have been removed altogether, but the circle still has quite a presence, doesn't it?'

Amy nodded.

'I've just read *Tess of the d'Urbervilles,* and she is captured at Stonehenge. It's not quite the same scale, but it's making me think of her.'

'Heavy stuff! I've not read it, but what I *can* tell you is that the view from here is amazing too.'

Amy stood in the centre of the circle and slowly turned round so that she saw the view from all sides. It was a picture of the Dales in all their glory: low snaking walls running away into the distance, rounded hills nestling up against each other, purplish patches of moor showing through the lighter snow.

She breathed it all in.

'It makes you wonder, doesn't it,' she said, 'what the people who constructed this were like.'

'I wonder what they'd make of us.'

Amy laughed. 'Hmmm. I'd rather not know. Probably that we lead very complicated lives.'

'Ready to make a move?'

'I suppose so.'

He glanced at her quickly, then looked away. 'We'll have to come another time. You need to see the stones in different lights and at different times of day. The snow's lovely, but dare I say it, it's even more spectacular in the summer.'

'Really? This will take some beating.'

They began to retrace their steps.

'Are your parents keen walkers?' Damian asked Amy as they headed back towards Grassdale.

'Dad is, Mum less so. He dragged us off on walks when we were on holiday. I didn't mind. I'd just trail along on my own behind them, daydreaming.'

'You're an only child?'

'Yup! Can't you tell? High achiever. Harshly independent.' She gave him a playful nudge. 'Potential to be over-sensitive. Bit of an all-round weirdo really.'

'Would you have liked siblings?'

'I don't know. I've always enjoyed my own company. Not sure if you can miss what you've never had, can you? But it did mean all the pressure was on me: every family needs a golden child, right? To be honest, I've always felt indebted to them in some way. My parents paid a lot for my education, and I was my own worst enemy. I had to ace everything to show them it was worth it. Does that make any sense?'

'It all came good in the end, though. They must be very proud of you now.'

'Oh, definitely. They love telling everyone I came top in my year group at university. Comes up more often in conversation than I'd like. Quite embarrassing really,' she admitted with a grimace.

'Oh, and the famous Sir Leonard Blackwell award?'

'Had you really heard of it before?'

'No, not until Mark mentioned it when he read your CV.'

Amy punched him playfully. 'I do sometimes worry that that's what I am to them – a high-achieving daughter they can show off to their friends. Except now, of course, I've gone and spoilt it all.'

Damian frowned, offering Amy a puzzled look.

'They can't understand why I'd want to be here. They seem to think of it as a demotion. But, hey ho, they're my parents and I can't change them. I suppose they only want the best for me. What about you? Are you close to your folks?' Amy was desperate to change the subject, fearing she'd divulged too much.

They were climbing a slope now. From the summit, they could see the snowy rooftops of Grassdale in the hollow, while radiating around it, the dark lines of walls and hedges gave the hills and fields a wonky patchwork appearance.

'Well then, I thought my parents were a bit odd but that was a lot to take in, Amy, jeez. My family? Dad's a bit old-school – he thinks girls should start a family and boys climb the career ladder. Mum's more relaxed. She wanted me to go to the local comp but he won in the end and they sent me to an independent school in Leeds as a weekly boarder. I struggled academically at first as it was a big jump from my junior school, and there were some clever kids there. I had to work really hard to get the grades I needed. I managed in the end though, but I don't think Dad has forgiven me for not making it on to the rugby team! That was his big thing.'

He was laughing when he said it, but Amy suspected it had been a big deal. She pictured the man she had met in the restaurant with her parents, and thought he might have been quite a fierce father.

'Any brothers and sisters?'

'An older sister with three kids. She lives in Hebden Bridge. We're very different but we're pretty close.'

'And you're the indulgent uncle?'

'I do my best!'

As the days were gradually growing longer, Lower Street was still bustling when they arrived back in Grassdale.

'You still up for tea and cake?' asked Damian.

'It's the only reason I came,' she joked. 'And my turn to buy, remember?'

They entered the bookshop, where Damian found them a table in The Snug.

'Any favourites?' Amy called from the counter.

'You choose. I trust you.'

She gawped at him in mock surprise before ordering a pot of tea, a rock cake and a piece of parkin. She had eventually discovered that the latter was a rich, dark type of gingerbread.

'Which do you fancy?' she asked as she set the tray on the table.

'Can't we share?'

Amy cut the cakes in half.

'I mustn't forget, I've got a book to pick up while I'm here,' said Damian, as they tucked in.

'What is it – if you don't mind me being nosy?'

'Oh it's not for me. Birthday present for my dad. A historical biography. I'm more of a thriller guy myself.'

'I never used to be but sometimes crime is just an easy read, isn't it? And with a satisfying ending.'

'And you don't need counselling, like after reading *Tess*,' he joked.

'No, but I do worry about all those murderers lurking in plain sight.'

'Fortunately, I don't think there are many in Grassdale.'

23

'You'll take part in the fell race, won't you?' Sarah asked Amy when she dashed into the bookshop one night after work. It was Mark's birthday the next day and she and Damian had ordered him a book. They didn't really celebrate birthdays at the practice, but it felt like a nice gesture.

'I don't know. I've never done one before.'

'All the more reason for taking part in ours!' said Sarah.

'I'm not so sure I've had the right training, surely I'd be out of my depth?'

'Not for this one. I suppose, strictly speaking, ours is more of a trail race. There'll be signs up so you can't get lost, and a couple of checkpoints along the way. It's early in the season so it's just a warm-up really, a bit of fun. But you can be as competitive as you want.' She added, with a teasing lilt, 'We know that we were holding you up when you came out with us.'

'Oh not at all,' replied Amy, though they both knew there was truth in Sarah's statement.

'Damian's taking part.'

'Oh.' Amy tried to sound uninterested.

'Well, you know … People have seen you together.'

'We work together!'

'I know. People are just terrible gossips, aren't they.' She grinned. 'No need to decide yet, anyway. Right, let me find your order.'

It wasn't just a fell race that was happening on Easter Monday. A poster in Sarah's window listed the other attractions that were taking place in the village that day. The church would be open for visitors, with guided tours provided by churchwarden Charles Brady and the vicar. There would also be a chance to climb the belltower, where the Major would give a short talk and bellringing demonstration. The community café ('Volunteers always needed!') would have extra tables and chairs on the green, and there would be a variety of stalls, including one selling bric-a-brac ('Donations required! No tat, please!'), a cake stall and a tombola as well as activities for the children. These were all in aid of the bells fund and the local food bank.

Amy also knew that Lauren, her landlady, was running a stall selling her baking in aid of Age UK, and that Sarah was hoping – weather permitting – to have a table of local interest books outside, including the works of Grassdale writer Tizz. Amy kept it to herself, but wondered if those books would be a big enough attraction to warrant displaying so prominently.

It seemed that the Easter Monday fayre was a long-standing tradition. Amy could sense excitement building in the village. Whenever she passed a group of people talking, they seemed to be discussing who was manning which stall, or reliving memories of previous years. Sophie said that her middle child was looking forward to singing at the fayre with her school choir.

It was a busy run-up to Easter as it coincided with the peak of lambing. Most lambing was straightforward, and the farmers experienced enough to treat the most common problems themselves, but Amy was called out to farms several times. While talking to the wife of farmer Keith of Yew Tree

Farm, she learnt that they had experienced a successful lambing season after the dog attack and that even 'Frankenstein's bride', as she called the poor ewe with the facial injury, had given birth to twins.

On the last day at work before the long Easter weekend, Mark handed them all a chocolate egg and Donna had made little cakes for everyone.

Amy woke up on Easter Day to glorious sunshine. A short while later, she heard the church bells ringing joyously. That must be the quarter peal that the Major had been talking about. Her parents would no doubt be going to their parish church, where her mother often read the lesson, her father restricting his church-going to feast days. ('He only goes for the hymns,' her mother complained.) As she drank her tea, she watched from her seat in the window as some of the locals headed down the road for the Easter service. She saw Fahimeh and Arad and a man who must be Salman, Arad's father. Arad was wearing a pair of black trousers and a long-sleeved shirt and tie. He looked very smart. Fahimeh, one hand in Arad's and one in her husband's, had her long hair hanging loose and was wearing the purple coat that Amy had admired.

She rang her parents to wish them a happy Easter and to thank them for the fancy chocolate egg that had been delivered. She had sent flowers to her mother, as well as to Aunty Liz, the neighbour she was so fond of.

'We wish you were with us, darling. Are they really working you over the Easter break?'

'No, the practice is closed, but I'm taking part in a fell race tomorrow.'

She had only made the decision to take part a couple of days earlier, though hadn't told anyone. She would spend the day eating nutritious food and resting, in readiness for it.

'You're doing what? Oh, Amy.' Her mother stretched out her name in disbelief. 'It sounds dangerous to me.'

'Less dangerous than road-running, Mum. We're on the moors, so nice and soft underfoot.'

'But what about the weather? I hear there's a storm coming your way.'

This was news to Amy, who rarely listened to news or weather reports. To keep her mother happy, she promised to check the forecast and to reconsider her decision if it sounded particularly bad. She opened her weather app as soon as she finished her conversation. Her mother was right, heavy rain and gusty winds were on their way from the west, but it looked as if most of Yorkshire would be spared, the more northerly counties facing the brunt of it. She hoped for the organisers' sakes that the events in Grassdale would not be affected. She supposed that most of the stalls could be moved indoors, and surely it would have to be pretty bad to cancel a fell race.

Today, it was warm enough to sit in the conservatory and watch the birds. The dawn chorus was starting to become louder and more insistent, sometimes waking her, a reminder that a new season was underway. Soon she would see her garden transformed like never before, with apple blossom emerging on the tree. Green spears of daffodils had begun to appear several weeks ago and were now almost ready to flower.

Someone was knocking on the front door.

'I don't know if I'm overstepping the mark here, Miss Ashton,' said the woman standing there. Amy recognised her face, but could not quite place her.

'Amy, please.'

'It's about Octavia.'

It was Katherine, Betty's daughter, holding a crate in her arms.

'You'd better come in.'

Amy showed Katherine into the kitchen and put the kettle on. Katherine put the crate on the floor.

'I don't know if you've heard that Mum's just gone into a home?' She didn't wait for a reply, but carried on, sounding anxious. 'She kept saying that you were going to find a home for Octavia should she ever need one. I did tell her it was far too much to ask of you, but she seemed to think it was all … decided?' She tailed off, apologetically. 'I mean, Mum being as she was, it was hard to tell sometimes. If her wires are crossed, then it's no problem.'

Amy's pause was brief, as she realised her mind was already made up. 'Your mum was absolutely right. And I'm so sorry to hear that she's not able to live independently anymore.'

Katherine pulled a face that was somewhere between a sad smile and a frown.

'Thank you. I suppose it will happen to us all one day. It's been a difficult time, but we've found her a lovely place and she seems to be settling in.' She added, examining the crate, 'There's an enclosure too, back in the house, with everything you could possibly need. Octavia had it all! Talk about a high-maintenance lifestyle! But I wasn't sure if you were keeping her yourself or if you had someone else in mind.'

Amy had been considering what to do with Octavia ever since her conversation with Betty. Her first thought had been Arad, knowing what an animal lover he was. But she had quickly dismissed that idea. Contrary to popular belief, tortoises were not cheap and easy pets, or even suited to young children. Octavia required an empathetic adult who would understand her very particular needs.

'I think I have the perfect home for her,' she told Katherine.

***

She had everything laid out ready for the next day. She wasn't exactly worried about the race, but something kept niggling inside her. She hadn't taken part in a race – let alone a fell race – since she left school. Sarah had assured her that it was a friendly occasion, with everyone looking out for each other, but knowing Damian as she did, she felt it might turn out to be more competitive. She wondered what he would think when he found out she was taking part. They had been getting on so well recently that she hoped he would be pleased. But she couldn't be sure of that.

After enjoying watching Octavia nosing around her kitchen, and feeding her some of the titbits that Katherine had brought – she had a voracious appetite – Amy left her for a few minutes and went to a cottage a few doors down the street. She hadn't been to this house before, nor did she really know its occupant, and even standing on the doorstep made her feel a little nervous. The man who answered the door was rather unkempt looking, in his T-shirt and jogging bottoms, rather as she remembered him from their first encounter. He regarded Amy uncertainly, waiting for her to speak.

She swallowed. 'I'm Amy, Colin. The new inhabitant at Ivy Cottage? You were very kind to me the day I moved in. I don't know if you remember, but ...'

He nodded now, his expression still serious.

'I wanted to talk to you, if it's convenient, about an animal that needs a new home. I thought you would be the perfect person to take care of it.'

It had gone well. On the shelves in Colin's living room, Amy had seen dozens of books about wild and domestic animals, even one about tortoises. When he had overcome his initial shyness, he had talked enthusiastically about some of the pets he once had. The look of joy on his face when she handed Octavia to him had made tears prick her own eyes.

They would be good for each other: he would give Octavia the care she needed, while she would supply him with companionship and a sense of purpose.

She would give Betty a little more time to settle, then she would visit her to tell her about the happy outcome.

24

She wondered what it was that woke her in the night. Something was howling outside her window. Ever since that first night, she had continued to leave a gap in the curtains – it gave her a hint of the time and of the weather outside – but there was nothing to see except darkness. The next time she woke, the gap was lighter. She got up and went to the window: grey clouds were racing across the sky at breakneck speed. Damn it! They hadn't escaped the wind after all. No rain, though – that was a blessing. But she thought of the stall-holders and felt sorry for them after all their work; most of them would have to move indoors.

She showered and had breakfast: a bowl of porridge and a toasted bagel with peanut butter, washed down with a mug of peppermint tea. She sat and ate it on her cosy kitchen window seat, partly so that she could see what was going on outside. It was still early but a few people were buzzing around. She watched John come out of the store, stand on the pavement for a few seconds, look up and down the street, then go back inside, clearly thinking better of putting out the sandwich board. Val arrived for work, linking arms with the Major who always bought his paper at this time, the pair of them fighting against the wind. Val had her free hand on top of her head, to protect her hairdo. She saw John rush to open the door for them.

A few other early visitors to the store stopped by to pick up their papers or groceries. There was no sign yet of the attractions or of the fell-racing team. The bunting hanging along the green blew crazily, stretched to its limit. An hour or so later, a car pulled up and two women emerged and unloaded a table and chairs from the boot along with some plastic crates. Amy recognised one of them as Chloe, Sarah's friend, from the running club. She decided to go out and find out what was going on. A sudden gust almost blew her off-course as she headed towards her.

'Hello, Chloe. Blimey! You've timed this well! Is the race still on?'

Chloe grinned at her. 'Not the greatest day, is it? We kept checking the forecast and thought we were going to miss all this.' She peered up at the skies. 'It'll probably put some folk off, unfortunately, but apparently it's going to clear up later.'

'I'll be back to register. Can I bring you both a coffee?'

'That's kind, but we're well supplied. Registration starts at eleven. We'll just get ourselves organised.'

The next time Amy looked out of the window, the table and chairs had been folded up and were lying on the ground, and the women had taken shelter in their car. The wind made shrill sounds in Ivy Cottage as it rattled round the windowpanes and down the chimney.

Amy had hated windy days in London; they made her feel uneasy, with rubbish flying in the air, but on the moors it was different. The wind made her feel connected to nature; it made her feel alive. She would have liked to scream into the open spaces around her, just for the sake of doing it. Being of a more cautious nature, however, she had been too much of a chicken, sure that if she ever did such a thing, someone would suddenly appear.

No doubt that someone would be Damian – he was the one with the habit of popping up like a bad penny! She smiled at the thought. Their relationship had undoubtedly changed in the past few weeks. It was peculiar, the things they had in common – pushy parents, competitive natures – as well as their jobs.

He was actually rather good-looking too, she had decided – what her mother would term 'dishy'. She glanced at herself in the mirror after changing into her running gear. Should she make a bit more effort today?

Come off it, Amy, you're going running, not on a date!

All the same, she had applied a touch of waterproof mascara and a smidgen of lip gloss.

The sky appeared heavy and grey and the trees were still shaking wildly when Amy saw a few people gathered by the table, which had been re-erected. She recognised Grace, the other friend of Sarah's she had been introduced to, and decided it was time to venture out.

'Are Sarah and Jenny coming?'

'Sarah's working – can't get anyone to cover – and Jenny's had a crisis at the guesthouse. Lucky them, eh?' laughed Grace.

'They're not stupid, are they?' Amy agreed. She had paid her entrance fee and was pinning on her race number when Damian appeared at her side.

'So you decided to take the plunge?'

'I must be mad. What a day!'

He started chatting to Chloe, asking after her parents. Amy remembered that their families knew each other.

'Chloe reckons there'll be quite a few drop-outs,' he said, then nudged her. 'Give you a fighting chance!'

'I'm just going for the fun of it!' *Who was she kidding?* She didn't need to win but she did need to give it her best, the way she did with everything.

The stalls weren't due to open until the afternoon, and there were few other people outdoors when a group of about twenty of them were shepherded to the starting point at the bridge.

When the clock on the church tower struck twelve, the disparate group of runners set off. Amy recognised a couple of women from Sarah and Jenny's running group. The rest of the runners consisted of men and women in their thirties and forties, plus a couple of men who looked much older and whose wiry bodies seemed to spring rather than run.

The race followed a circular route of about seven miles, the way marked with yellow flags. It began on fairly level ground, on the minor road that led to Bottom Farm. From there it moved onto the moors, picking up a rough track running alongside a drystone wall.

It didn't take long before some of the stronger runners, including Amy and Damian, began to leave the others behind.

Damian seemed to know where he was going even without the signs. Amy was determined to keep him in her sight, though it meant pushing herself as he was quicker than her with his long powerful legs. The wind pummelled her in all directions – it had been behind them at first, almost carrying them, but now it buffeted her side as if trying to force her off the track. As the path started to climb Amy saw a flag fluttering on a post by the wall. When she reached it, she saw that it marked a stile, and that Damian was waiting for her on the other side of it. She was surprised, but gratefully took the hand he offered, gripping it tightly for just a second as she jumped the last part.

It had started to rain, softly at first but gradually growing more and more heavy. On this higher ground, low cloud swirled around them. The wind felt even fiercer here, but at least it was at their backs again. They were on Grassdale

Moor. Skirting the edge of a scar of weathered limestone, they came to the top of a small waterfall that dropped off the end of the cliff. The route followed a narrow stony path down the side of the falls. Immediately, Amy noted that it looked very slippery. Running would be dangerous here, so Amy took the descent slowly and carefully; she had no desire to hurt herself – it had been bad enough twisting her ankle on the edge of the village. She lost sight of Damian several times but again he was waiting for her at the bottom.

'No sign of the others?' he asked her when she reached him.

They couldn't see anyone at the top of the falls, but someone coming down the path might have been hidden from view.

'Do you think they've given up?' she said. 'I'm not sure that we should have been using that path in this weather.' She had a sudden thought. 'In fact, do you even think we were meant to come down this way? It can't be an easy route at the best of times.'

She realised that her feet were sopping wet, as was the rest of her. She watched a large drop of rain trickle down Damian's face and fall off his chin.

'I can't see any flags down here,' she added. 'And weren't there supposed to be a couple of marshals on the route?'

'Maybe they've given up,' said Damian, and started running again.

Amy followed him as she had no desire to be left on her own, but she was bothered by the lack of signs and the absence of other competitors. The wind howled in her ears and the rain almost blinded her at times. She called out to Damian to stop, feeling the hammering of her heart against her chest and a rising sense of anxiety. She had to shout his name a few times before he heard her.

'This feels wrong to me,' she said, catching up with him when he finally stopped. 'Surely we should be heading more that way,' she pointed over her shoulder, 'so that we start doing a loop round Grassdale. Otherwise, aren't we just getting further and further away?'

'Grassdale is that way, not this way. We're already on the return stretch.'

'Are you sure?'

'Of course I am.'

Amy usually had a good sense of direction, but in this weather, with driving rain and low cloud, there were no distinguishing landmarks to help her get her bearings. Damian knew the area better than she did. As for the lack of race signs, which had been plentiful earlier on – Sarah had assured her that the route would be well marked – she reasoned that some of them may well have blown away.

It's such a shame about this weather, she thought, as she followed Damian. *The views would be terrific on a clear day.* As it was, all she could see was a heavy grey pall of mist and rain, obscuring all the features.

Damian wasn't running so quickly now. Amy wondered if he too was doubting his navigation. Irritation was beginning to bloom within her panic. If he didn't know where he was going, why didn't he just say so?

She wanted to get back safely to enjoy some of the other activities that were taking place in the village. She knew that Arad, who was one of the children who would be singing with his school, was helping his mother at Sarah's stall, and she had promised she would see him later. Mary was running the bric-a-brac station ('I've got so much of Mum and Dad's stuff to get rid of,' she had said) and she had been looking forward to seeing Lauren again too. She wanted to be there to support them all, but at this rate, she and Damian would be returning to Grassdale long after everyone had packed up and gone home.

Ahead of her, Damian came to a stop under a large tree. There was little cover, as the tree was not in leaf, but it gave them some respite from the rain.

'I don't suppose you've got a compass, have you?' he asked her.

'Er, no.'

'Hmmm.'

'So we're lost?'

'I didn't say that.'

'It sounds like it.'

Amy pulled her ponytail round and wrang it out, producing a long trail of water.

'My feeling is that we go that way.' Amy pointed. 'Or we retrace our steps, but I'm not sure that's really a good idea at this stage. I don't know about you, but I don't want to spend the night on the moors.' When Damian didn't reply, frustration drove her onwards, 'I'm off then. Go your own way if you want to.'

She sprinted off in a far more lively fashion than mirrored her mood. This was miserable. She really wished she hadn't agreed to take part in the first place. *Why had she*? Races weren't really her thing, she was only ever determined to beat her own records. The wind was in her face now, though it had dropped a little from earlier. But the rain was relentless. She looked over her shoulder. Damian was a few paces behind her. Phew. She didn't really want to be out here on her own. She thought of what she had brought in her lightweight running backpack – a light waterproof jacket, a snack and drink. Perhaps she should have followed the extreme advice she had read on one of the fell-running websites and included a bivi bag – having to take shelter for the night seemed more of a possibility than ever.

She saw a shape looming out of the mist. As she got closer, she could see that it was a stone building with a slate roof. Did someone live out here? Or was it another abandoned shepherds' hut, a fairly common sight on the moors? She heard Damian shout something so she stopped and waited for him.

He caught up with her. 'It's one of the buildings from an old lead mine. The Dales are full of them. Just mind where you go. It should be safe but we probably shouldn't be running.'

'Do you know where we are then?'

He hesitated. 'It's hard to say. They all look the same in this weather. There's a big set-up not that far from Hettie's place, but this one looks smaller. I said don't run!'

Amy had set off again, fed up. 'Well I want to get home one day! And you're not being much help.'

'And you'll never get home if you fall down a mine shaft.'

Amy wasn't sure if he was kidding or not, but stopped running. They were now on a rough manmade track. Piles of stone and rubble lay on either side, some of them appearing to be the foundations of other buildings.

'If we stay on this path ...' began Damian, before tailing off.

'If we stay on this path, what?' snapped Amy.

'Well, if it's the mine I think it could be, the old miners' cottages aren't that far away. I'll be able to get my bearings once we're there.'

'And if it's not that mine?'

'Then who knows.' He sounded annoyed. 'You're making me feel as if this is all my fault, Amy. You're— ' he broke off. 'Did you hear that?'

He held a finger to Amy's lips to prevent her saying anything else. The sound of a sheep could be heard, but it didn't sound like the regular baaing they were used to hearing; this was the high-pitched bleating of a sheep in distress.

Vision was still awful, and the rain still fell in sheets, even though the wind was dropping. They followed the source of the noise, though neither could agree at first which direction it was coming from. They had left the lead-mining track and were back on sodden moorland. Every view was indistinguishable from the next. The sound appeared to be coming from a small tree, toppled by the winds, that lay ahead of them. It wasn't until they were right beside it that they saw what had happened. A sheep lay on her back underneath one of the branches.

'Oh, the poor thing!' Amy gasped.

Seeing them, the ewe became more agitated, striking out with her legs, grunting and snorting. They realised that though she was totally covered by part of the tree, the branch that lay across her was not a heavy one, and in fact was barely touching her. The problem was that on either side of it lay far weightier branches which did not allow her the space to free herself.

'Ssshh, girl.' Amy crouched down beside her and gently touched her head. She baaed, sounding more angry than distressed this time.

'Ssshh, sssshh. I've come to help you. Do you think she's hurt?'

Damian crouched down too so as not to intimidate her. 'She's moving her legs OK, so I don't think so. I think she's just well and truly stuck.' He looked at Amy over the sheep. 'Good job we came along.'

But there was another problem confronting them.

'Look at the size of her udder,' said Amy. 'And, hmmmm.' Inspecting the sheep further confirmed her own suspicions. 'I think she's going to give birth very soon.'

'We need to get her out of here and find somewhere safe for her to deliver. If we free her, her instinct will probably be to scarper, but it's so awful out here, the lambs won't have much chance. If I can lift the branch, can you try to restrain her?'

The larger branches of the fallen tree were far too heavy for one person to lift, but fortunately it wasn't necessary. Damian raised the branch that lay over her and shifted it slightly. It took the sheep a few seconds to realise that nothing was holding her down, but when she did, she pulled herself onto her side and climbed to her feet surprisingly quickly.

Amy held the ewe firmly under the jaw with one arm, the other around her middle, pressing her towards her own body. She seemed agitated, pawing at the ground with her front legs.

'Damian, we are running out of time, she's going to deliver any minute. We've got to get her somewhere more sheltered.' She muttered, 'It would help if we knew where we were. She's not going to want to walk miles in this state.'

Damian now stood on the other side of the sheep, so that they had her firmly between them. She was strong and determined, even in her heavily pregnant state.

'If I'm right about where we are, there's an abandoned lead miner's cottage about a hundred yards away. It's been used in recent years as a very basic sort of bothy. We could take her there.'

'What about the buildings we've just passed? At least we know where they are.'

'I don't think they're safe, Amy. The bothy would be a better bet. If you trust me to get us there?'

She wondered if there was a hint of humour in his question.

'I'll even carry her,' he volunteered.

'You can't carry her. She's far too heavy. But she seems OK. I suggest we walk her. As long as we've got a firm grip, she won't have much choice in the matter.'

As if just to prove Amy wrong, the ewe had other ideas. She had now decided that she didn't want to go anywhere.

'I think we're going to have to drag her,' said Amy. 'If I pull her from the front and you shove her from behind, she might get the message. Where are we going?'

Damian pointed, and they set off on their slow journey. The sheep was very wilful. She allowed herself to be propelled a short distance, then stopped. Amy was always surprised by the sheer heft of these creatures, and this particular one, with one or two – maybe even three – lambs inside her was heavier still. The rain was blowing straight into their eyes so that it was hard to see where they were going. They had to shout at each other to make themselves heard.

'I think that's it, ahead,' called Damian, and Amy felt a wave of relief as she caught sight of a stone building with a small chimney at one end of its roof, set within the remains of a drystone wall.

The ewe stopped once more. Her body was twitching and she pawed again at the ground.

'Come on, girl, not far to go. The cottage hospital awaits.'

A sudden gust blew her voice away.

A door had never looked so welcoming. *Gosh I hope it opens*, Amy thought, but it opened easily. They went inside with their patient and closed it behind them. With its small windows and the poor light outside, the interior was dim. If Amy had been expecting bunkbeds and a little kitchen, she was disappointed. The room was almost totally bare. At the end where the fireplace was, some ancient-looking pans hung on the wall, while hanging from hooks on the ceiling were a couple of cotton bags, perhaps used to keep food away from rodents on the floor. There were two rickety wooden benches, a bale of straw and the odd bit of rubbish in the form of a tin can and an empty paper bag. Although the cottage had an upstairs, the staircase was broken and there was no longer access to it.

'They haven't exactly gone to town, have they?' joked Amy. It was all feeling rather ludicrous now. She had an urge to laugh at the strange direction the day had taken. At least they were out of the wind and rain. 'We could get a nice fire going in no time.'

'If we had matches.'

'You weren't a Scout then? They wouldn't need matches.'

'I was, but I think I missed that meeting.'

The sheep, happy to be out of their grasp, trotted off to the farthest corner where she promptly lay down. Amy and Damian broke up some of the hay and laid it down beside her.

'I think we got here just in time.'

'She looks like an older mum. Hopefully she won't need any assistance.'

'Got anything to eat?'

They pooled their resources. Amy had a cereal bar and Damian had a bar of chocolate. They both had water.

Amy shivered but there seemed little point in putting on her waterproof jacket. For a brief second, she thought wistfully of her beautiful Christmas gift, that hung – pristine and unworn – on a coat-hanger in her wardrobe. They sat on one of the benches, eating their scant supplies, and surveying their patient.

'I hope she doesn't mind being watched like this,' said Damian.

'Sorry about the private room being booked, old girl.'

'Aaagh!' Damian, who had leant back, pulled himself up again. 'That wall is like a block of ice!' He looked at Amy. 'Do you want my jacket?'

'I'm fine, thanks. I've got one if I need it. Do you think anyone's missed us yet?'

He didn't reply.

'My neighbour and my landlady are both running stalls at the fayre. Then there's Arad …' She was feeling sorry for herself now. 'They'll all have packed up and gone home by the time we get back.'

'We've plenty of time to get there.'

'I admire your confidence.'

Amy realised that although the bench was wide, they were sitting very close together. Hadn't one of their bags been in between them just a minute ago? One of them must have moved it, though she hadn't been aware of it. Her upper arm accidentally brushed against Damian's and she quickly straightened up, but not before feeling a sudden jolt of electricity pass through her. When had she last felt like that? *A long time ago.* Probably not since the early days of Jake. She wondered if Damian had felt it too. It was hard to know, as he was studying the sheep intently.

The sheep's tongue was flicking in and out of her mouth. She was lying on her side now and was straining. It was clear the birthing had begun. She stood up, strained again, took a few paces in a circle, then sat down, forelegs first. More of the lamb appeared. The ewe's tongue continued to flick. The newborn was a dark elongated shape, still not fully out of her body.

'Do we need to help her?' asked Amy. She realised she was whispering.

Damian put a hand on her arm, and kept it there. 'Just give her a bit longer.'

The ewe stood up again, paced a bit more, then the back legs emerged and the lamb landed in the pile of straw. Both Amy and Damian waited nervously in anticipation. The lamb didn't move until the ewe bent her head and nuzzled it, when its legs wiggled, it shook its head and seemed to come to life. The ewe left it for a few seconds, then returned and started licking it clean, the lamb twitching and shaking as it acknowledged its freedom.

'She's a great mother,' whispered Amy, aware that Damian's hand now covered hers.

'Yes, she knows what she's doing.'

The lamb looked almost ridiculous. Its front legs, stuck out at strange angles, looked too big for its body, while its ears, too, appeared comical and outsized.

As the mother continued to clean it, the lamb started trying to stand, but fell instantly back down again. A few minutes later, it managed to stand for a couple of seconds on all four legs, wobble hopelessly, and collapse again. It felt wrong to laugh, but hard not to. A few more times it rose, its bottom too high and its back legs sticking out awkwardly, so that each time its legs gave way and it fell again. It started searching for milk, but every time it got closer to the udder, the ewe moved to lick clean a different part of her newborn and in doing so moved further away.

It was all hugely touching.

Then the mother began to strain again. She lay down, the lamb still nosing around for milk. The pointed head of another lamb became visible.

'I can only see one leg coming, it might be a tougher one this time.' Amy retrieved her hand from Damian's now, in readiness to help the ewe if she needed it. A correct presentation was with the head and forelegs first; one leg caught up behind could cause problems.

The ewe stood up. Her lamb was baaing peevishly.

'Be patient, you'll get fed soon,' said Damian.

'I think we need to intervene. The lamb is going to need to breathe before the ewe pushes her out,' said Amy.

They both approached the ewe, who backed away and baaed angrily, except that there was nowhere for her to go. Amy took hold of her head and, with her knee against the sheep's hip and her other hand on the other hip, gently turned her head towards her tail. This move put the ewe off balance and made it easy to get her to lie down again. Once the ewe was down, Amy pulled on the emerging head. It came out a bit further, still with only one leg showing. She reached to locate the other foreleg, and a few seconds later, the whole body slipped out smoothly. She gave the lamb's face a cursory wipe before holding it by its forelegs and presenting it to its mother, who began to clean it as thoroughly as she had done to the first born. The older twin, now confident on his feet and clearly deciding that Amy was a better bet than his mother, started to follow her.

'Much as I'd love to adopt you, I think you'll be happier with your real mum,' she said, as she nudged him back towards the ewe. The sheep's udder was now displayed at her side, and soon the lamb was enjoying his first feed while the ewe continued to clean the other twin.

Amy and Damian surveyed the scene like proud parents.

'So, they're all fine, now it's just us,' said Damian. They were standing so close together that Amy felt as if she was leaning into him. All the drama of the moment, combined with the fact that she was cold, wet and running on a cereal bar, made her feel weak all of a sudden.

She turned her back on the touching scene to fetch her jacket from her backpack. As she did, she saw that the rain had stopped and the sky was lighter.

'Look! Timing, eh? Why couldn't it have stopped earlier?'

She opened the door and stuck her nose out. 'It actually feels a few degrees warmer. In fact, I think it's warmer outside than in.'

Damian followed her.

'Maybe we'll be able to finish the race after all,' she said. 'Even if we are hours behind the others.' She paused, seeing a funny expression on Damian's face. 'What?'

'I was thinking,' he began, taking a step towards her, 'that it might not be so awful to be stuck here together for a little longer'.

'Is that so?' Amy asked with a smirk. Looking up into his eyes, she hoped he'd continue to close the distance.

25

Amy disengaged herself from Damian's arms after their passionate kiss seemed to last forever, her heart fluttering wildly. She heard someone shouting her name.

Hettie was coming towards them on her quad bike. The wind had dropped to a gentle breeze and the sky was a pale lilac.

'Well this is a cosy little scene,' said Hettie, as she stopped the bike in front of them, and Amy wondered if she had seen their embrace – she must have done, surely – or was simply commenting on the sight of them in front of the old cottage.

'We might have something of yours here,' said Damian.

'Three things, actually,' said Amy.

'She was trapped under a tree,' Amy explained, as Hettie stepped inside with them. 'It was pretty wild at the time, but we managed to free her and get her in here in time to give birth.'

The ewe gave a gentle baa. She seemed happy to see Hettie, who gave her head an affectionate rub.

'Silly girl, what were you playing at? What a stroke of fortune that you found her. Did the births go OK?'

'The first one was pretty straightforward. Amy had to give her a hand with the second one,' said Damian, while Hettie listened and nodded.

'Thank you. Thanks to both of you. All three are looking pretty good now, aren't they. What I'll do is, I'll whizz them back to the maternity barn on the quad and then I'll come back for you two.' She cast a look at Amy. 'You look freezing, duck. Would you rather come first?'

Amy shook her head. 'No, definitely not. Take Mum and the twins home and get them settled. They've had quite an ordeal. In fact …' She tailed off, and looked over at Damian to see what he thought. 'I was thinking we might finish the race? I don't think I'll be running, but we could walk home. I feel the only way this day can end now is if we cross the finish line together.'

Hettie threw back her head and laughed. 'You are a glutton for punishment. I don't think I'll ever understand what pleasure you get from this running lark, but I have to say, I'm glad you pair of barmpots were doing it today.' She shook her head in bemusement. 'Well, if you head off soon, you might catch John and Andy's barbecue. I hear that Barry's sausages are worth trying.'

The mention of food made Amy suddenly feel very hungry.

Hettie left with her charges, after pointing them in the right direction. They both washed their hands and arms at an outdoor tap. Not quite the usual post-birthing cleanse but as good as they could get on the dales. The air felt almost balmy as a hazy sun finally started to break through the cloud.

'What are you thinking?' asked Damian, considering Amy's thoughtful face.

'I'm wondering what it was like to live here, no mod cons, out on these moors all those years ago.'

'A hard life. We've got it easy.'

They set off. Now that the low cloud had lifted, familiar landmarks were visible. They could see Hettie's farm on the hill ahead of them. Amy had approached it from the other direction the day she had encountered the lost goat. She smiled at the memory of her first meeting with Hettie. After her foot skidded on a patch of mud, Damian offered Amy his hand, and she kept her hand in his. Further on, they passed the ruined farm buildings she had seen before, followed by the semi-detached houses where she had spotted the boy on a swing. He wasn't in his garden today, but perhaps he was at the fayre.

When they reached the road at the bottom, they heard the slightly discordant sound of a lone bell ringing.

'Sounds like the Major giving a lesson,' said Amy. 'I might go up the tower, if there's time.'

'But we must say hello to Arad first.'

'Of course. Arad first. And we'll need to spend some money on the other stalls.' She glanced at her watch. 'There's still time. But they might not recognise us in this state. What must we look like?'

She said it with a laugh. They were both spattered with mud all over, their shoes squelching, their clothes, though they had rung them out, still soaking.

'You always look beautiful, Amy,' said Damian.

Amy laughed, and punched him lightly with her free hand. 'Yeah, right!'

He uttered an embarrassed cough. 'I've wanted to tell you this for a long time, but, well, here goes … Remember that night when I saw you in the pub?'

'Ages ago? In the Fox and Ferret?'

'Yes, I think you were meeting people there.'

'And weren't you with a big crowd?'

'Dad and a few mates, I think. Well, when I looked up and saw you, you had your hair loose – I'd never seen you like that before, and I couldn't take my eyes off you. You looked so beautiful, smiling and laughing with the others. I think that was the night something changed, and ever since then I've been falling for you.' She felt his head turn towards her before he looked away. 'I was surprised by it. I didn't know where that feeling had come from. And I didn't think I had a chance – I mean, I thought you couldn't stand me! I actually hoped the feeling would go away!'

'I'm sorry, Damian.' Amy squeezed his hand. 'I didn't make it easy for you, did I? I'm still not sure why I was so pig-headed when I hurt my ankle. My stupid independent streak, I suppose.'

'I did check you got back OK that day, you know?' Seeing Amy's puzzled expression, Damian added, 'I was worried about you. I waited for a while until I could see that you were on your feet, then I was lurking at Woody's garage to make sure you managed the final stretch.'

'No!'

'I'm a big softy really.'

They were almost at the edge of Grassdale now. A surviving race flag fluttered on a footpath sign. The bells dinged again, more melodically this time.

'Hopefully the Major has found a few more volunteers,' said Amy, still taken aback by Damian's revelations.

'Sorry, if I've embarrassed you.'

'No, I'm not embarrassed. I'm just … well, I'm happy!'

They stopped walking and looked at each other. Amy put her hands on Damian's chest, tilting her face up to look at him. Meeting her eyes, his head moved towards hers. His kiss tasted of the rain and the moors.

**

They could hear music and voices as they grew closer to the junction, and could smell the barbecue. A couple of people were standing talking at the crossroads. The woman glanced at them over the shoulder of her companion as they approached, then looked again. Amy recognised her as one of the women who had invited her to join the Women's Institute several months ago.

'Heavens! Don't say you completed the fell race! Didn't you know they called it off hours ago?'

Her companion turned round. It was Mark, their boss.

'Good God, look at the state of you both.' He kept his eyes on them keenly. Amy realised they were still holding hands.

'One of the marshals was supposed to intercept you,' said the woman.

Amy and Damian looked at each other and laughed.

'I think fate had other ideas,' said Amy.

'Let me get you both some food,' said Mark, and they thanked him and said that they would take him up on the offer after they had crossed the finish line.

To their surprise, they saw that some of the stalls were now back on the street. It was almost as if the storm had never happened. People were floating around in the weak sunshine. Upper Street looked quiet, but Lower Street was busy with people wandering from table to table, perusing the goods for sale, or catching up with friends.

Extra tables had been placed outside the community café and others put out on the green, where John and Andy were manning their barbecue. A small queue waited for the next batch of burgers to be cooked. Amy thought that frying meat had never smelt so wonderful.

As they headed down the street towards the pub, which marked the end of the race, Amy saw many familiar faces. It gave her a warm feeling. She realised it was the feeling of being part of a community, something she had never experienced before.

Mary and Lauren had stalls next to each other. Amy saw that Mary's table was covered in miscellaneous objects, a large china owl dominant amongst them. She was talking to Woody, but broke off her conversation when she saw Amy and Damian. She looked as if she wanted to say something, but Amy wanted to finish the race first.

There appeared to be very little on Lauren's stall, so Amy guessed that her baking had proved popular.

A little further down the road, Fahimeh and Arad stood at a table in front of the bookshop. When Arad saw them, he grew very excited, jumping from foot to foot as he tried to attract the attention of his mother, who was speaking to Sarah. When he finally was successful, Fahimeh picked up a bag, and after checking that the road was clear, she and Arad crossed and hurried towards the pub. Between them, they held out a ribbon, one at each end, marking the finish line.

Still holding hands, Amy and Damian broke into a gentle run towards it.

'I knew you would win! I knew it!' called Arad, looking as excited as if he had won the race himself. He and Fahimeh let the ribbon fall as they ran into it.

'I'm not sure that it counts as winning,' laughed Damian, ruffling the boy's hair.

'It does, it does, and we've got your medals!'

Fahimeh passed them to him. With a broad grin, he held out a medal to Damian, who crouched down so that Arad could put it round his neck.

'Chloe left Arad in charge,' explained Sarah, who was now standing beside them too, along with some other villagers who were wondering what on earth was going on.

'I've been so worried,' said Mary, who had also rushed over. 'I thought we should send mountain rescue, then we got a message from Hettie saying that you were fine.' She gave Amy a meaningful look. 'And making the most of your solitude.'

Amy caught sight of Donna and Sophie coming towards her, both of them grinning broadly. Sophie had her two youngest children in tow, the ten-year-old in her school uniform after performing in the choir. She thought how, just a few months ago, she hadn't known any of these people. Everything had started with a job application. To think that it had been done on a whim, with little expectation of success! But how pleased she was now that she had trusted her instincts! It had changed her life.

Damian whispered something to Arad, who then handed him the other medal.

'Amy Ashton,' said Damian, as he held the medal in the air for everyone to see before placing it round her neck, 'no longer a city girl, but a true Daleswoman.'

A few people cheered, while Donna put her fingers in her mouth and whistled loudly.

'Welcome home!' said Arad.

Acknowledgements

My thanks to everyone who supported and encouraged me in the writing of this book. Stephanie Lonsdale, Jack Dixon, Joseph Fox, Emma Gray, Rob Quinn, Dave Morris and Thomas Fox all provided valuable information or inspiration.

Thank you to my editor, Megan Jones, and to all at HarperNorth. It's wonderful to have a publisher devoted to northern writers and stories!

Huge thanks, as always, to my agent Sallyanne Sweeney of International Creative Agency.